NEWHAM COUNCIL
THE HEART OF EAST LONDON

19 SEP 1995
11 NOV 1995
14 DEC 1995
23 DEC 1995
-9 FEB 1996
16 MAR 1996
22 APR 1996
10 MAY 1996

LEISURE SERVICES — LIBRARY SERVICE

green street

FOREST GATE LIBRARY
081 534 6952

This book must be returned (or its issue renewed) on or before the date stamped above

NEWHAM LIBRARIES

NOT TO BE TAKEN

There will always be something sinister about the third of September to Douglas Sewell, for on that date he saw his friend, John Waterhouse, dying in agony. According to the medical certificate Waterhouse died of gastric ulcers, but his estranged brother Cyril demanded that the body be exhumed because he suspected that his brother had been murdered. It was proved to be death by arsenic poisoning, which could have been been administered in various ways at various times. But the answer to the mystery lay in the 'why'—and by carefully considering all the motives and knowledge of the characters involved, Sewell finally arrived at the startling answer.

NOT TO BE TAKEN

Anthony Berkeley

BLACK DAGGER CRIME

First published 1938
by
Hodder & Stoughton
This edition 1995 by Chivers Press
published by arrangement with
the Society of Authors

ISBN 0 7451 8658 0

Foreword copyright © John Kennedy Melling 1995

British Library Cataloguing in Publication Data available

Printed and bound in Great Britain by
Redwood Books, Trowbridge, Wiltshire

FOREWORD

THE FIRST TWO Berkeley titles to be reissued in the Black Dagger series were *Top Storey Murder* (1990) and the classic *The Poisoned Chocolates Case* (1991). Berkeley (1893–1971) was also A. B. Cox and Francis Iles; he was a journalist, comic novelist, mystery book reviewer for the *Daily Telegraph* and *Sunday Times*, founded the Detection club in 1928 and was an innovator in the genre.

As Francis Iles he had written *Malice Aforethought* in 1931—the 'inverted' story of a doctor wanting to murder his wife, based on the Armstrong case. *Before the Fact*, which appeared in 1932, became a magnificent Hitchcock film, *Suspicion*, with the elegant Cary Grant and award-winning Joan Fontaine. Some authorities, such as Eric Quayle, maintain that these two titles are crime novels 'with little or no mystery' yet must be studied as part of the development of detective fiction.

Berkeley used real people in his books such as the wickedly funny sketch of Dorothy L. Sayers in *Before the Fact*, and he parodied Allingham's Campion and Bailey's Reggie Fortune in *Top Storey Murder*. As an innovator Berkeley followed E. C. Bentley, author of the parodic *Trent's Last Case*, and was in turn followed by Richard Hull whose innovative books include *My Own Murderer* and *Last First* with the last chapter coming first, for the benefit of those readers who peruse the last chapter first.

Not To Be Taken, first published in 1938 (US title *A Puzzle in Poison*) is a poisoning murder, by arsenic. Set in a Dorset village, written in the first person by Douglas Sewell, it centres on an octet of characters—Sewell and his wife, the doctor and his intellectual sister, a shadowy young woman and her gossiping bachelor friend, and the powerful John Waterhouse and his irritating, invalid wife Angela. Waterhouse dies suddenly, his brother forces an exhumation, gossip runs rampant, Angela's German secretary-companion vanishes and Nazism appears. Surprise after surprise is sprung at the inquest with solution after solution collapsing. What, not who, are the Waterhouses?

The reader is shocked into action. You are told you have all the facts—so what is the answer and is there a Dominant Clue? As in the first eleven Queen books, Christie's *Ten Little Niggers* and Dennis Wheatley's *The Crime Murder Dossiers*, the reader has the opportunity to solve the crime.

The 1938 Haycraft-Queen first list of Cornerstone's best seventy-six titles included *The Poisoned Chocolates Case* and *Before the Fact*. Read *Not To Be Taken* and find out why!

JOHN KENNEDY MELLING

John Kennedy Melling, one of the first editors of the Black Dagger series, specialises in the history of crime fiction. He has recently been a Celebrity Lecturer on the QE2 and his next book, *Murder Done To Death*, is the first survey of parody and pastiche in the genre.

THE BLACK DAGGER CRIME SERIES

The Black Dagger Crime series is a result of a joint effort between Chivers Press and a sub-committee of the Crime Writers' Association, consisting of Marian Babson, Peter Chambers, Peter Lovesey and Sarah J. Mason. It is designed to select outstanding examples of every type of detective story, so that enthusiasts will have the opportunity to read once more classics that have been scarce for years, while at the same time introducing them to a new generation who have not previously had the chance to enjoy them.

CONTENTS

		Page
I	Strong Medicine	7
II	Conversation Piece	21
III	The Funeral Will Not Take Place	41
IV	Misbehaviour of a Lady	56
V	Enter the Police	73
VI	Disappearance of a Nazi	90
VII	All About Arsenic	107
VIII	International Interlude	124
IX	Scotland Yard Is Not So Dumb	140
X	Shocks for the Coroner	157
XI	Secret Cupboards and Secret Ladies	172
XII	Revelation to a Fruit Farmer	189
XIII	Unrepentant Sinner	201

CHAPTER I

Strong Medicine

1

Is it my imagination, or have other people noticed too that there is something slightly sinister about the third of September?

It is a date I shall never be able to overlook; and now when it comes round I observe that it is one of those decadent days, half dying summer and half autumnal, with the worst features of both—sudden sharp and inexplicable gusts of wind that yet do not seem to relieve the oppressiveness of thunder lurking somewhere just round the horizon, sunlight slanting under heavy dull clouds, a drip-drip unseen but persistent from the last night's rain, battered flowers, prematurely yellowing leaves and a general sense of foreboding and decay.

I suppose it is my imagination, but I know that particular third of September was just such a day. I can remember every detail of it. I can even remember that we had filleted herrings for lunch, and that the mustard sauce was a shade on the strong side. I can remember that the tea tray had a smear of jam on the underside, which got on to the table and thence on to a rather austere patchwork quilt that Frances was making with a black-and-white design, and how cross she was, and how inexplicable the smear was at all, because there was no jam at our tea and no jam, apparently, anywhere except on the underside of the tray. I can remember, too, that the maid was wiping the table with a damp cloth when the front-door bell rang, and she had to leave the table to answer it.

She came back and told me that Miss Bergmann wanted to speak to me, and I told her to bring Miss Bergmann in. Fräulein Bergmann acted as a sort of companion-secretary to Angela Waterhouse.

"She's brought those records Angela promised me," said Frances.

But the girl had brought no records. She hurried into the room looking so distraught and wild that Frances exclaimed aloud:

"Mitzi! What on earth is the matter?"

"Oh, Mr. Sewell! Mrs. Waterhouse says will you please come at once. Mr. Waterhouse is so ill, and we can't get Doctor Brougham on the telephone."

I jumped up.

"You mean he's had an accident?" So much the embodiment of robust health had John Waterhouse always seemed to me that for the moment I just could not connect him with plain illness.

"No, no. He is being sick. It is terrible. Please come."

"Of course I'll come. Frances . . . ?"

"Yes, of course, if there's anything I can do. You run on with Mitzi. I'll just tell them in the kitchen that we may be late for dinner."

Mitzi had already gone. Frances and I looked at each other significantly.

"So it was a gastric ulcer after all," she said.

No, I am not likely to forget the third of September. To see a man dying in agony is a thing one does not forget.

2

I must explain the Waterhouses.

They had settled in Anneypenny seven years ago, on their return from Brazil, and had taken the big house at the end of the little lane in which we lived—the first lane you came to on the left after Anneypenny village, on the west. Oswald's Gable was the name of the house, and it was reputed to be built upon an extremely ancient site, though the existing building dated only from the period of the first George. The Waterhouses were thus our nearest neighbours, for there were no other houses in our lane.

Anneypenny lies in Dorset, not far from the Somerset border, and its choice had been that of Mrs. Waterhouse. Angela Waterhouse was something of an invalid, though I don't think anyone knew exactly what was the matter with her except perhaps her doctor. Speaking as a fruit farmer, I am afraid I should diagnose her case as hereditary; for you cannot expect a vigorous bud if you graft it on worn-out stock, and Angela's stock though prolific had already shown signs of being worn out over which it would be kinder to pass in silence. The appearance in the dock of men with ancient and once honourable names may gratify a base element in a certain type but makes any decent person feel uncomfortable.

However that may be, all along that particular part of the border between those two counties were to be found first, second, third and even fourth cousins of that excellent but now somewhat decayed family from which Angela Waterhouse came. After the uncivilised wilds, as represented by a small coastal town in Brazil, which had struck her with helpless bewilderment the first moment she saw it and had kept her in that state for two whole years, Angela must have felt she had come home at last.

Waterhouse himself had been well enough content.

An electrical engineer by profession, he was one of those Englishmen who in a perfectly unobtrusive way are doing more for their country than all the statesmen and professional patriots combined. It is an industrial age, and pioneers of industry now fill the niche once occupied by the Raleighs, the Clives and the Captain Cooks. The fame is less, but the work is even more useful.

It was not long before we gathered something of Waterhouse's history and began to realise that we had in our small community a man of some distinction.

The history was an interesting one. A first-rate man at his job (that was obvious), possessed too with the faculty of handling men and full of the urge for adventure, Waterhouse had first served his term with a firm of repute

and learned everything they had to teach him. Then, with
their recommendations and backing behind him, he had set
out as a kind of roving contractor, with a preference for
queer jobs in the more inaccessible parts of the world.
He became known, particularly in the East, as the man to
send for when any native ruler with plenty of money and a
yearning for the bright lights was contemplating an electrical
installation in his jungle capital.

Goodness knows what queer jobs Waterhouse carried
out during those early years, or what imbroglios he got
himself into. He was no man to talk about himself, and
there was little but an occasional stray hint to go upon;
but I do know that before he was forty he had installed
electric light in a world-famous temple in India, done work
in Indo-China, Baghdad and Tibet, been captured by
bandits while on a job in China and escaped; and to crown
his career he had landed a million-pound contract for the
building and equipment of a series of power stations up the
Amazon extending more than a thousand miles into the
interior. It was this task which had procured for Angela
her two years' purgatory in Brazil; but it had, too, by
yielding a profit handsome even beyond the contractor's
expectations, made possible the retirement to Anneypenny
and something like luxury. As Waterhouse could not but
agree with his wife, an income of nearly five thousand a
year and no children was enough for any man to retire on.

Angela Waterhouse took up life in the English country
again with a sigh of relief; she knew it, she liked it, and it
seemed to suit her. For the first eighteen months or so her
health appeared to improve beyond all hopes.

Waterhouse, on the other hand, was bored. Country
life and country pursuits, to none of which he had been
brought up, struck him as excessively dull. The house
that his wife had persuaded him to buy, though not
enormous, was too big for his simple tastes, more used to a
tent and a camp bed. He tried a little half-hearted farming
on the hundred-odd acres that went with the house, but

the land was too poor and too hilly. Frances and I had got to know the pair fairly well by that time, and to like them, and I tried to interest Waterhouse in my own line, fruit farming; but somehow it did not appeal to him.

Then at last he found his hobby: building. It was an ideal hobby for a man with his urge for construction.

His fields bore a richer yield of stone than they ever had of crops. It was good building stone, too, with square corners and always one straight face. Waterhouse had some of it collected and built a little stone summerhouse in a sunny corner of the lawn, where Angela could recline in her long chair on warm afternoons. He built the whole thing with his own hands, and told me afterwards that he had enjoyed it more than anything since he came back to England. It turned out a good job, too, a workmanlike job that gave Waterhouse more pleasure to contemplate than his whole chain of powerhouses on the Amazon.

From that point he had gone on. Luckily the house was a stout concern and was able to withstand the onslaughts made on it. For Waterhouse gave it no peace. Having tasted mortar, he let himself go. He excavated cellars, underpinned the old walls, pierced them, propped them and grouted them. Half the outbuildings he had down completely and rebuilt. He dotted the garden with small erections and the fields with sheds for the cattle he had long since sold. Each little erection and each shed embodied some new experiment in spanning, some new mix for concrete or some new method of reinforcement. You could not visit him without coming across his burly form bending over some doubtful foundation, or seeing his big, red face, rising triumphant like the morning sun above a heap of wet concrete; and when he was not building the last, he was intently drawing his plans for the next.

This hobby was referred to by his wife and his friends as the Works, and it came in for a good deal of chaff. But it kept Waterhouse happy, gave a fair amount of local employment (he no longer mixed his own concrete and carried his own stones, though he continued to wield a mason's trowel), and consequently made him very popular in the village.

For that matter John Waterhouse was popular throughout the whole neighbourhood; for there was a great deal to like in the man and, so far as any of us could discern, nothing at all to dislike. He was free with his money, too, pressing unsolicited sums from time to time on the vicar, for any purpose that the latter might see fit; any case of hardship in the village had only to come to him to get relief, and in service as well as cash, which is much rarer; and Frances and I had some reason to believe that he was even ready to oblige his wife's cousins with a small loan from time to time, down to the fourth generation.

Waterhouse was indeed (again so far as any of us knew) a simple and kindly man, of a type that is becoming old-fashioned: a good fellow of the old school, though not necessarily of the old school tie; and it was a shame that he should have had to die as he did.

3

I think really that Angela only sent for me to console herself rather than minister to John, for when Frances and I arrived there, we were not at all sure at first who was the actual patient. It was John himself who met us in the hall, and Angela who was lying prostrate on her bed upstairs. By a tacit understanding Frances and I divided our attentions. She went up, with Mitzi Bergmann, to look after Angela; I stayed downstairs in the library with John.

John certainly looked bad, his usually red, full face positively pale and with a sunken appearance about it; and I noticed that, conceal it as he tried, his hands were inclined to tremble. He was obviously feeling weak, too, and I made him sit down at once. Of course he pooh-poohed my concern and apologised for the message which had brought us over.

"I'd have stopped it if I'd known," he smiled, "but Angela gets so fussed."

"Well, what *is* the matter with you in any case, John?"

"Eaten something that's disagreed with me. Nothing more or less than that. Biliousness, my boy. Haven't had a touch of it since I was a child, but here it is, curse it."

"You have been having a bit of trouble with your digestion lately," I suggested tentatively.

"Oh, a twinge or two. Nothing. I must expect that sort of thing at my age. Only wonder is that it hasn't set in before." John, like all hale men in late middle age, was a trifle touchy about his health and could never be induced to admit that anything might possibly be the matter with him.

"Well, what are the symptoms of the present trouble?"

John grinned, though a little wanly. "What are the usual symptoms of biliousness? Though they do seem to get a bit more severe as one gets older. I feel as if I'd eaten a couple of hundredweight of your green apples."

"A lot of pain?" I asked with the awkwardness that seems inseparable from this kind of conversation between males. Women treat pain more straightforwardly; they see no reason why they should feel ashamed of it.

"Oh, a bit. Seems to come on in spasms. I——" He broke off and got hurriedly to his feet. "Sorry, I must leave you for a minute. Another symptom, that won't take no for an answer."

After he had gone I took up the current copy of *Night and Day* from the library table. To tell the truth I did not take John's trouble very seriously. As Glen Brougham, our local doctor, had told him only a week or so ago in my presence, John had played the devil with his digestion for years, and must expect it to come back on him. In fact Brougham had suspected something in the nature of a gastric ulcer; though if that was the case, I thought John certainly ought to be in bed.

I did not disturb myself for some time. There was a fire

in the library, and the big leather armchair was very comfortable. Only when at last I looked at my watch did I realise that John had been gone for nearly twenty minutes. I felt I had better see that all was well.

When he did not answer my knock I did begin to feel some alarm. I listened and could hear him groaning. For John to groan meant that things were pretty serious.

I wasted no time then. Within ten minutes I had got him upstairs and into bed. He scarcely protested. He was indeed too weak to protest.

Sending a discreet message for Frances, I told her to go downstairs and telephone quietly for Brougham again.

"Is he bad?" she asked anxiously.

"Not too good," I whispered. We were standing in the passage outside the bedroom door. "A bilious attack, but a bad one. I should keep Angela away."

Frances nodded understandingly. In any sickroom but her own Angela was likely to be more hindrance than help.

She went down, and was up again in a minute or two to say that Brougham was still out and had just telephoned to say that he would not be back even for surgery. He was on a confinement case that was proving difficult, and half-a-dozen miles away.

"And Rona?" I asked. Rona Brougham is Brougham's sister, and there are not a few in Anneypenny who affirm that she is a better doctor than her brother for all that she has no qualifications. They are wrong, of course, but Rona, like most people who come of medical families, certainly has more than a smattering of medical knowledge.

"I asked," Frances said. "She's gone to Torminster for the day."

I looked at my watch. It was just past six o'clock. "If you could find out where Glen is, I could telephone through to him and get some sort of instructions perhaps."

"Yes," Frances said and hurried away. It was curious how completely the two of us had taken possession of the Waterhouses and their home.

Just as Frances reached the bottom of the stairs there was a knock at the front door. She went to answer it herself, and I hung over the banisters to see who it was. To my immense relief I heard Rona Brougham's distinctive, quiet, rather deep voice.

"Hullo, Frances. I haven't time to come in. Will you give this parcel to Angela and tell her I couldn't match the stuff exactly but this isn't so bad. Oh, and the Vaughan Williams record isn't in yet."

"Rona, you must come in. John's very ill, and we can't get hold of Glen."

There was no mistaking the astonishment in Rona's voice.

"John? What's the matter with him?"

"We don't know," I heard Frances answer. "He's been very sick, and all that sort of thing. And I think he's in pain."

"Good God!" For one usually so calm and quiet Rona spoke in something like consternation. "You can't get Glen? I'll go up at once. He's in bed?"

"Yes. Douglas is with him. I don't know whether Angela ought . . . ?"

"Keep Angela out of this," said Rona briefly.

She hurried up the stairs, and I met her on the landing, but with no more than a quick nod she passed into the bedroom. I followed her.

"Well, John," she said, "this is a bad business. I'd as soon expect the heavens to fall as to see you ill in bed. Tell me what's happened."

Somewhat sheepishly John told her. He was looking rather better now, and his voice was stronger. To get him into bed had obviously been the right thing.

Rona listened, her lips compressed. Then she felt his pulse. Frances was sent for a thermometer from Angela's room, and Rona carried out what seemed to me a thoroughly professional though rapid examination.

"Humph!" was all she said when it was finished.

John looked at her still more sheepishly. "I don't know whether you could get me anything to relieve the pain, Rona. It comes on in spasms, and it's—well, it's pretty bad."

Rona nodded. "It's more than biliousness, John. I think you must have eaten something that's poisoned you. Glen——" She broke off and seemed to be thinking hard, the toe of one shoe tapping on the floor. "No, we can't get Glen. I'm going to wash out your stomach myself."

John began to protest in a half-hearted sort of way, but Rona, having made up her mind, was out of the room at once. I could not help feeling relieved at the way she had taken things in hand. There was but one other doctor within a dozen miles, and as it was now surgery time, the probability was that he would not be able to come within the next hour.

John exchanged a rueful glance with me, and I wandered idly out into the passage.

Rona was telephoning below, in her usual calm yet somehow compelling way, and I could hear her explaining to the maid at the other end exactly what she wanted. Rona did all her brother's dispensing, so that she knew the position of each jar in the surgery.

"Listen carefully, Alice. I want you to find some things out of the surgery for me and bring them over here at once. It's urgent, you understand." I heard her detailing the stomach pump, and drugs such as bismuth, morphia tablets, magnesii oxidum and ferri hydroxidum (which I hoped the maid understood), and making the other write each item down on the pad beside the telephone.

Mitzi Bergmann appeared as Rona was hanging up the receiver, and asked if there was anything she could do.

"You can," Rona replied briskly. "Fill every hot-water bottle in the house, and bring them to me. And you, Frances," she added, catching sight of my wife, "ask Angela where the brandy's kept, and bring me the bottle."

I intercepted her before she reached the head of the stairs, out of earshot from John's room.

"You're going to give him morphia?" I asked in a low voice.

"Just a small injection, to relieve the pain. Angela has a hypodermic syringe."

"It's all right?" I asked doubtfully. "I mean, you're not a qualified practitioner, Rona."

She looked at me with an impatience unusual to her. "Damn qualifications. I can administer a shot of morphia as well as any qualified doctor."

"You think it's serious, then?"

She looked at me again, rather queerly. "I don't know. But it might be, my friend. Damnably serious."

4

Perhaps (I thought) women have a tendency to exaggerate. Certainly Rona has a very slight tendency at times toward the dramatically impressive. At any rate her brother, when at last he arrived over an hour later, took a very much less serious view.

Rona had certainly given poor John a strenuous time. She had dosed him with a compound from her bottles, given him the promised shot of morphia, then plied the stomach pump on him (during which process I preferred to leave the bedroom), and finally surrounded him with hot-water bottles and made him swallow a large dose of brandy—which I should imagine he was by then not unwilling to do.

By all these strenuous methods Glen Brougham was no more than mildly amused. Having made his examination, he pooh-poohed the diagnosis of food poisoning which his sister had voiced, confirmed a suspicion of an incipient gastric ulcer and pronounced the case one of epidemic diarrhœa, of which there had been several instances in the village during the summer. He assured Frances and me that there was no danger and no need for us to stay any longer.

"Oughtn't he to have a nurse?" Frances asked.

"No need," Glen replied laconically. "He can afford one if he wants the luxury, but Mitzi and Angela can look after him well enough." Glen was the Waterhouses' and our friend as well as our doctor—one of my oldest friends in fact, for I had been brought up in Anneypenny with Glen and Rona—and he was therefore able to be rather unprofessionally outspoken. Glen always had been rather unprofessional, for that matter.

"Angela!" exclaimed Rona. "No, if Angela will let me, I'll nurse John myself. I look on him," she added with a rather forced smile, "as my patient, you see."

Glen guffawed. "I believe you still think your diagnosis was the right one."

Rona shrugged her shoulders and turned away.

Unsnubbed, Glen spoke to us. "The old idiot deserved to have a tummy-ache, and I told him so. I made him up a bottle of medicine this morning—one tablespoonful to be taken every four hours—wrote the label myself as plain as I'm speaking to you now: and what does he do? Goes and swigs off half the bottle at a go. Says he had a pain and thought it would take it away. What can you expect with a chap like that?"

"Then that's what made him so bad?" Frances cried.

But Glen shook his head. "No, couldn't be. There was nothing to hurt—luckily!"

"What was the medicine?" I asked.

"Oh, just a mild sedative. Bismuth, and a spot of morphia."

"Morphia!" exclaimed Frances. "But you gave him morphia too, Rona. You don't think . . . ?"

"No, no," Rona answered impatiently. "That couldn't have done him any harm. There was no morphia to speak of in the medicine." But she looked exceedingly worried all the same.

There was rather an awkward little silence.

"Well, I'll run up and say good night to John," Frances remarked suddenly, and she did so, literally.

"No respect for the profession, your wife," Glen commented humorously. "Never asked the patient's doctor's permission, you see."

We chatted desultorily during the five minutes that Frances was upstairs. Rona still looked worried and preoccupied; Glen was more concerned in wondering whether Angela would sufficiently recover from her prostration to offer us a drink before we went. It was past nine o'clock, and he had had a hard day and no food.

Angela, however, did not appear, and the three of us left the house drinkless, Rona staying behind to keep an eye on the invalid. Glen walked down the lane with us but refused Frances' invitation to come in and share our belated dinner. He was expecting another message and would have time for only a couple of mouthfuls at home.

Frances came into my dressing room as I was brushing my hair.

"Douglas," she said, "Rona's worried."

"I know she is." Privately I thought we could very well leave things to Glen, but the sex loyalty which afflicts even the most reasonable of women would have driven Frances to combat this if I had said so out loud.

She did not need the provocation, however, for she went on at once. "I'd sooner trust to Rona than Glen."

Her tone was both defensive and pugnacious, so unusual a combination with Frances that I looked round in surprise.

"Frances, what's in your mind?"

"I believe Rona's afraid there was something wrong with that medicine."

"But she makes up the medicines herself."

"She didn't to-day. She was catching the nine-forty to Torminster, I know, because she asked me to go in with her. Besides, didn't you hear Glen say he made it up himself? .... I wouldn't let Glen make up a bottle of medicine for *me*," Frances added defiantly. "He's far too casual."

"My dear girl, what on earth are you hinting at?"

"Why, that Glen made some stupid mistake or other and put the wrong drugs in. Anyhow"—Frances suddenly whisked into view an object which she had been holding behind her back—"anyhow, here it is."

I stared at the half-empty medicine bottle.

Then I laughed. "Well, prevention's better than cure. You mean to make sure that John doesn't get another dose?"

"I mean more than that," Frances said soberly. "I'm all for standing by one's friends and that sort of thing, but doctors oughtn't to make careless mistakes. Can't we have this stuff analysed or something?"

5

We were thus in the affair, as it were, from the beginning.

Actually, however, I do not date that first evening of John's illness as the beginning. In my own mind I always put the beginning at a little dinner party which the Waterhouses had given about a week earlier. That was the first time, for instance, that I heard any mention of the gastric ulcer. In any case, whether the link is a real one or not, there is certainly a link of irony; for the conversation took a somewhat morbid turn after dinner was over, and what could be more ironical than a man's discussing murder and sudden death only a few days before his own?

CHAPTER II

Conversation Piece

1

It is a queer feeling to reconstruct the intimate past and bring the dead to life again in all the trivial details of everyday life; but I must try to do so if I am to fill in a full background for the picture which I have set myself to paint. And perhaps all the details were not so trivial either. Or alternatively, if they were genuinely trivial, efforts were to be made later to give them a sinister ring. In either case I will set them down just as they happened.

The Waterhouses had six guests that evening. In addition to Frances and myself there were Glen and Rona Brougham, brother and sister; Harold Cheam; and Daisy Goff, whom everyone had been trying for years to pair off with Harold, including Daisy herself.

We were late, I remember, and only just had time to swallow our cocktails, with the uncomfortable feeling that dinner was being held back especially for us. It is a curious thing that the less distance one has to go, the more likely one is to be late. It was only three minutes on foot from our front door to the gates of Oswald's Gable, but I think that each time we dined there, and that was fairly often, we ran it fine. The Waterhouses generally ran it fine when they came to us, too; but that may have been due to Angela, one of those women who seem to find it physically impossible to be punctual for anything. She has her invalidism to excuse her, of course, and she never fails to make use of it; but to my mind there is never any excuse for being late, even when I am the culprit.

Nothing very much remains in my memory of the dinner itself, nor of what we men talked about after the women had left the table. But of a conversation in the drawing room later (Angela Waterhouse retained the old-fashioned

.d, and certainly the big, rather formal room deserved it) have the most vivid recollection.

We had split somehow into two groups. Angela had a new batch of records down from London, and she had collected Daisy to help her listen to them and Brougham to put the records on the machine for her. Angela was always rather good at collecting people against their wills; for I am sure that neither Daisy nor Brougham wanted in the least to hear the kind of music which Angela professed to admire. Frances, however, did want to hear it, and joined the others to do so. Their group was scattered over the main part of the room, Angela on her couch near the fire, and the others near her. Waterhouse himself, Rona Brougham, Harold Cheam, and I were gathered round the smaller fireplace in the short arm of the L-shaped room, out of sight of all the others except Brougham at the gramophone, where we could talk without disturbing the listeners.

The August evening was not particularly chilly, but a fire was usually to be found throughout the summer in the Waterhouses' drawing room except on the very hottest nights, and often enough two. Angela averred that a fire was necessary to her; and her husband, after a life spent mostly in hot countries, had no objection. Not that he would have voiced it if he had. Where his wife's whims were concerned it was John Waterhouse's habit quietly to give way.

How our talk got on to capital punishment I can't say. We were all old friends, and among old friends talk has a way of drifting over totally unrelated subjects, through the oddest of links; but probably Waterhouse had led it there, not without malice, in the hope of teasing Rona a little. For Rona held strong views on this matter, as indeed she did on most matters. But if this were so, Waterhouse ought to have known quite well that he would fail, for Rona is quite unteasable. To be teasable, one must mind what people say. Rona never minded.

Rona, indeed, is an exceptional woman. In appearance she is striking, with her wavy black hair parted in the centre above a very white, high forehead, her rather broad face, her full but upright figure, and the air of reposeful dignity which always envelops her. Rona is one of the few people I know who are thoroughly efficient and yet placid. The chief niche that she occupies in our village community, however, is that of our local intellectual. We are proud of Rona. She has been up at Oxford and done exceedingly well there; she had held high office in a feminist society in London: and she has to our knowledge been approached by more than one commercial firm with an offer of a responsible post at a high salary. When on the death of old Dr. Brougham she threw up all these activities and came back to Anneypenny to keep house for her brother, we were ready to welcome her but we could not help feeling that she was wasting herself; she would have done us more credit, we felt, by staying in London.

As to her views, which are advanced, there are some of us who deplore them and more who are puzzled by them; but most of us, I imagine, have an uneasy conviction that if Rona holds them there must be something in them.

2

I must repeat that Rona is an exceptional woman. Unlike most people, for instance, who hold strong views, Rona never seems to have any wish to convert others to them. It is not easy to persuade her even to state them at all; though those of us who know her really well can usually persuade her into argument, Waterhouse perhaps better than most. Again, most of the people who hold strong views on capital punishment are those who wish to abolish it. Rona, however, thought otherwise.

"But, John, *why* keep them alive?" she asked in her gentle, even voice, when Waterhouse had finished dangling a series of provocatively humanitarian assertions in front of her. "We don't really want them. They're no good to us. Why not put them out of the way?"

"Hang the lot, in fact?" suggested Harold Cheam.

"Oh, I mean humanely, of course. Hanging's barbarous; though I suppose it has its uses as a deterrent. But to be humane doesn't require one to be sentimental; so just give me one solid, practical reason, John, for keeping them alive."

"Yes, come on, John," Harold urged. "I can think of plenty of reasons myself. It's a serious matter, and I think we ought to convert Rona." He looked at the other two with the funny little half-smile that just quirked the corners of his mouth, obviously hoping to be asked his reasons. That little half-smile and the word "serious" are the two things that I particularly associate with Harold. One would meet him walking sedately, as he always did, down the village street, his tall figure erect as a flagpole, and he would tell you that three hymn-books were missing from the church and he was looking into the matter for the vicar, adding with the little half-smile that it was a pretty serious thing; so that one never quite knew whether Harold really thought it serious or not. Not that Harold was a fool by any means, but he did enjoy niggling little importances; and he enjoyed talking still more. It is all nonsense to pretend that only women gossip.

Rona obliged him.

"All right then, Harold," she said, also with a little smile. "You tell me the reasons." There are smiles and smiles. Harold's has a deprecatory tinge; Rona's, for all I know, may be completely innocent. But Rona's little smile always makes me a shade uneasy. It gives me the feeling that she knows exactly what I am going to say next, and is gently smiling at it in advance.

Harold, however, does not seem to be affected by it. At least he is never timid of arguing with Rona, or even of breaking into an argument that she is having with someone else. When Rona is arguing I personally am content to sit and listen.

Harold quirked the corners of his mouth. "Why keep them alive, Rona? But why not? I thought you judged everyone by his or her use to the community rather than by their private ethics? Well, a murderer may be a model citizen, except for the one unfortunate lapse. And you'd have him put out of the way, and his value to the community destroyed, just because he once lost his head— perhaps only for a few seconds. I call that most unpractical."

"A point to you, my boy," observed Waterhouse. He was the oldest of our little circle and would sometimes assume the airs of a patriarch. He was, as a fact, fifty-two. Harold and I are much of an age, in the middle forties, and Brougham two or three years younger. The women averaged thirty-three or -four, except Daisy, who was, I believed, twenty-eight.

"Oh, murderers," said Rona. "I wasn't thinking so much of them. I was thinking of the habitual criminals, the useless nuisances. Or criminal lunatics. And of course it isn't so much a matter of capital punishment as of elimination."

"Elimination?" said Harold doubtfully. "Well, that's a pretty serious thing, you know."

There was a little pause, while Waterhouse puffed lazily at his pipe and seemed to be listening to the Bax symphony which was coming from the other part of the room. He was a big, burly man, with hair that was beginning to fall out and what had not fallen turning grey, and a rather large, rather red face which did not seem to accord at all with a Bax symphony. At the moment his face wore a half-quizzical, half-tolerant expression; but whether this was for his companions or for Bax there was no saying.

"Elimination, eh, Rona?" he said at last. "Well, that's a nice, big, efficient word. But the result seems to be much the same as capital punishment."

"The result perhaps," Rona agreed, "but not the logic—if it's logic you want, though I'm afraid it's only sentimentality."

Waterhouse stretched his feet a little nearer the fire and shifted his large frame comfortably in the big armchair which he had bought especially to contain it.

"You Communists are so ruthless," he complained.

"Ruthless," nodded Harold. "That's the word exactly."

Rona laughed. "But am I a Communist? I'm sure I don't know. The only practising Communists I've met seemed to me rather half-baked. But if you mean, as Harold said, that I judge people first and foremost by their value to the community—yes, I do. And I'm not afraid to admit that I believe in the elimination of the community's useless members: most certainly in the elimination of those who are a drag on the progressive ones."

"Dear me!" Waterhouse knocked out his pipe and felt in the pocket of his capacious dinner jacket for his tobacco pouch. "Then I suppose I should be one of the first to go? I've done my work in the world—I'm finished. And Douglas, sitting there as silent as an owl and living on his unearned increments——"

"Owls aren't silent," I interrupted. "At any rate the ones in your woods that make our nights hideous aren't. And I'm not an idle rich. I'm a fruit farmer."

"Douglas, living on his unearned increments and wasting half of them on the expensive hobby of fruit farming. And what use is Harold to the community, if it comes to that? So what would you like to do with us, Rona? Make a bonfire of us and pile all the true-blue Conservatives in the district on top? Poor old Sir Charles Fenchurch. But don't forget that he'd have all his yokels round him on the pyre. There's no one so rigidly conservative as your agricultural labourer."

"You're just trying to confuse the issue, John," Rona smiled. "And anyhow, I'll exempt you from my pyre, if only because your work in the world isn't finished. One day you'll find you can't stand this idle existence any longer and go out to do a job of work again."

"I've never been able to understand how he's stuck it here so long," Harold put in provocatively.

Waterhouse finished ramming tobacco into the bowl of his pipe and began to light it. "Circumstances," he said between puffs. "Besides, I've settled down for good. Anyhow, who's confusing the issue now? What I was going to say is, no, Rona, you're not a Communist, so you can stop flirting with the idea. Communism belongs to the towns. No one can live in Anneypenny and be a Communist."

"I'm not so sure of that," Rona replied reflectively. "In fact I believe you're a bit of a Communist at heart yourself, John. I'm sure you are. A Christian Communist. Every intelligent person must be."

"Am I intelligent?" Waterhouse pulled at his pipe. "I know you tell me so, Rona. But I don't think I'm convinced."

"And that from the man whose name, I understand, is now almost synonymous throughout the Far East with electricity. Besides, electricity is a thing I've never been able to understand, so I'm naturally convinced that anyone who does must be intelligent. In any case, fiddlesticks, my dear John! You and I are the only two intelligent persons in this village," asserted Rona equably, "and you know it as well as I do. Except Harold, of course."

"Thank you, Rona," said Harold. "I've no false modesty either. I am intelligent, and I know it."

"But not Douglas. No one could be intelligent and a fruit farmer."

"Not without a little more protection, which I suppose you wouldn't allow us," I said, not without bitterness.

"You mean not without the common sense to combine and market your own produce, instead of allowing the retailer to treat you like a lot of milch cows," Rona retorted.

"In any case, Rona," Waterhouse interposed, "I don't hold with too much intelligence about the place. You, for instance, are far too pretty to be intelligent. Pretty women oughtn't to be intelligent, you know. It upsets the balance."

"Really, John, I can't let you scrape out of the argument by paying me compliments. That's the unfairest type of the *argumentum ad hominem* when it's directed against a woman." But Rona was obviously delighted by that same compliment nevertheless. I found myself wishing that some remark of mine could bring such a look of pleasure into her face; for I think we all liked to please Rona. I remember reflecting, too, how odd it is that women should attach so much importance to the spoken word, for Rona could scarcely have been unaware of her own looks. Not that she looked much younger than her thirty-four years, or anything like that; but she did look as if thirty-four was exactly the age which suited her best—an impression which she had conveyed, as I had had every opportunity of knowing, at every age since she was sixteen. Anneypenny tongues had taken much exercise in speculating why Rona had never married, but they were agreed that it could not have been through want of chances.

"What was it you took at Oxford, Rona?" Waterhouse bantered. "A first in classics, was it?"

"I took a first in Greats, if that's what you mean. And they taught me logic too, John. Not that I need logic to know that you're not nearly so stupid as you pretend and that you really think much the same as I do on any subject that matters. But I won't try to explain why you should think it necessary to make out that you don't."

"Do I, though?" Waterhouse took his pipe from his mouth and rummaged in its interior with a match stalk. "No, I'm not so sure about that. I'm afraid I'm not ruthless enough. I suppose it takes a woman to be really ruthless."

"It takes a woman to pretend to be ruthless," Harold

said. "You don't believe Rona really means what she says, do you?"

"I'm not sure that she doesn't." Waterhouse eyed Rona doubtfully, and she gave him her gentle smile, with its faintest hint of mockery. "No, you can call me a sentimentalist if you like, Rona, but I can't subscribe to your ideals of treating mental patients, for instance, with prussic acid instead of psycho-analysis. Nor, I'm sure, does Glen."

Rona glanced at her brother, who was turning through an album of records on top of the grand piano with undisguised boredom.

"Glen's very conventional, of course," she said, her smile deepening. "A doctor has to be."

Brougham, catching his own name, looked up. "Eh? What's that about me?" He uncoiled his sinuous length from the extraordinary position into which it had been twisted and sauntered over to our side of the room.

"I can't make that chap Bax out," he went on, ignoring his own question and any possible answer to it. "I've managed to educate myself up as far as Beethoven, but that seems to be about my limit."

"Well, this sounds like the end," Harold pointed out.

"Thank God," said Brougham simply and went back to stop the machine.

The interruption had broken up our talk, and one by one we followed him back into the main part of the room.

Frances smiled at me. "Well, Glen?" she said. "Did you enjoy it?"

Brougham yawned. He has appallingly bad manners, but curiously enough one does not seem to mind them in him. Both Frances and I detest bad manners, but we agree that in Glen they play no small part in his undoubted charm.

"I'm afraid Angela's taken on too much of a job," he grinned, "trying to cram Bax into me. There doesn't seem to be room."

"Oh, but, Glen, you must try. He's wonderful. Really

he is." Angela has a plaintive voice, as befits an invalid. It is her custom to appeal for support in any assertion to the nearest person. "Isn't Bax wonderful, Rona?" she appealed now.

"Well, you know I'm not very musical, Angela," Rona said gently. "I can't pretend to understand Bax myself, but if you tell me he's wonderful I'm quite ready to believe you."

"Oh, but he is wonderful," Angela repeated, and looked helpless.

As is in response to a cue Waterhouse lumbered over to the couch on which his wife was lying. He had a curious rolling gait, more suited to a sailor than to an electrical engineer.

"Not feeling tired, dear, are you?" he asked, looking down at her.

"Well, perhaps . . . a little." Angela looked at the rest of us apologetically.

"Come along, Glen," said Rona. "Time for us to clear out."

"Douglas," said Frances.

"Oh *no*!" Angela wailed. "Rona, you *know* I didn't mean that. You make me feel horrible, breaking things up. It's terribly early, too. I'll just slip off, and you can all go on talking. John, give them some drinks and make them stay."

"Of course they'll stay," John assured her.

"I can't," said Daisy. "I promised them I'd be back by eleven. If you don't mind I'll go and put my things on. It's all right, Angela; don't you bother." She bustled out of the room. The door banged behind her. I had known it would. Doors invariably banged behind Daisy.

Angela looked round with an apologetic little smile. "Then if nobody minds, I think I'll . . ."

"Like me to carry you upstairs?" Waterhouse asked.

"That's sweet of you, darling, but I'm not quite helpless yet, you know."

Angela rose gracefully from the couch, a slim, straight figure in her exquisitely cut black evening dress, conveying an ethereal effect as much by the extreme pallor of her ash-golden hair as by the general delicacy of her colouring. A greater contrast to the robustness of her husband it would have been hard to find. Angela, I knew quite well, was thirty-six if she was a day, but unlike Rona she looked, at any rate in the heavily shaded light of her own drawing room, no more than twenty-five. Persistent ill-health since she was a young girl at least had not destroyed her looks.

She hovered now in the middle of the room, smiling vaguely at all of us and conveying, as somehow she always managed to do, a kind of mild surprise at finding herself where she was and an inability to get elsewhere without help.

Then Daisy came back in her cloak, and I even welcomed the bang of the door behind her in spite of the patent suffering which it brought to the invalid's delicate nerves; for when Angela looks like that, I always feel a fool. I don't know why I do, and there is no reason why I should; but I do.

"Well, good-bye, Angela, and thanks for a topping evening. It's all right, John, don't you bother; Harold will see me home, won't you, Harold?"

"Certainly, Daisy," said Harold.

I like Daisy. She is what is called a real country girl. That is to say, she goes out in all weathers, uses the slang of the last generation, always means what she says but can't always say what she means, and gets her man in the end.

3

I suppose I am becoming introspective as I grow older. For instance I don't think I used to be so much interested in the workings of my inferiority complex as I am now. It amused me that evening, after Harold and Daisy had gone, to notice that there was not a single person left in the room who did not call this inconvenient appendage into play.

I am not a particularly humble person, but it may be that I am too quick to discern qualities which I do not possess, and too quick to assess them at a higher value than my own. On the other hand, I am equally quick to recognise my mental inferiors; though perhaps too apt again to despise their powers compared with my own. However it may be, there is the cut-and-dried division, and everyone I know has his or her place clearly defined on one side of the line or the other. Harold Cheam, for instance, is a person who never gives me any feeling of inferiority, and I am in consequence decided that I am Harold's superior in everything that matters (put like that, the criterion sounds rather a negative one, and perhaps it is); but that is not to say that I do not sometimes envy Harold's temerity in rushing in where I would hesitate to tread—though here again I consider it a mark of superiority to know and observe one's own limitations.

There are certain attributes which at once set my own inferiority in action, and I do not suppose I am in any way unique. Feminine beauty, for instance, leaves most men slightly tongue-tied; feminine intelligence is notoriously and still more alarming. Achievement is another thing which makes me feel rather humble, never having achieved anything myself—not even a really good peach crop. And before notoriety I feel exasperatingly unimportant. Still more exasperatingly, I cannot resist a feeling of inferiority in the presence of someone better born than myself; against all reason, for my own stock, though undistinguished, is a sound one, and I am convinced with my intelligence that, individual for individual, I am a good deal better than most persons of more distinguished birth. Few things are more irritating than when instinct is at odds with reason.

To the six persons left in the room after Harold and Daisy had gone, each of whom was to play some part in the drama which, little as we knew it, was even then upon us, I was ready to take sixth place.

Of Frances I need say nothing more than that any proper man who has the kind of wife I have will feel a slight depression at his end of the balance. Rona Brougham represented female intellectuality, and so went at once to the head of the list. Waterhouse stood for achievement, and ran her a close second. I resented having to admit Glen to a higher place, for I had known the Broughams all my life since we had been children together, and a couple of years' superiority in childhood is an advantage not easily to be sacrificed; but I had had to give way for some years now to his superb nonchalance, his complete disregard for the other person, so devastating as to be positively kind. To anyone who is over-sensitive for the other person, that is impressive. Glen had quite a local reputation, too, as an extremely clever surgeon; and I am not even a good fruit farmer.

As for Angela, I think that, like county cricketers and industrial barons, she would set the inferiority complex of any man working.

I must try to give a picture of Angela, for in view of what was to happen later it is essential that her outlines should be as clear as one can make them, though descriptions are at best vague and unsatisfactory things. To begin with, she was not beautiful. "Beauty" is a strong word, and, like most strong words nowadays, much misused. But she was very pretty: quite pretty enough for a man to pull any string to get an introduction to her, and then, having got it, not know what to say to her. She had that kind of fragile prettiness which appeals most to men; but there was not enough character in her face for beauty.

I have mentioned her peculiar air of bewilderment. Strangers meeting Angela for the first time were apt to be disconcerted by this, and to ascribe it to a disinclination on her part, courteously but by mischance not completely veiled, to have anything to do with one so alien. If they knew something of her background, and the excellent and ancient family from which she came, this feeling would be intensified; for, after all, there is nothing like social snobbery to set the inferiority complex in motion. I know I am not unique in that—which annoys me all the more.

Waterhouse himself, who was well aware of this effect of his wife's, having suffered from it at one time himself, had once confided to Frances that he always wanted to explain to the victims that her manner meant nothing at all beyond a vague apology for something of which she was not quite certain, that she had been an invalid since she was seventeen, and that if there was an inferiority complex anywhere in the offing it was probably her own. But whether Waterhouse was right in this estimate or not is another question. He ought to have known his own wife, no doubt. But how many of us really know our own wives? Do I even really know Frances?

4

I may have dealt at too great length with the trivialities of that evening's talk, but I feel that I ought to show exactly what led up to that momentous conversation about which each of us was questioned and cross-questioned later so many times. Not that it was a conversation so much as a series of desultory remarks and retorts. Certainly I imagine that none of us attached any more importance to it at the time than that it was perhaps a little bit awkward.

It began with John's return from the front door, after seeing Harold and Daisy out. I have had my memory sharpened by the police, and I can recall that Angela had turned back from the door to ask Rona something about the next meeting of the Literary Society, of which Rona was the honorary secretary. It was pretty obvious, therefore, that so far as Angela was concerned the thing was unpremeditated; for she could not have known that John would be back so soon.

For that matter it must have been unpremeditated by everyone, for it began quite by chance with an attack of indigestion on the part of John; and that could certainly not have been foreseen by anyone. I believe I myself vaguely noticed that John seemed to hesitate as he came into the room and then went forward again, but I have heard it stated so many times since that I cannot be sure. Frances says she had her back turned to him and saw nothing. As it happened, only Rona was standing in such a place that she could see John's face; and it was an exclamation from her that precipitated the whole incident.

"John! Whatever is the matter?"

I do remember that John's voice was a little gruff as he replied: "Nothing. Why?"

"You looked for a moment as if you were in agony."

John laughed. "Oh, just a twinge. Indigestion. I've been having a bit lately."

"You must get Glen to overhaul you," Rona said.

"No need," Glen put in, in the lazily drawling voice which I believe his female patients find so attractive. "I can diagnose it from here. Incipient gastric ulcer, caused by eating too much rich food, drinking too many pegs during too many years, and smoking that foul pipe of yours too much and too often. Give up all three for six months, and no more twinges."

"Thanks," John smiled. "I'd sooner have the twinges."

"Oh, John!. . . . He won't take care of himself," Angela appealed to us.

"A gastric ulcer sounds rather serious," Frances suggested.

"As Harold would say," I could not help adding.

Rona turned to her brother. "Can't you prescribe something for him?" she asked with an unwonted touch of impatience. Rona naturally would have little patience with failure to look after oneself properly.

"Oh, I could, of course," Glen answered. "But what's

the use? He'd never take it. The man's a Christian Scientist."

"Well, that's nothing to be ashamed of."

"Who said it was, my dear girl? Who said it was? But as a business-man as well as a doctor, I can hardly be expected to approve."

"Oh, I'm sure John isn't a Christian Scientist," Angela contributed. "You're not, are you, John?"

"But why not?" Rona wanted to know. "It's a very sensible thing to be."

"If I'm a Christian Scientist, Rona's a Communist." John had flushed faintly at the term, and spoke as if defensively.

"But he won't take medicine, ever," Angela lamented. Anyone who would not take medicine must indeed have seemed strange to Angela, who regarded it almost as part of her normal diet, if not the best part.

Rona disregarded her and nodded approval of John's last remark. "Exactly. You mean you approve of the principle but can't quite swallow the practitioners—any more than the other side's medicine. Well, I think you're quite right. Christian Science seems to offer by far the most logical theory of illness that I've seen, and certainly the most interesting."

Glen snorted. "Logic! I'll tell you what logic is. You swallow a pin, and you get a pain under the pinny. That's logic. Cause and effect. But John here will tell you there isn't really a pain at all; what you feel is only——"

"No, John won't, because he doesn't know anything about it," John interrupted in a tone that was light enough. "But I'll tell you this: I won't take any of your rotten medicines, my dear chap, so don't waste your time prescribing one. I warn you, if you send a bottle round I'll pour it straight down the sink."

"Oh, John, what a waste," Angela reproved; and she really looked as if she thought it was not so much a waste as sacrilege.

"My dear fellow, I haven't any intention of sending a bottle round," Glen retorted, "and I wouldn't care what you did with it if I did. Go on with your twinges, and let your gastric ulcer increase and multiply. I don't mind."

There was a little pause. I for one had an uneasy feeling that despite the lightness with which both John and Glen had spoken, there was a hint of bigger issues, almost of antagonistic principles, underneath the words.

If that were so, Angela effectively dispelled them.

"That reminds me, Glen," she murmured. "*My* indigestion's been rather worse lately, too. I wonder if we can both have been eating something that disagreed with us?"

"I'll call in and examine you to-morrow morning," Glen promised.

"Oh, will you? Well, perhaps it would be best, just to be on the safe side . . . And you could examine John, too, if you could persuade him to leave the Works for ten minutes," Angela added, rather perfunctorily, I am afraid. "Well, perhaps I'd better . . . No, don't bother, Douglas . . . If you don't mind me just slipping off by myself . . . I'm sure they're dying for drinks, John . . . Yes, well, good-night . . ."

Angela got herself out of the room at last; John shut the door behind her and busied himself with decanters and syphon; the rest of us dropped easily into chairs near the fireplace.

"What are the Works at present, John?" Glen asked. The slight feeling of constraint had quite gone.

"Oh, we're still pulling down the stables. Would you believe it, there are no foundations at all. Stones laid just six inches below the surface. Simply disgraceful. It's a marvel to me that the walls have stood up all these years."

"Look here, John!" Rona spoke so abruptly that all of us turned to look at her. "You have been looking rotten lately, you know. Let Glen overhaul you. You may have leanings to Christian Science, just as I have; but you haven't any hard-and-fast principles. You needn't drink his medicine, but at least let him examine you—for our satisfaction, if you like."

"Oh, all right, if you make a point of it, Rona." John looked slightly sheepish. "But there's really nothing wrong with me, you know. There never is."

"Not a day's illness, man and boy, these sixty years," Glen scoffed. "Yes, my son, and those are just the ones who go off quickest in the end. I bet the state of your colon passes description."

"You need a holiday, John," Frances said. "I know for a fact that you haven't left here for three years. That's the worst of next-door neighbours. They notice that sort of thing."

"Why don't you cut loose from the whole bag of tricks and go off to put electric light into the Temple of Angkor or some equally weird place, as in the old days?" asked Glen.

For a moment quite a wistful look came into John's most unwistful face. "Well, it's funny you should say that, because I was approached only last week . . ."

"Then go, man. This place is getting you down."

"And it wasn't so far from Angkor either. Well, within a thousand miles."

"Then go, man!"

"No, I had to turn the offer down. I couldn't leave Angela, you see, and the climate wouldn't have suited her at all."

Glen made a rude noise with his lips.

That was all, I think, that turned out to be relevant. Only trivialities, you can see, but how they were to be raked over and sifted later.

5

There is no time more convenient for discussing our friends than in walking home from their houses.

The Broughams left when we did, and hardly were we halfway down the drive before Frances said:

"You were quite right, Rona. John hasn't been looking at all fit. Do you really think he has a gastric ulcer, Glen?"

"I shouldn't be surprised. Or gastro-enteritis in some form."

"Dangerous?"

"Not in the least, provided he takes the ordinary precautions."

"But can you persuade him to do that?"

"I doubt it," Glen said carelessly. "He's infernally touchy about his health, like all these ex-sahibs with livers like leather and insides like a sanitary inspector's nightmare. He'd suffer agonies rather than admit that he doesn't feel exactly as fit as he did at seventeen. Mind you, I don't say John's in a bad state. He's probably in very sound health, for his age. He takes a fair amount of exercise, and any insurance company would be delighted to have him on their books. But he's got to begin taking care now, and he just hates the idea."

"He promised to let you overhaul him," I reminded Glen.

"And a fat lot of good that'll be, if he doesn't do anything I tell him afterwards."

"You don't think he will?"

"Not he. It's become a sort of point of honour. You were wrong about the Christian Science, Rona. He may think he approves of the principles, but what the old idiot really feels, though I dare say he doesn't know it, is that he's never needed a doctor in his life yet and he's dam' well not going to begin needing one now. Well, it's no business of mine."

"It's a pity, if he's going to be stupid," Rona said a little absently.

We turned out of the gates and into the lane which led to the village. Our house, the only other except Oswald's

Gable, the big place where the Waterhouses lived, was only a few yards further.

Before we reached it Glen suddenly laughed.

"Did you notice Angela? Green with jealousy, poor girl. John had something wrong with him for a wonder, and she wasn't the centre of the sickroom picture."

Frances smiled. "Poor Angela! Yes, I'm afraid she's become rather fond of her ailments. And indigestion, too—almost her pet one."

"I've noticed before that Angela is getting inclined to look on indigestion as her prerogative," I agreed.

"That's what was making me laugh," said Glen.

We were still taking the affair lightly, you see, in spite of the ominous sound of the words "gastric ulcer." I wonder what our reactions would have been if someone had advanced the theory then that John's twinges were not due to natural indigestion at all but to minute doses of arsenic: and not only that, but that the poison was being administered to him by one of the very persons who had sat at his dinner table that night.

We should probably have received the idea with an almost amused incredulity—just as we did when, in due course, the contention was actually made.

CHAPTER III

The Funeral Will Not Take Place

1

JOHN WATERHOUSE died a painful and a messy death, but he died gallantly.

His death was quite unexpected, not least by his own doctor. He was ill for five days, but seemed to be getting better all the time. The diarrhœa and sickness both abated, though they did not disappear; there was much less pain than at first; the temperature was never more than a few points above normal; but of course there was great weakness following the physical strain, and the pulse was weak. In the end he dropped quietly into unconsciousness and never came round.

His doctor, Glen Brougham, was surprised, but not astounded. He gave a death certificate without question and stated the cause as epidemic diarrhœa.

"The poor old chap really died of heart failure," he told me a few hours afterwards. "His heart must have been a bit groggy all the time, though he never knew it. That's often the case with these big, fleshy men. When the strain comes their hearts can't stand up to it."

We were all very much upset, for we had a strong affection for John. Frances, of course, had been in and out of the house during his illness, and had been able to help Angela and to take a good deal of responsibility off Mitzi Bergmann's shoulders. For it must be admitted that Angela had not been very helpful herself, and but for Frances all the domestic arrangements would have fallen to Mitzi. Rona Brougham had taken complete charge of the sickroom and had even succeeded in getting herself installed in the house as nurse; so we had been satisfied that everything was right in that department. Rona did all that possibly could be done to save John, and his death was a bigger blow to her than to anyone; she was really quite knocked out by it, and one could hardly recognise the old imperturbable Rona in the weeping, almost distraught woman who cried for an hour in our drawing room on the evening that John died, and would not be consoled. Indeed, what with Rona there and Angela in a state of semi-hysteria at Oswald's Gable, Frances and I had such an evening as we are not likely to forget.

It may have been the strain of it which caused Frances to burst out when we were at last alone. She had borne up remarkably well so long as there was any need, as one could trust Frances to do; but once Glen had taken Rona home, and Angela had calmed down sufficiently to be left to the almost equally agitated Mitzi, Frances began to cry herself. She had been very fond of John, as all in our little circle were, and his death was a terrible shock to her.

"Douglas," she cried as I tried to comfort her, "there's something wrong. I know there is."

"Darling, what do you mean?"

"Rona knows there is too. I'm certain she does."

"What's wrong?"

"Rona seemed to be blaming herself for John's death."

"Frances," I said sharply, "you're talking nonsense."

"I'm not. Oh, I don't mean blaming herself literally. But she kept saying, 'I ought to have saved him, I ought to have been able to save him.'"

"My darling, you mustn't attach any importance to what anyone says in these conditions. Rona's been under a terrible strain. She nursed John most devotedly, and she knocked herself up. I know for a fact that she didn't go to bed at all for the first two nights. Besides, you know what Rona is. She can't bear failure, and she'll be feeling that somehow she did fail. She didn't, of course, and to-morrow she'll have recovered her balance."

But Frances was not convinced.

"You can say what you like, but I believe that Rona was

right from the beginning, and Glen wrong. I'm sure John didn't die of epidemic diarrhœa."

"Pull yourself together, Frances."

"I know what I'm saying. What have you done with that bottle of medicine?"

"It's quite safe," I hedged.

"Well, don't throw it away," said Frances ominously. "It may be needed yet."

2

How do rumours arise in a small village community such as ours? Nine times out of ten when you read of an exhumation taking place in a country churchyard, with all the melodramatic accompaniments of lanterns and secrecy, the act is the result of rumours with which the place has been seething for weeks.

Frances based her suspicions (which, I must admit, appeared to me then of the wildest nature) on nothing but a medicine bottle which she and I alone in Anneypenny knew to be in our possession. No enquiries seemed to have been made for it; no one had appeared in the least interested in it; no one, outside our own small circle, had even heard of its existence. Yet I know now that within a few hours of John's death people in the village were saying that there was something queer about it. What had they to go on? So far as I can see, nothing at all. Perhaps there are some people who say this over every death that occurs, and only cease to do so when no one takes any notice of them.

I have often wondered whether Cyril Waterhouse was given some sinister hint by one of these rumour-mongers before he ever set foot in Anneypenny, which caused him to adopt the extraordinary attitude he did adopt, and take the otherwise almost inexplicable action he did take. There was an anonymous letter writer at work, the usual trouble-loving pest. Did Cyril receive some communication from that source? Or had he other, more sinister reasons of his own?

Cyril Waterhouse is John's brother and the last sort of man to be brother to bluff, simple-souled John that the ordinary person would expect. I write "the ordinary person" because the ordinary person rarely peers below the surface of character; but it may be that a psychologist would have used the tortuosities of Cyril's mind as a clue to the possibility that John was not altogether the simple soul he appeared. And in that case, as will be seen, the psychologist would not have been far wrong.

Cyril is a business-man, engaged, I believe, in the import and export trade. He is in a prosperous way of business, has offices in the city of London, and lives in a big house in one of the wealthier suburbs. He is tall and thin and rather bald, and he wears pince-nez and that kind of striped trousers which denote a certain professional standing. He is a sharp man, is Cyril, and he knows it.

It is queer on what little things enormous issues depend. If Angela, with a fecklessness that was really absurd (*I* put it down as fecklessness, mark you, though Cyril had a different explanation)—if Angela had not omitted to notify Cyril at once of John's death and invite him down for the funeral, quite possibly we should never have heard anything more about it, and Anneypenny would never have got into the headlines. As it was . . .

The funeral was a very quiet one. Angela had spent the intervening three days in a state of collapse, in bed, pronouncing herself incapable of doing anything at all. All the necessary arrangements were made by Glen and myself. In a half-hearted way Angela seemed to want John's body to be cremated. Both Glen and Rona agreed with her. Frances, however, opposed the idea. She has never told me why, but I know the reason. She was right, of course, from one point of view; but I can't help feeling it a pity . . .

Anyhow, the suggestion came to nothing. Angela,

although protesting that this was what John had wanted, seemed unable to make her mind up; Glen seemed not to care either way; Rona was apathetic and did not press the point; Frances carried the day. Buried John was, therefore, in the ordinary way, in the little cemetery across the road from Anneypenny Church, and in the presence of no more than three or four of his wife's relatives, of us his closest friends in the neighbourhood, and of a fair number of genuinely mourning villagers. His own side of the family was not represented at all.

It was Frances who discovered that Cyril had never been told.

Commenting after the ceremony was over on the absence of any relative of John's, she asked if his brother, of whom we had heard vaguely once or twice, was not still alive. Angela answered that he was, but that John had never cared for him and had not seen him for years, and she let out that Cyril had not yet been informed of the death. Frances, who is strict about matters of that sort, was horrified and made Angela sit down and write to him there and then.

The next day Cyril arrived, preceded by a wire which put Angela in a flutter of nerves and exasperation. She seemed genuinely not to understand why Cyril should be coming down at all; she did not want him; and she was plainly a little frightened of him. She actually came running down to our house herself instead of sending Mitzi to ask Frances if she would go up to Oswald's Gable, and made Frances promise to help her through what she obviously expected to be an ordeal. Frances told her that she and I would dine at Oswald's Gable that evening if she liked, and Angela almost kissed her with gratitude.

And that is how Frances and I, having already been in at the beginning of the first stage, came to be present when the curtain went up for the second act.

And go up the curtain did, in the most dramatic way.

For as we were sitting rather awkwardly with Angela in

the drawing room, not knowing quite what to talk about over our cocktails and waiting for Cyril, who had arrived late and was still upstairs dressing, the parlourmaid came in and spoke to Angela with an embarrassment not generally to be seen in so perfectly trained a maid.

"Excuse me, madam, may I speak to you a moment?"

"Yes, Pritchard," Angela replied petulantly. "What is it?"

"The sexton is here, madam. He wishes to know if it will be convenient for him to fill in the grave to-morrow."

"Convenient?" Angela looked bewildered. "How can I know whether it's convenient for him?"

"I think he means after your telegram, madam."

"Telegram? What telegram?" As usual Angela appealed to the nearest person. "What does she mean, Douglas?"

A sudden feeling of uneasiness invaded me. "Would you like me to go and speak to him, Angela?"

"Oh, would you? Thank you so much, Douglas."

I went out. The sexton, who combined that post with those of village carpenter, joiner and undertaker, and only became a sexton when duty commanded, was waiting at the back door.

"Yes, Blake?" I said non-committally.

The old man touched his cap. "I only wanted to know if Mrs. Waterhouse would like me to fill the grave in to-morrow, sir, or shall I put it off any longer? By rights it ought to have been done to-day, but when she sent me that telegram . . ."

"Yes, of course. By the way, have you the telegram on you?"

"Yes sir, I believe I have got it in me pocket. Let's see now." He dragged out an enormous collection of very dirty pieces of paper and began to sort them through with maddening slowness. Of course Blake knew just as well as I did that Angela had sent him no telegram, but the decencies had to be preserved; and for sheer instinctive tact, commend me to any West Anglian countryman.

THE FUNERAL WILL NOT TAKE PLACE

At last the telegram was found, and I read it through quickly. It ran:

> DO NOT FILL IN GRAVE PENDING INSTRUCTIONS FROM ME.
> WATERHOUSE.

It was addressed to "The Sexton, Anneypenny, Dorset," and it had been handed in at ten twenty-seven that morning in London.

I gave it back to the old man.

"I think, Blake," I said, "that I shouldn't bother Mrs. Waterhouse this evening. I'll see that she sends you the instructions to-morrow."

3

I thus took a dislike to Cyril Waterhouse before I had even met him.

This dislike was confirmed during dinner. The man's appearance I have already described; his manner was unpleasing in the extreme. Toward Frances and myself he was coldly civil but let us see plainly that he considered us inconvenient interlopers; toward his sister-in-law he was cold and curt to the verge of rudeness, and over it. Dinner that evening was not a happy meal.

When the two women had withdrawn and Pritchard had served us with our coffee, Waterhouse broke through the laboured small talk with which I was trying to ease the situation and said abruptly:

"I'm not at all satisfied about my brother's death. I understand that you and your wife saw as much of his illness as anyone. Please give me some account of it."

I complied, of course, with as good a grace as I could muster. The illness had followed the usual course of summer diarrhœa, I told him, and death had been due to collapse following the intense physical strain. Everything, so far as I understood, had been perfectly normal.

"He had been expected to die?" Waterhouse asked.

I answered no, his death had been a surprise and a terrible shock to all of us.

Waterhouse began to peel a peach from one of the Gable glasshouses in a scientific way, as if he were dissecting a fact.

"I don't understand," he remarked. "Why was no second doctor called in? Can you tell me that?"

"I suppose Doctor Brougham saw no necessity."

"He did not consider my brother's condition dangerous?"

"So far as I know, he didn't. Serious perhaps, but not dangerous. . . . Though this sort of question," I added, a little stiffly, for I was becoming nettled by this examination, "would surely be better addressed to him."

He took no notice of my intended snub. "And why was no professional nurse sent for?"

"Miss Brougham very kindly undertook the nursing. She is a most competent woman."

"Is she a trained nurse?"

"Technically, no," I replied a little lamely. "But she is certainly the equivalent in value, and more than the equivalent."

He sliced his peach in two and flipped the stone neatly onto his plate. "This fellow Brougham. What's he like? Is he any good?"

"Doctor Brougham is considered one of the ablest surgeons in the county," I replied with distaste.

"No doubt, but it isn't his surgery that's in question. What use is he as a physician?"

"I'm sorry, Mr. Waterhouse," I said at last, "but you must make enquiries of this sort elsewhere. Brougham is one of my oldest friends, I have full faith in him, and I can't listen to the innuendoes contained in your questions." I paused for a moment and then added: "I think, nevertheless, that it might be better if you were to tell me exactly what is in your mind. I know of the telegram you sent to the sexton here, which seems to me frankly a most outrageous thing to have done unless you have the strongest grounds for suspicion. But what is it you suspect?"

The man's answer was certainly frank.

"Very well. Perhaps it would be best. I suspect that my brother was poisoned. Can you honestly tell me that the same suspicion has never occurred to you?"

"But good heavens," I began, "the idea is . . ." I hesitated. I could not help myself. The thought of that bottle of medicine now lying in a locked drawer in my desk came to me as a sudden, horrible shock. For why had Frances removed it if not out of exactly the same suspicion as I was now being taxed with? "The idea is preposterous," I concluded.

Unhappily my hesitation had not passed unnoticed. "I see that the same thought has occurred to you," Waterhouse commented drily.

"You mean food poisoning, of course?" I asked, feebly enough.

"No, I do not mean food poisoning."

"But who could have a motive for poisoning your brother?" I protested as warmly as I could. "We were all very fond of him. He was——"

"It's you who are going too fast now," Waterhouse interrupted with a chilly little smile. "I'm not accusing anyone of having poisoned him. I merely say that the suspicion is in my mind that he died as a result of poison, and I feel it my duty to verify or disprove that suspicion. If my suspicion were to prove correct there is nothing at present to suggest to me that the poison might have been administered to him by any other person. It might have got into him by accident, or it might have been suicide. That would be a matter for the police."

I felt that somehow I ought to be able to dispel the man's suspicion there and then. I knew that now if ever was the time to do so. I was not at all sure that, in spite of his rather repellent manner, he was genuinely hoping that I could and would. But all I found myself able to do was to ask:

"But what do you intend to do?"

He answered briskly, as if in some way I had made his mind up for him.

"I intend to insist on a post-mortem." He saw that I was about to protest, and forestalled me. "Why not? There can be nothing to lose by it. We all want to get at the truth, I suppose—even my brother's closest friends."

"But it will make such a lot of talk," was all I could find to oppose the idea. "It would be most unpleasant for Angela."

"Not at all." He favoured me again with the chilly little smile. "The request, of course, must come from Angela herself. I propose to put the suggestion to her now, if you've finished, and I shall look to you to support me. As a man of the world you can see that it's a very reasonable one. And as for talk, you may be sure there's plenty of that going already.

"And you must admit"—again the chilly smile was in evidence—"you must admit that telegram of mine to the sexton was a good idea. It's saved us the extreme unpleasantness of an exhumation."

4

If I had at first been inclined to ascribe Cyril Waterhouse's determination to make trouble to resentment over Angela's remissness in not letting him know at once of his brother's death, I soon saw that I was wrong. He was resentful, no doubt, and equally without doubt he had no liking for poor Angela, but his conviction that there had been something wrong in his brother's death was a perfectly genuine one.

There was a painful scene in the drawing room, of course.

Angela wept and had hysterics and refused for a long while to have anything to do with the idea of a post-mortem. She protested and she appealed, but neither tears nor pleas had the least effect upon Cyril. Never losing his temper, never even departing from his demeanour of cold calm, he insisted and continued to insist. I could not advise Angela that his suggestion was altogether an unreasonable one, and Frances, after taking some time to make up her mind, decided, too, that if anyone had any doubt, however ill-founded, such a doubt ought to be cleared up before it was too late. Neither she nor I hinted that we at any rate had some reason to believe that the doubt might not be so ill-founded.

Angela was therefore in a minority of one; and of course in the end she gave in. There was really nothing else she could do.

Then she tearfully announced an intention of going at once to bed.

But that, it appeared, did not suit her brother-in-law.

"Not just yet, please, Angela," he said with an assumption of authority which irritated me. "If Mr. and Mrs. Sewell will excuse us, there are one or two things which it is imperative to do as quickly as possible."

"We'll go home," Frances said quickly, and rose.

But Cyril had a use for us. "If you and your husband would be good enough to stay a little while, I think it would be advisable."

Even Frances seemed nonplussed before the man's evident determination to arrange matters exactly as he saw fit.

"Well, if you want us to stay . . ."

"I should be grateful. Both Angela and I, you see," Cyril said with deliberation, "may be looked upon as prejudiced parties. It might be useful later to have had two independent witnesses. You will understand perhaps when I add that I wish to ask about John's will." He turned to Angela. "I imagine you have no objection to my examining the document, Angela?"

Angela looked her most helpless. "Of course I wouldn't. But I haven't seen it myself."

Cyril looked really flabbergasted. "You haven't seen

it? But aren't you in touch with his solicitors? Haven't they produced it? What on earth is all this?"

"Oh, Mr. Ventnor rang up," Angela explained, beginning to weep again, "but he said they haven't got John's will. He said John didn't make a will with them. I don't see why you should blame me, Cyril."

"I'm not blaming you, Angela. I only want to find out the facts. Did Mr. Ventnor give you to understand that John died intestate, then? I must say it seems most improbable."

"What does that mean, Douglas?" Angela appealed to me.

"That he never made a will."

"Oh no. At least I don't think so. You see, Mr. Ventnor said that John told him there was a will. He told me, too, a long time ago. Before we went to Brazil."

"You know what its contents were?"

"Yes, John told me, of course."

"Well, what were they?"

"Oh, he left everything to me."

Cyril's face did not change. "Have you any idea where the will is now?"

"No, I don't know. How could I? But I expect it would be in John's desk, wouldn't it?"

"You haven't even looked?" Cyril asked incredulously.

"No, I haven't," said Angela, beginning to cry once more. "You don't expect me to rummage through poor John's papers almost before he's buried, do you? I think it's horrible."

Cyril looked at me. "I think perhaps if you'll come with me, we ought to do this at once. Angela, please get us John's keys."

I had to show him the way to the library, for he did not know his way about the house, and he at once tried the drawers of the big mahogany desk where John had spent so many hours drawing his plans and elevations. Only one drawer was locked. A key from the ring which

Angela brought fitted it. Cyril drew it open and lifted out half-a-dozen folded documents. There were five insurance policies and the will.

Without more ado Cyril opened the letter and glanced through it. I could not help seeing that it was very short. I noticed, too, that Cyril's jaw seemed to tighten rather curiously as he read.

"Exactly," he said tonelessly. "Everything is left to you, Angela. Well, I congratulate you. You will be a wealthy woman."

"Oh, Cyril, how can you be so heartless?"

"I'm only stating the fact. I see, by the way, that there is a codicil apportioning his life insurance. Five thousand pounds is set aside for the payment of death duties; forty-five thousand pounds is left to you outright; and the income of a further fifty thousand is left to you, the capital to revert to Maurice on your remarriage or death. Five, forty-five, fifty . . . good heavens!" He snatched up the insurance policies and began to look through them with something more like agitation than I had yet seen in him.

Laying them down again, he stared at Angela.

"A hundred thousand pounds! And taken out only five years ago. Why, the premiums must have been colossal. Did you know that John had insured his life for a hundred thousand pounds, Angela?"

"I knew he was insured, of course," Angela fluttered. "I don't think he ever told me how much it was. Why? Is it a lot?"

Cyril looked at her with compressed lips. "A remarkably large amount."

"Oh well, that's a good thing, I suppose," Angela said vaguely. "Oh dear, my head is aching so. I'm not very strong, Cyril, you know, and all this has been a terrible strain. I think I'll go to bed now."

"In just a few minutes," Cyril demurred. "Sewell, if you'll take Angela back to the drawing room, there is something I wish to do before I rejoin you. Angela, where can I find Miss Bergmann?"

"Mitzi? Oh dear." Angela held her forehead in both hands, as if the effort to think was almost too much for her bursting brain. "Well, I expect she's in the sewing room." She described its situation in vague terms, which I amplified.

Cyril held the door open for her and disappeared up the staircase.

On the way back to the drawing room I asked Angela who Maurice was, and learned that he was Cyril's only son and John's only nephew.

"A pleasant surprise for him," I remarked.

"Oh, I don't think it was a surprise, was it?" Angela said absently. "I mean, John had written to tell Maurice about it a long time ago. I remember he said so when he told me."

"You knew about the hundred thousand, then?"

"Oh dear, what does it matter?" Angela said petulantly. "I knew John had insured himself, and I knew I was to get it all while I was alive, or the income or something, and Maurice wouldn't get any till I was dead. What *does* it matter?"

Privately I thought it might matter a great deal, but I did not say so. I also found time to admire Cyril's control. He must have heard of the provision for Maurice, and perhaps he hoped for a substantial legacy for himself; yet his face had not altered at all in the drawing room when Angela told him so casually that she was to have everything.

Cyril's three minutes lengthened out to half an hour, and then to three quarters. It was not until nearly fifty minutes later that he reappeared and intimated with great politeness that Angela might now go to bed, and we might take our departure—which we did, not unthankfully.

It was not until a day or two later that we learned how that fifty minutes had been employed: in a careful search, assisted by a Mitzi willing or unwilling but no doubt intrigued, of Angela's bedroom, rest room and bathroom.

What he expected to find was pretty obvious; what he did find was detailed in the coroner's court later. But the inference to me was that, if he had been speaking the truth when he told me after dinner that he had suspicion of no definite person, the discovery of the will and its provisions had quite altered that.

5

Frances and I did not talk much on our way home that evening.

Only after she had gone upstairs and I had locked the house up and followed her did she call me in from my dressing room.

She was sitting in front of her mirror, a pot of cold cream in her hand, and she continued to rub it into her face while we talked. I remember that, for it struck me as such a good example of the way the trivial combines in life with the significant.

"Douglas, I can't help feeling worried. We backed that man up, you know, about the post-mortem. Were we right?"

"I think we were."

"Wouldn't it be much better to leave things? After all, there's no *real* suspicion of anything, is there? I mean, it's all so impossible. John . . . us . . . Angela . . . Why not leave things?"

"When things go over a certain line it's impossible to leave them."

"Yes, I suppose so. But . . . Douglas, I'm frightened. This post-mortem—what are they going to find?"

CHAPTER IV

Misbehaviour of a Lady

1

I MET Harold Cheam in the village the next afternoon.

I had put in a hard morning grease-banding the pear orchard against a bad invasion of winter moth and, while not deliberately avoiding Oswald's Gable and all its complications, had not been sorry to put it out of my mind for a time. Angela had all my sympathy, but it was no place of mine to constitute myself her guardian.

I had therefore heard nothing of any further developments, and I am afraid it had slipped my memory completely that I had promised old Blake to let him know about the grave.

Harold's first words, however, showed me that any message of mine to Blake would have been superfluous.

"I say, you know, this is getting pretty serious, Douglas, don't you think?"

"What is?"

"Why, what this brother of John's is doing. Haven't you heard? He got hold of Blake first thing this morning, before breakfast, and told him to lift the coffin and take it to the mortuary. Blake told him that he couldn't do that now without an order from the Home Office (exhumation's a pretty serious thing, you know), but Waterhouse said that the body hadn't been buried yet, so the exhumation rules didn't apply. Rather a nice point, don't you think? Anyhow, he told Blake that if *he* wouldn't take it on, he'd hire a couple of labourers from the village. So Blake agreed. Pretty forceful sort of chap, I should say. You've met him, haven't you? How did he strike you?"

I told Harold that Cyril Waterhouse had certainly struck me as a pretty forceful sort of chap, and one quite capable of cutting through a legal or any other sort of tangle instead of wasting time in unravelling it. I also asked Harold how he had come to hear of the proposed post-mortem at all.

"The late post-mortem, you mean," he said with a little snigger. "It's over. How did I hear of it? My dear chap, we haven't all got our heads buried under gooseberry bushes, you know. Why, the whole place is seething with it. I can tell you, some pretty serious things are being said, too."

Harold proceeded to regale me with some of them as we walked along together.

The remarkable thing about Harold is that he is not only the first to know what people in our own lot are whispering, he has the general gossip of the village at his finger tips too. I never know how he manages this, for Harold comports himself with great propriety and would never dream of discussing any of his friends with, let us say, Miss Cornish, the postmistress—any more than Miss Cornish would dream of such an error of taste as attempting to discuss "the gentry" with one of them. And yet Harold always seems to know just what Miss Cornish and her friends are saying, what the neighbouring farmers are saying, and what the humblest farm labourer is saying to his mates in the fields. I am in contact with them myself and employ four men on my fruit farm, but I never have the least idea what they are thinking. Our conversation on outside topics is limited to boxing matches and foreign affairs, concerning which the farm labourer of to-day is remarkably well informed and takes a surprising interest. I often think that it would be salutary for the Prime Minister or the Foreign Secretary to have a chat with my men. They would be surprised at the vigour of the opinions held in rural districts and the force with which any weakness in our foreign policy is deplored.

Harold continued to discuss the post-mortem, which seemed to excite him as much as, secretly, it excited me.

I learned that Cyril Waterhouse had telephoned early that morning to a well-known surgeon in London to come down and perform it, and to his own doctor in the fashionable suburb to come and assist. According to Harold, he had expressed his determination that no local surgical talent was to be employed.

"It's a direct insult to Glen," Harold bubbled. "Probably all against professional etiquette, too. I must say this chap Waterhouse doesn't seem to care a damn for anything. *I* wouldn't have liked to take the responsibility of lifting the body out of the grave like that. I'd like to know what the authorities will have to say about it when they hear."

"Confronted with a *fait accompli*, they'll probably say nothing."

"Yes, that kind of chap always gets away with it," Harold said admiringly. "And of course if they *do* find anything, he'll get any amount of credit."

"I don't see how they can possibly find anything," I said firmly.

"Well, frankly, no more do I," said Harold in a tone of regret.

We had come to the entrance of our lane, and I asked Harold if he would come along and share my tea, Frances having taken the car into Torminster.

Harold, however, had other intentions.

"No, I thought of dropping in on the Broughams. You come along too. Glen might have some news."

"About the post-mortem, you mean? I thought you said he wasn't present."

"Oh no. He was there all right. Rookeway—that's the London chap—invited him to attend, of course. That's always done."

"Oh, I see. Still, I shouldn't think the Broughams would want to be bothered with us."

"I'm going," said Harold simply.

Curiosity struggled against good taste, and lost.

"All right," I agreed. "I'll come with you."

As we went I pondered on some of the things Harold

had told me. I had been sorry to hear them, but not surprised. Where there is an English village there will always be gossip; and where there is gossip there will always be a hint of malice. The easy camaraderie which existed between the Waterhouses, the Broughams and ourselves, had apparently not gone unremarked. But even so I think it would have surprised Glen (though it might not have distressed him much) to learn that in less than twenty-four hours after John's death the chances of his stepping into the dead man's shoes were being freely discussed—and that, it seemed, not only among the village people. It would certainly have infuriated Rona to know that considerable sympathy was being felt in the same quarters for herself, with the view freely expressed that she would rather have lost the wife than the husband. Not the least infuriating part would have been that this was undoubtedly true. Though we tolerated her, none of us had a very high opinion of Angela. I don't really think that we liked her very much; though it is sometimes difficult to say exactly whether one likes a person in the country or not. Rural friendships are formed by propinquity, not by attraction.

I also wondered, somewhat uneasily, if these things were being said about the Broughams, what nonsense was being talked about Frances and myself. But that I hardly liked to ask Harold.

2

The Broughams lived in a house of fair size on the main road a few hundred yards beyond our lane, one of those whitewashed, rough-cast houses of indeterminate period which seem to crop up at each end of any West Country village.

Harold asked for Rona, and we were shown into the sitting room. We had timed our arrival nicely, for Rona was sitting behind the big silver tea tray, and Glen was sprawling in the most comfortable armchair—from which characteristically he did not rise when we came in. Rona, I thought, looked listless and greeted us apathetically.

"Hullo, here come the vultures," Glen remarked. "Well, you'll get nothing from me, my lads. Professional reticence, seal of secrecy, and all the rest of it."

"I don't know what you're talking about," said Harold. "I only want a cup of tea, if Rona's got one to spare. And I brought Douglas along because Frances has deserted him for the giddy whirl of Torminster."

Rona smiled wanly.

"Blah!" said Glen.

We sat down.

Harold helped himself to a piece of bread and butter.

"Well?" he said blandly. "Have they struck you off the register yet?"

"Blah!" said Glen.

"Come on," Harold persisted. "You know you'll have to tell us sooner or later. Was it epidemic diarrhœa, or wasn't it?"

"Read your newspapers and see," said Glen.

Harold pricked up his ears. "Newspapers, eh? That means something."

"It means nothing. This fandango's bound to get into the newspapers, isn't it? You can't go snatching bodies out of graves and carving them up without a newspaper smelling something in the wind."

"Don't be coarse," Harold reproved. "Have any sealed jars gone up to London for analysis?"

"Wasn't that rather the object of the proceedings?"

"They have. Thank you."

The maid brought in the extra cups, and I took advantage of the break to change the subject; for to tell the truth Harold's shameless questioning made me feel a little uncomfortable.

"Look here, while we're together . . . oughtn't we to do something about Angela?"

"What about her?" asked Glen indifferently enough.

"Well, I'm afraid she's in a rather awkward position." I detailed the events of the preceding evening. "I think this fellow Cyril has his knife into her, goodness knows why. He hasn't accused her of anything, but what he thinks is pretty plain—or what he's pretending to think. She ought to have proper advice."

"She's got a solicitor, hasn't she?" Harold asked.

"Goodness knows. I suppose there must be a family solicitor somewhere. She must get into touch with him."

"I'll see that she does," Rona said. "I'll go up there at once after tea."

Glen laughed lazily. "I don't think you need worry much about Angela."

I suppose we looked our questions, for he went on:

"Whatever complications John's death leads to, and however much we miss the poor old chap, one thing's certain: it's going to be the making of Angela."

"Glen," said Rona, "what *do* you mean?"

"You'll see. From this moment Angela will begin to bloom like a flower in spring. Her health will reappear miraculously; she'll become positively sturdy; we shall all be mightily astonished."

We gaped at him for a moment, and then Harold cried delightedly:

"*I* see. You mean there's nothing wrong with her? Never has been. She's a *malade imaginaire*. Eh?"

Glen lit a cigarette. Neither his sister nor the rest of us had finished our tea, but Glen never noticed things like that.

"She took you all in?" he said with a sardonic smile. "Well, no wonder, poor girl. She took herself in. Been taking herself in for years. Neurotic case. Interesting psychologically."

"Well, I'm glad to hear there's nothing organically wrong with her," I said; a little blankly perhaps, for it was difficult to realise that Angela, whom we had treated, humoured, and sympathised with all this time as an incurable and pathetic invalid, was just as fit as Frances herself, and that all our sympathy had been wasted on a neurotic case.

"Most interesting," Harold chimed in with a knowledgeable air. Harold has read a little Freud and is inclined to be proud of it. "A subconscious excuse for sexual frigidity, I suppose. Yes."

"Blah," said Glen.

"Eh?" Harold looked taken aback.

"Keep the party clean. And keep Freud out of it too."

"Well, that's pretty good, coming from you," Harold retorted hotly. "Keep the party clean, indeed. Did you hear that, Rona? In any case it's pretty common knowledge amongst ourselves that Angela wasn't altogether a satisfactory wife, in the usual meaning of the term, for a full-blooded man like John. You realised that, didn't you, Rona?"

"Oh yes. I should think everyone did." Rona spoke listlessly, as if the subject did not interest her very much.

"Well then," Harold pursued truculently, "I suggest my explanation for Angela's invalid pose is the right one. If you've got a better one, Glen, let's hear it."

"I've not only got a better one," Glen drawled. "I've got the real one. Angela's an almost pure leptosome type. She has the long egg-shaped face; she looks taller than she is; long neck, flat breasts, pointed chin and all the rest of it. She's a bit of a schizophrenic, too (and you'd understand what that means, Harold, if you'd ever read any psychologist a bit less out of date than Freud). But first and foremost she's a self-constructive egocentric. She wants prestige, and she'll go to any lengths to get it: even lie on her back in bed for the rest of her life, if that was the only way.

"This invalid pose of hers doesn't date from marriage, as according to your theory, Harold, it would. You've heard her tell us a hundred times what a frail, delicate girl she was, and how much time she had to spend resting and so forth when her brothers and sister were out playing, and how she used to lie and long to join them, and what a miserable childhood she had in consequence. Well, the pose was there then. She had no more the matter with her as a child than she has now. But her brothers were strong and athletic; her father was a beefy old rider to hounds known through three counties as a grand sportsman; her mother was an exceptionally beautiful woman; her sister was older than herself and had some brains. She was, in that society, the dud. And she couldn't stand it. So she took to her bed and became the most interesting member of the family, and the most unusual: there'd probably never been an invalid in it before.

"But marriage brings no change. Instead of marrying some weak personality whom she could dominate, she marries a man with a world-wide reputation, who, furthermore, by his beefiness and physique reminds her all the time of her father. Once more she's in danger of being a nonentity: just the wife of a well-known man and of no interest in herself. So the pose is brought into play again.

"Then she comes back here and finds herself among all sorts of people who knew her and esteem her, simply on account of her birth, at a higher value than her husband. It's she who is to the fore now, and John drops into the background. That sets her on her feet, and a surprising improvement in health is the result. But after a bit John begins to edge forward. People like him; they find him interesting; at dinners he is becoming more of a draw than she is. Result, health suffers a sad relapse.

"Now John's out of the way; father's dead; one brother's abroad and the other in jail; sister married a nonentity and has sunk out of sight; and Angela—she's going to be a rich woman and a beautiful woman and an altogether wonderful, desirable, entrancing woman. Unless she goes and marries another John (which you can bet she won't) she'll never have another minute's ill-health in her life. You see."

"Oh!" said Harold.

"Well I'm damned," I remarked.

There was a little silence. Glen tossed his cigarette into

the fire and lit another. It was Rona, not he, who offered the box to Harold and myself.

She looked closely at her brother as she put the box down again on the table by his chair.

"You've never told me any of this before, Glen," she said quietly.

"I don't discuss all my cases even with you, my dear girl."

"You're gossiping about this one now," Rona retorted quite nastily.

"Not a case any longer," drawled Glen. "Ex-case. I'll never be called in to Angela again. We-ell, not after the next fortnight. Give her that to get over the present spot of bother."

"Well, I think it's abominable," Rona suddenly flared up, to my intense surprise. "Here you've been leading me, and all the rest of us, to believe that Angela was an invalid, and—and waste our sympathy and time on her; and you were laughing up your sleeve all the time."

"Here, steady on," returned her brother. "Professional secrets is secrets, you know."

"Then why are you giving them away now?"

"The case is altered, eh?" Harold sniggered.

"Precisely," said Glen. "Besides, there's more to it than professional secrecy. You observe my sister's reaction now, gentlemen? Exactly. Her efficiency sense is outraged. And that's exactly what would have happened if I'd given the show away before. She'd have girded up her loins, gone straight up to Oswald's Gable and informed our pseudo-invalid that there was nothing at all the matter with her and the best thing she could do would be to take up her bed and walk. And *that*, gentlemen, would have been the worst possible treatment that could be applied. These cases have to be humoured. Rough-and-ready methods, honesty and all the rest of it don't pay at all. Not at all. It would be quite on the cards for a woman like that to do herself some really serious injury, just to show. No, my dear girl, it's no good getting your tail up. So long as she was in that state no one could be told she was shamming, not even her own husband; and last of all you."

"Absurd," said Rona, but less heatedly.

"Well, it's queer to think of," I put in, trying to turn the conversation a little, "but if it had been Angela who had died suddenly like that, and not John, I suppose you'd have insisted on a post-mortem. Exactly the opposite of what all of us thought."

"Exactly," Glen nodded.

My intervention had been unfortunate. With the subject brought back to the post-mortem again, Harold began unblushingly to try to get information out of Glen. I don't think he necessarily wanted it to pass on and so gain a transitory importance, like your born scandalmonger; he was just illimitably inquisitive.

Glen, however, was giving nothing away, and even added a word of warning about what he had just told us.

"It's not for publication, mind, so try to restrain yourself for once, Harold. Rona won't give it away, and Douglas is as close as an oyster; if it gets out I'll know you've been blabbing—and I'll never tell you another thing."

Harold was beginning some indignant reply when the entry of the maid cut him short.

"Miss Bergmann," she announced, and Mitzi Bergmann followed close on her words, looking even more worried than usual.

"Oh, excuse me, please, Miss Brougham. It's a note for Mrs. Sewell." Mitzi had been four years in England and spoke excellent English.

"Mrs. Sewell isn't here," Rona told her. "Only Mr. Sewell. Have you had tea, Mitzi?"

"Oh yes, thank you." Mitzi turned to me. "Please, Mr. Sewell, would you open it? I think it is important."

I took the note, somewhat battered from Mitzi's hot grasp, and tore it open. It was much as I expected.

Frances, please come at once. Something terrible has happened. I don't know what to do.

A.

Something terrible was always happening to Angela; and whenever it happened she implored Frances to go and console her.

"All right, Mitzi," I said with a little smile. "I'll come."

"No, please, Mr. Sewell," Mitzi said earnestly, "it is dreadful. Really, this time she means it. I don't know what is happening."

"Very well. Tell Angela I'll be there in ten minutes—or thereabouts."

With somewhat incoherent thanks to me and apologies to Rona, Mitzi retired. I rose reluctantly.

"The usual SOS from Angela," I explained. "I suppose I'd better go up and see what it's all about."

To my surprise Glen rose too.

"I'll stroll a little way with you," he said. "I want a mouthful of air before surgery."

Knowing Glen as I did, I suspected some motive beyond the wish for a breath of air. Nor was I wrong. We had hardly gone fifty yards before he began to grin and said:

"I thought we'd keep Harold on tenterhooks a bit longer, but I expect you'd like to hear about the post-mortem."

"I certainly would. But it wasn't fair to ask you."

"That's why I'm telling you," said Glen. "Well, it's a washout. Nothing doing. Friend Cyril can pack up his nasty suspicions and take them back to Mincing Lane with him."

My voice probably sounded as relieved as I felt.

"John died of epidemic diarrhœa?"

"Absolutely. No sign of any other disease, no sign of anything else at all. Nothing (if you want the technical details) but a bit of reddening of the duodenum and a very slight reddening of the jejunum. Precisely what one would expect, in fact, after epidemic diarrhœa."

"Thank goodness," I said.

It seemed that Cyril had had his trouble for nothing. I hoped, somewhat viciously, that the Home Office might have something to say about his body snatching after all.

"Then that's the end of that," I added. "And now, presumably, John really can be buried at last."

"Less certain vital parts of him," Glen replied with professional callousness. In answer to my look of enquiry he went on: "Oh yes. The bigwig surgeon was satisfied, I was satisfied, the assistant was satisfied, but dear old Cyril isn't satisfied. He's insisted on the usual organs being sent up to some hospital or other for analysis."

"What on earth for?" I asked, mystified.

"Seems almost as if he'd got inside information, doesn't it?" Glen said.

"Your taste in jokes, Glen, like your manners, is deplorable," I told him.

3

It was, therefore, without any anticipation of ill that I made a comparatively blithe way to Oswald's Gable.

Angela was in tears and had sought her usual refuge: bed. She received me there with the aplomb of the habitual invalid—and one who knows, at that, that she looks very nice in bed. She seemed to think it deliberate malice on the part of Frances to be in Torminster when she, Angela, wanted her.

"Oh well, I suppose you'll do," she told me peevishly. "You're not very sympathetic, are you, Douglas? But after all, it's advice I want, not sympathy. . . . Douglas, what am I to do? Everyone's against me."

"Nonsense, Angela," I soothed. "No one's against you."

I sat, a trifle gingerly, on the end of the bed where I

had been bidden, and confronted Angela, looking very young and pretty and pathetic, in a pale silk dressing jacket with her hair just untidy enough to be charming. I knew quite well that the effect was calculated, as all Angela's effects were; but the knowledge, instead of putting me at my ease, only seemed to embarrass me the more.

"Oh, indeed?" she sniffed, dabbing at her nose with an absurd little handkerchief—and being very careful not to disturb the powder, as I saw with fascination. "Well, if *your* parlourmaid took your most private letters and gave them to your horrible brother-in-law, and *he* opened them, wouldn't you say they were against you?"

"What are you talking about, Angela?" I asked.

Angela explained. She had written a private—a *most* private—letter that morning, and given it to the parlourmaid to post. And the parlourmaid, instead of posting it, had carried it straight to Cyril, who had opened it—and found himself well rewarded.

"Cyril opened it?" I repeated incredulously.

"Yes. He's like that, you know."

"But whom was it to?"

Angela actually bridled.

I will not recount the twists and mental wrigglings in which Angela indulged during the next ten minutes, obviously anxious to tell me about the letter and ask my advice, and yet at the same time unbearably coy about it. In view of the importance which was attached to this letter later I will give its text now, just as it was read out in the coroner's court a fortnight afterwards:

DARLING BOY:

I am in great trouble and very unhappy. Please come at once and tell me what to do. You know that John died last week—most unexpectedly!—*of some internal trouble from which he had been suffering for a long time.*

Now his brother is down here, acting very strangely. He seems to think there was something wrong about John's death and has insisted on a post-mortem. I am so frightened. He is treating me as if I were a criminal. If he finds out about us, I don't know what he might do. For God's sake don't say anything to anyone about the François—and remember, I wasn't in London at all that week; I was in Bournemouth all the time.

You could come and stay in Torminster, and Peters could drive me over. Nobody could know, and I must have your advice, now more than ever.

All my love, darling boy, still,
Your distracted
ANGELA.

And the letter was addressed to Philip Strangman, Esq., St. Joseph's Hospital, London, E.C.

The gist of this precious communication I gathered then from Angela, and it did not need a fool to see that if Cyril's suspicions, whatever they might have been, had not proved groundless and appearances at the post-mortem had been ominous, the information which this letter afforded might have been capable of a most sinister interpretation. Even as it was, I thought the lack of taste was bad enough, and I scolded Angela suitably.

She hung her head and tried to look ashamed, but there was a curiously triumphal glint in her eye which made me feel a little disgusted. Nor was this disgust lessened when I learned, in answer to further questions, that this Philip Strangman was not, as I had imagined from the "Esq." after his name, a surgeon on the hospital's staff, but a mere unfledged medical student.

"Were you mad, Angela?" I said without sympathy.

Angela bridled. "Don't take that tone, please, Douglas. I know I'm older than Philip, if that's what you mean; but age isn't everything. We love each other."

"You mean you're lovers," I said somewhat brutally.

"We're that, in the vulgar sense of the word too," Angela answered, not without dignity.

"And what would John have thought about it? I wonder," I demanded a little hotly, for I resented the silly woman's betrayal of my friend.

"John knew. And he quite understood."

"John knew?" I echoed.

"Certainly he knew. I told him. Only a few weeks ago. I didn't wish to deceive him, and offered to leave here. We talked it over. He was fond of me, in his way, but he knew he'd never suited me—any more than I'd ever suited him. He advised me to stay here with him, on a purely friendly basis, until Philip was earning enough to keep us both. It was very generous of him, and I was grateful and agreed. John always was very generous, you know."

"He certainly was," I agreed, rather nonplussed. The gesture did undeniably sound like John. And yet . . .

"So, seeing that the whole thing had John's approval, will you please get into touch with Philip for me (since apparently it isn't safe to write a letter while Cyril's still in the house) and ask him——"

"No, I won't," I cut Angela short; for to tell the truth the complacency with which she brought out John's acquiescence in the role—for, after all, that was what it amounted to—of *mari complaisant*, irked me very much. "Nor, I'm sure, will Frances. And my advice to you, Angela, is——"

"Oh well, if you won't help me I don't want your silly advice," Angela pouted—yes, literally pouted. "Will you go away, please, Douglas?"

"I certainly will, Angela. And in view of your incredible idiocy in writing such a letter, I think I'd better congratulate you about the post-mortem. If they *had* found anything——"

Her manner completely changed as she darted forward and caught at my arm.

"You mean—they haven't found anything?" she asked breathlessly.

"Apparently not."

"John *did* die of epidemic diarrhœa?"

"According to Glen, there's no reason to doubt it."

"Glen . . . oh!" She frowned. I noticed that she no longer looked like a spoiled and helpless child. "But Cyril practically said that . . ."

"What did Cyril practically say?"

"Oh, nothing." All of a sudden the old appealing look came into her face. Her voice went up at least two tones. "Oh, but Douglas . . ."

"Well?"

"Before you go, if you *do* happen to see Cyril, please try to find out what it is he's been searching the house for ever since last night. He and the servants have turned everything simply upside down. *Do* try to find out, and tell me. Will you?"

"I'll ask him," I said, and escaped.

Cyril was in the hall as I came down the stairs. I had the feeling that he had been lying in wait for me.

Cyril evidently believed in direct methods, for his question was certainly blunt.

"I suppose Angela sent for you. What did she want?"

I believe in direct methods myself at times, and I used them then.

"That's her business. What have you been searching her house for?"

Cyril stroked his little moustache and smiled, unpleasantly.

"I might answer, that's my business. But I won't. I'll tell you: I've been searching for a half-empty bottle of medicine which, as I understand, was prescribed and sent round by Doctor Brougham to my brother, but now seems unaccountably to have disappeared. Can you throw any light on its whereabouts, Sewell?"

I kept my composure.

"If you have any problems of that sort, I suggest you take them to the police," I said shortly.

He smiled again.

"Oh, but I've already done *that*."

I let myself out of the house.

I had made an enemy, but that did not worry me. I thoroughly disliked the fellow in any case.

But I could not help reflecting, as I walked home, how very fortunate it was that the post-mortem had proved abortive—for all of us. As for that wretched bottle of medicine, I determined to bury it under the next tree I planted.

4

Just ten days later Harold came round to see us at ten o'clock in the evening, in a state of dithering excitement. There was no need for him to apologize for the lateness of his call. The news he brought fully justified that.

"I say, what do you think?" he broke out, almost before the door had closed behind him. "I thought you'd like to know at once—they've found arsenic in John's body!"

CHAPTER V

Enter the Police

1

FRANCES and I stared at Harold.

"*Arsenic?*" I repeated stupidly, stopping dead in my movement to pull a chair up to the fire for him. "Nonsense!"

"Not nonsense at all," retorted Harold. "I happened to be at the Broughams' this evening, and the report came through to Glen on the telephone. As a matter of fact I believe it was that fellow who did the autopsy, tipping Glen off."

"And Glen told you?" asked Frances.

"He said it would be all round the place to-morrow, so I might as well be the first to know," Harold said ingenuously. "I thought you'd like to be the second. Arsenic! That's a pretty serious thing, you know."

"That's a mild way of putting it," I muttered.

To tell the truth I felt quite dazed. I don't know if anyone reading this has ever had an intimate friend die from the effects of poison, but if so he will know that at first the news sounds quite incredible; and the closer the friend is, the more incredible does the news sound. Other people, other people's friends, people of whom one reads in the newspapers, may die perhaps of poison, but one's own friends never. The thing seems impossible.

Harold pulled his own chair up to the fire. I leaned back against the mantelpiece, still staring at him. Mechanically I noticed that the book Frances had been reading had fallen on the floor, apparently without her noticing it, and mechanically I stooped and picked it up and laid it very carefully on the arm of her chair.

"Arsenic!" breathed Frances again. She looked at

me in a peculiar way. I realised at once what was in her mind: that cursed bottle of medicine. More than ever I wished that she had not seen fit to meddle with it.

"There'll be an inquest, of course," Harold said, not without a certain relish. "And pretty quickly too, I expect."

"What does Glen think?" I asked abruptly.

Harold shrugged his shoulders. "Can't account for it, of course. Flummoxed."

"Yes, yes, but what does he *think*? You know—accident, suicide or murder?"

"Oh, not murder," Frances put in with such assurance that Harold looked at her.

"Why not murder?" he asked with (I would swear) something like disappointment in his voice.

"Who could possibly want to murder John?" Frances replied simply.

Harold prepared to be argumentative. "How do we know? We can't possibly say. All sorts of things might have been going on."

"Nobody could ever want to murder John," Frances returned with the same conviction.

I felt she was right.

"John was such—such a grand fellow," I amplified, searching for the right phrase to describe John and finding them all either inadequate or banal. "Nobody but a fiend or a lunatic could have thought of murdering him."

Harold quirked the corners of his mouth in that mannerism which has always slightly irritated me. "Well, how can we say? It might have been a lunatic. Or a fiend."

"The idea's out of the question," I snapped.

Harold's quirk deepened. "Is it? It would have been out of the question, I should have said a month ago, that we could be sitting in this room discussing John's death from arsenical poisoning. But we are. After that, nothing seems impossible."

I **did** not wish to pursue the argument.

"Did Glen say how much arsenic they'd found?"

"I gathered it was a measurable quantity. Glen seemed to think that meant a good deal."

"More than just traces?"

"A lot more. If you're thinking of arsenical wallpapers or minute traces from cooking utensils," Harold said knowledgeably, "it's nothing like that. Death was directly due to arsenical poisoning, and for a measurable quantity to be found after an illness lasting several days, with all the eliminations that took place, a good deal more than a fatal dose must have been swallowed."

"You seem to know a lot about arsenic all of a sudden," I said suspiciously.

"Don't be silly, darling," Frances told me. "Glen's been coaching him."

"As a matter of fact," returned Harold, "Glen hasn't. He didn't seem to know very much about arsenic himself. We looked it up in one of his textbooks."

"I believe Glen positively despises drugs," Frances remarked. "Surgery's all he cares for. Why does a man have to be a physician and a surgeon? He may be rotten at one of them and brilliant at the other . . . well, like Glen."

"This will look pretty bad for Glen, by the way," I said to Harold, disturbed by the thought.

"He doesn't seem worried."

"No, I don't suppose he is. And if he were, he wouldn't show it. But it can't do a doctor much good to have a patient die of poison under his nose and give a certificate that he died a natural death. They won't break him, of course, but he'll come in for some very nasty criticism."

"It's a shame to put all that responsibility on one man," Frances observed with some heat.

"Oh, Glen seems to think he's covered all right," Harold said carelessly. "Rona was asking him about that. He says no one can tell the symptoms of arsenical poisoning from natural illness, or very rarely. After all, it happens over and over again with these arsenical poisoning cases."

There was a little silence.

"How the devil did John get arsenic inside him?" I burst out. "That's what I can't understand." It still seemed an incredible horror that John, whom we had known so well, should have died from arsenic poisoning. It made me feel foolishly and uselessly angry; and the anger, as I dimly realised, sprang from an irrational sensation of guilt, as if in some way I could have prevented the thing and had not done so. Of course I could not have prevented it.

Harold quirked again. "Well, you and Frances seem agreed that it can't have been murder, and I imagine that John was hardly the person to commit suicide, so it must have been accident."

"But how?" I demanded helplessly. "How could anyone, John least of all, have taken a large dose of arsenic by accident? One simply doesn't do such a thing."

Harold spread out his hands. "One doesn't. But the only presumption is that he did."

There was another uneasy silence.

Finally Frances broke it.

"It needn't have been an accident on John's part," she said quietly. "It might have been someone else's."

"It must have been someone else's," Harold affirmed.

I avoided Frances' eye.

2

After Harold had gone I tackled her.

"Things have gone too far now," I told her. "We must hand that infernal bottle over to the police."

"I suppose we must," she agreed reluctantly. "Oh, Douglas, I wish we needn't. I wish I hadn't taken it. At first I wanted to have it analysed, but now . . ."

"If the arsenic was in that," I said gloomily, "it'll

break Glen. A mistake in diagnosis is one thing, but a mistake in a prescription is serious. I should think they could have him for manslaughter if they wanted. Glen is so confoundedly careless, too. It really was the devil's own luck that he should have been doing the dispensing on that day of all days. Rona would never make a mistake like that."

"You feel sure that's where the arsenic was, then?" Frances asked almost fearfully.

"Where else could it have been?"

"That wretched man Cyril Waterhouse seems to think Angela . . ."

"Absolute nonsense," I snapped. "Can you see Angela poisoning anyone? He dislikes her and he seems to have some sort of grudge against her, and he's taking this dirty way of paying it off."

"I think he really believes it. Oh dear," Frances wailed suddenly, "life's going to be simply *beastly* for the next few months, with everyone suspecting everyone else and all of us suspecting each other. If the arsenic isn't in the medicine, I mean. But of course it is."

"I wish to goodness you'd left the bottle where it was," I could not help saying.

"Oh, darling, so do I. But I was sorry for John. He looked so ill and awful. I was sure Glen had made a mistake in the medicine, and I meant to show him up." Frances burst suddenly into tears. She is not a woman who cries easily. "Oh, poor, poor John! We all liked him so much. What a dreadful way to have to die . . . and so unnecessary. Who could ever have——"

She stopped crying and looked at me fixedly.

"Douglas," she said, "how did Cyril Waterhouse *know* that there was anything wrong at all? How did he know there was anything worth having a post-mortem and an analysis for?"

"I don't think he did know," I said a little awkwardly. "I think he was only being vindictive and troublesome

at first, and just carried the thing through to the end.
I've no doubt he was as surprised by the result of the
analysis as we were."

Frances shook her head. "He acted as if he *knew*,"
she said obstinately. "I believe he did know."

3

I don't know why I did not hand the bottle of medicine
over to the police first thing the next morning.

That is not true. I do know. It was the instinctive
wish to put off a distasteful task, when any excuse can
be found for doing so. My excuses were fairly good
ones, as it happened. For one thing I took it for granted
that a journey into Torminster would be necessary, for
I did not fancy entrusting the thing to our own local and
somewhat bucolic constable; and that would take up a
lot of time. For another I had been much worried during
the night over Angela and the extremely awkward position
in which she must now be finding herself.

I had said nothing to Frances about the letter of which
Angela had told me. That was Angela's secret—or
should have been. Besides, I saw no reason why Frances
should be involved any further in the affair. Nevertheless
I felt that someone else, possibly wiser than myself, ought
to be consulted: and having meditated over a plan for
approaching Angela's solicitor in confidence, and rejecting
it for a number of excellent reasons, I had decided before
morning came to lay the trouble at the feet of the two most
level-headed persons I knew, Glen and Rona, and let them
see what they could make of it. Immediately after
breakfast, therefore, I gave a few hurried directions to my
men for the morning's work and then set out for the
Broughams' house, hoping to catch them before Glen's
surgery.

I caught Glen actually before he had begun his breakfast.
Ten minutes was the time he allowed for that meal, and I

arrived one minute early. While he despatched eggs and bacon with professional skill, and Rona plied him with coffee, I told the two of them what I had to say.

They received it in their respective ways.

"The confounded young ass," remarked Glen benevolently.

"You're right, my friend," said Rona seriously. "This makes things look unnecessarily bad. What do you want us to do?"

That was characteristic of Rona, I thought. She took it for granted that Angela's indiscretions had no bearing upon John's death, she took it for granted that she and Glen would do what they could to help, and she knew that I had some sort of a scheme in mind. Rona certainly made things easy for one.

"I'll tell you," I said gratefully. "You know what Angela is. There may be nothing organically wrong with her, as Glen told us the other day; but she's pretty spineless. That fellow Cyril Waterhouse, to whom, by the way, I've taken a strong dislike, is going to do what he likes with her unless we interfere. I think he's made up his mind that she poisoned her husband. We know that's absurd, but that's the bee he's got in his bonnet. We've got to put a buffer between him and Angela, or he'll probably drive her right off her head. There's only one person who can act as a buffer, and that's you, Rona. My idea is that you should go up there (at once: there's no time to lose) see Angela, and get her to let you install yourself in the house again as nurse—her nurse this time. And tell her why, if you like. She'll be delighted to have you. In fact she'll clutch at you. And no one could keep Cyril at bay better than you. I would ask Frances, but . . ."

Rona nodded quickly. "No, no. It's my job, of course. Admirable. I'll go and get my hat on at once."

Glen gulped down the end of his last cup of coffee. "Some hustler, aren't you?" he asked ironically.

"You're in on this too," I retorted. "Surely you can fake up some medical excuse to prevent Angela from being badgered."

"Oh, I'll have a shot, of course," Glen answered casually. "Though I've an idea that my stock isn't too high with friend Cyril just at present."

"Look here," I said awkwardly. "Harold came round to us last night. Is it true that they've discovered arsenic?"

"Perfectly," Glen said with complete equanimity.

"But—but how the devil did he come to take it?"

Glen shrugged his shoulders as he rose from the breakfast table. "How is a victim usually persuaded to take it? Disguised in something else, I suppose."

"A—a victim?" I stammered. "You don't mean John was murdered?"

"Of course he was murdered," Glen retorted with complete calm. "And damn cleverly too. I'll admit I was taken in, properly."

"But it's out of the question," I felt compelled to expostulate. "My dear chap . . . oh no, it can't be murder."

"Murder—or criminal carelessness," came Rona's voice from the doorway, so bitterly that I looked round at her in surprise. "It's the same thing. . . . Are you ready, Douglas? Then let's go."

4

"Mrs. Waterhouse can't see you," said the parlourmaid with lofty contempt. "She's engaged." The swelling importance of her information made her suddenly human. "It's the p'leece," she added with undisguised gratification.

"Oh, damn the police," said Rona, and walked in.

I followed.

"Oh, miss," twittered the now alarmed parlourmaid

ENTER THE POLICE

as Rona made straight for the stairs. "Miss, you're not going *up*, are you?"

"Naturally," Rona answered her. "Is Mrs. Waterhouse in her room?"

"Yes, miss. She's in bed."

"Are the police in there too? . . . In the bedroom, girl?" Rona added sharply as the maid hesitated.

"Yes, miss. Some of them. The others are still searching the house."

"What are they searching for?" I asked.

"For the rest of the arsenic, sir. We've all been looking for it."

"They haven't found anything?"

"Not yet they haven't. But if she didn't use it all they'll find what's left. Trust the p'leece."

I felt myself go quite cold with anger inside my clothes. I took a step or two toward the girl.

"You're the woman who betrayed her trust and handed a private letter of your employer's to another person, aren't you?" I said; and I know I spoke quietly, for I forced myself to do so.

The girl, a tall, handsome creature in her way, fell back a step or two. Then she looked defiant.

"And a good thing I did, too. We don't all want to be murdered in our beds."

I felt at a loss in spite of my anger. I am not used to bandying words with maids (especially other people's maids), and it was disconcerting to see the training peel away from this one like the shell from an egg, to show the spiteful, vindictive human being beneath it.

It was Rona who finished off the encounter.

Coming down the stairs she had mounted, she spoke very quietly and gently.

"Listen . . . Pritchard, I think your name is. I heard you assert just now, in the presence of two witnesses, that Mrs. Waterhouse poisoned her husband with arsenic. I shall report that statement to Mrs. Waterhouse in accordance with my duty as her friend; and if she sues you later for criminal libel, and you spend six months in prison, you will have only yourself to blame.' In a situation like this, Pritchard, we all have to be very, very careful what we say. We may think any foolish thoughts we like, but we would be advised not to speak them out loud—especially to those who may repeat them to others. I think you will be more careful in future. Very well, that will do. You need not show us up."

The girl withdrew without another word, looking a little frightened.

"The servants have made up their minds," I said, not without bitterness.

"Oh, I think it's only excitement," Rona said wearily. "And hope. She probably didn't really mean it; though that kind is always the first to turn on the hand that feeds, clothes and pays it."

We began to ascend the stairs again.

"The police here already," I said uneasily. "Somehow I hadn't thought of that. They don't waste much time."

"From their point of view they haven't much time to waste," Rona pointed out. "But I'm afraid there may be trouble."

"Trouble!"

"I mean, we know what the police are. That silly letter—they'll take it as a motive, of course. And with the police, motive often simply spells fact."

"You mean they'll take Angela's guilt for granted?"

"Not if I can stop them, they won't," Rona returned grimly. And with a quick "Wait for me here" over her shoulder to me, she walked without knocking into Angela's bedroom.

As the door opened I could hear the rumble of male voices. Rona left it open behind her, and what followed was clearly audible to me as I lingered, somewhat uneasily, in the passage outside.

"Good morning, Angela," came Rona's voice. "I've

just come round to see if there's anything I can do for you." Her voice was as calm and ordinary as ever. I judged that she had simply disregarded the presence of the two policemen.

"Oh, Rona!" I heard Angela exclaim with a kind of sob in her voice. "Thank heaven you've come. Awful things are happening. You *must* help me. I——"

"Pardon me, madam," a male voice interrupted, respectful but firm. "I'm afraid I must ask you to withdraw. We are police officers, and Mrs. Waterhouse is being good enough to answer a few questions which it is our duty to put to her."

"Police officers?" repeated Rona thoughtfully. "Yes, I think I've seen you before. You are . . . ?"

"I am Superintendent Timms, from Torminster, Miss Brougham. This is Detective Inspector Carson. Your brother will know us." He waited evidently for Rona to withdraw.

"And you are questioning Mrs. Waterhouse?" Rona asked coolly. "About her husband's death, I take it. Have you given her an opportunity to send for her solicitor?"

"No, they didn't, Rona," Angela moaned. "They never even suggested it."

"Mrs. Waterhouse could have had every opportunity, if she had expressed any wish to have her solicitor present," returned the superintendent austerely.

"Then I strongly advise you to send for him, Angela, my dear," counselled Rona cheerfully, "and not answer any more questions until he's here."

"But they wouldn't let me have him. Cyril wouldn't let me. I know he wouldn't."

"I'll settle with Cyril," said Rona. She appeared at the door and spoke to me. "Douglas, see if you can find Mr. Waterhouse and ask him to come up here at once."

I was about to do so, not without joy in the forthcoming battle, when quick steps sounded on the stairs behind me, and the next moment Glen brushed past, bestowing an irreverent wink on me as he disappeared into the bedroom. Instead of going on my errand I waited to hear what would happen.

"Good morning, Angela. Hullo, Rona, you here already? Why, Timms, what are you doing here? And Carson?"

"You must know what we're doing here, Doctor," came the superintendent's voice, now distinctly huffy. "In view of the information known, I make no doubt, to you as well as us, it's our duty to ask Mrs. Waterhouse what information she can give us that may throw any light on the matter."

"All right, all right, you needn't work your set speeches off on me," Glen returned easily. "In other words, you thought you might be able to twist something damaging out of her before anyone could get in and warn her."

"You've no right to say anything of the kind, Doctor," retorted the superintendent angrily—and, indeed, with perfect justice. "The questions I've been putting to Mrs. Waterhouse are pure matters of routine, as you know perfectly well. And you know, too, they have to be answered."

"Not at present, they don't," replied Glen equably. "Because it's *my* duty to warn *you* that Mrs. Waterhouse, who is my patient, is in a dangerous condition and on the verge of a nervous collapse, and she's certainly in no fit state to answer any questions of yours. If you persist in worrying her after my warning you do so on your own responsibility."

The superintendent admitted defeat.

"I'm obliged to you, Doctor. In that case, of course, we'll defer our interrogation. . . . It can wait," he added with bitter ominousness, "until after Mrs. Waterhouse had had an opportunity to consult with her solicitor."

"Quite so, my dear chap. Then if you'll be good enough to make yourself scarce, I'll examine my patient."

The sound of heavy, sulky footsteps suggested to me that it might be more tactful if I were to make myself scarce too. I hurried down the stairs and paused, not knowing quite what to do next, in the hall. It was possible that Glen or Rona might want me again, and I did not like to go home and leave them to fight alone. After a moment's thought I turned into the library.

The next instant I regretted my choice, for as I closed the door behind me Cyril Waterhouse rose from a chair by the fire, *The Times* in his hand, and looked at me enquiringly.

"Yes?" he said politely. "Oh, it's you, Sewell. You wanted to see me?"

5

It is difficult to tell a man to his face that he is the last person one wanted to see.

"Actually," I said stiffly enough, "I came round to see if there was anything I could do for Angela."

"Ah, Angela, yes. I'm afraid she's engaged at the moment. In fact the police are interviewing her."

"Not at the moment, no," I retorted crudely. "Brougham's just turned them out of her room. Angela's in no fit state for police interviews, as anyone might have known."

The man's face flushed faintly. "You appear to concern yourself very closely with my sister-in-law and her affairs."

"Naturally. We are her friends here, as your brother was when he was alive." Some extraordinary impulse drove me on to add: "To us the idea that she could have poisoned John seems nothing short of fantastic."

"As it would, of course, to anyone," replied Cyril smoothly.

"I should have imagined," I told him, "that nothing short of a suspicion just as grave as that could possibly excuse the intercepting and opening of her private letters:

a thing which in the ordinary way could only be regarded as the act of an unspeakable cad."

Waterhouse regarded me thoughtfully. He did not appear angry. I had never met a man with more complete control over himself.

"You speak very bluntly, Sewell," he said at last, in the mildest way.

"Sometimes blunt speaking clears the air."

"I think it does. Well, I'll be equally blunt. I did suspect my sister-in-law of poisoning her husband, and I do still so suspect her. And I believe that any measures which may bring her guilt home if she is guilty—or equally, establish her innocence, if she is innocent—are defensible. I'm telling you no secret, by the way. Both Angela and the police are fully acquainted with my belief."

"And you had formed this idea almost before you even knew your brother was dead?" It was remarkable how calm we both were considering the extraordinary nature of the conversation. We might have been discussing the weather for all the outward show we made of it.

"How do you mean?"

"Why, you seem to have left London with this *idée fixe*."

Waterhouse appeared to reflect. "Not exactly left London, nor arrived here. But I must admit that, as soon as I heard the circumstances, the conviction jumped into my mind that my brother's death, so unexpected and so inexplicable, had not been a natural one. I could never have rested until I had proved or disproved my suspicions. The fact has justified me."

"And you're convinced that it was murder?"

"I'm convinced."

"And not only that, but that Angela is the guilty person?"

"Candidly, I have the gravest doubts of Angela's innocence. Let us put it that way."

I found the forced calm slipping from me. "Simply

because you think she had a motive. But if it's only a question of motive . . ."

"Well?"

"Well, you must allow Angela's friends to be equally candid. I think your family would benefit considerably under John's will in the event of . . ."

"Yes?"

"Of anything happening to Angela."

For the first time the chilly little smile which had so annoyed me before appeared on his lips.

"Angela's friends are of course at liberty to draw any strange conclusions they can find. But I think candour has gone far enough now, hasn't it? Except that . . ."

"Well?"

"You remember I mentioned a bottle of medicine to you? It is still missing. I wonder if any of Angela's friends can suggest an explanation?"

I turned away. The truth was that a disquieting reflection had just occurred to me. Supposing that wretched bottle did contain arsenic, what was there to prevent the police and Waterhouse from saying that it had been put there by Angela and was no mistake of Glen's at all?

As if divining something of my thoughts, Waterhouse spoke again.

"By the way, Sewell, concerning this matter of Angela's friends, I think if I were you I should hint to Brougham that it would look rather better if he were to advise Angela to put herself in the hands of another doctor."

"Why would it look better?" I asked somewhat truculently.

"Because I'm afraid I have no faith in him as a doctor; and it would certainly look better for him to retire from the case than be, so to speak, dismissed."

"Well, really," I began indignantly, "one would think that you were already in possession. I must remind you that Angela, unless or until your misguided efforts get her arrested, is still mistress of this house; and if it comes to appearances, wouldn't it look a great deal better if you were to remove yourself to the nearest pub instead of staying here on Angela's hospitality and working against her as hard as you can?"

"You must allow me to be the judge of that," he answered stiffly. "The position is not a pleasant one, but I feel that justice will best be served by my remaining here—as the guardian of John's interests, if you like to consider it that way."

"But not as the guardian of John's wife," said a nonchalant voice from the doorway. "You took the words out of my mouth, Douglas; though perhaps I might not have put them so forcibly. . . . No, my dear chap," Glen continued to Waterhouse in the most cheerful of tones. "Sorry, and all that, but you must clear out. I'm speaking as your sister-in-law's medical man. Your presence here is having a most disturbing effect on her. She can't be expected to get right again in these conditions. Besides, you needn't worry. The police will do all the snooping for you now."

I must say I have never known anyone who could be so offensive as Glen when he was minded to be, and in such a careless way, too, which made it all the worse. For the first time that I had seen, Waterhouse flushed to the roots of his hair.

"And if I say that I have no faith in you as Angela's medical man or anyone else's, and refuse to go?"

"In that case," said Glen cheerfully, "I shall advise Angela to hire a couple of toughs to throw you out: and I'll volunteer as one of them. Now then, go upstairs and get packed, and don't be silly."

Waterhouse glared at both of us for a moment, then turned on his heel and went out of the room.

"I don't really like that merchant," said Glen unnecessarily, and followed him.

I decided it was time to go home.

As I went I pondered the conversation I had had with Waterhouse. Had he or had he not answered Frances' question as to how he had known from the beginning that something was wrong? In any case one thing was certain. As I had told Frances last night, that bottle of medicine must now be handed over to the police, whether it contained arsenic or whether it did not, and irrespective of the interpretation which might be placed on the fact that it did. The police would almost certainly be coming during the day to interview me, as one of the persons who had seen Waterhouse when he was first taken ill. I would give them the bottle then.

As soon as I got indoors I went upstairs to the drawer where I had hidden it under a pile of handkerchiefs.

The handkerchiefs were still there, but the bottle was not. It had gone.

CHAPTER VI

Disappearance of a Nazi

1

IF this account of John Waterhouse's death is to be considered as a detective story, I suppose I am telling it quite wrongly. After all these pages I have only just reached the point at which a detective story usually begins: with the mysterious death and the inevitable problem of accident, suicide or murder. All the various events which I have already set out would be brought to the reader's notice later, under the questioning of the detective.

But I cannot view John's death as a detective story, in spite of the fact that the problem it presented was as complicated and as baffling as that to be found in any work of fiction. Anyone who has lived on the inside of a suspected murder, and yet outside the confidence of the police executives, will understand what I mean. Just as at a sensational trial it is said that the spectator quite loses sight of the issues of guilt or innocence in watching the game as it is played between the opposing counsel, so in a way we tended to overlook the huge question of who, if anyone, poisoned John Waterhouse, in the excitement of wondering what was going to happen next. Our point of view was, in fact, quite different from that of the readers of the newspaper sensation; we were as much in the dark as they were, and yet we could not help feeling that we ourselves were a part of the sensation. And we were, of course. None of us knew on whom amongst us police suspicion, when once it had veered away from the unlikely person of poor Angela, would next alight. It was an uncanny and a most uncomfortable feeling.

Another reason why I cannot look on this tale of mine as a detective story is the simple one that there is no detective: that is to say, no detective as the central figure whose investigations, discoveries and suspicions the reader is allowed to share. I may have known more or less what was going on in the minds of the local police; but into those of the Scotland Yard men later I was not given a glimpse. And as for a central figure, I suppose the central figure of this story is John himself. I at any rate have no wish to usurp that position. I was only a very small cog in the general machinery, given a transient importance greater than I deserved by the mere accident of propinquity; and I have been at some pains, therefore, to tell my story as impersonally as possible. I have indeed only one justification for telling it at all. For strangely enough in the end it was I and not any of the official detectives who eventually solved the mystery of John's death; and I solved it entirely out of my own knowledge of the case and of the people involved in it. For a pretty dull, stolid fruit farmer that was not so bad.

We in Anneypenny were a sensation, true enough; but I do not want to make sensations where none existed. Within ten minutes I had discovered the secret of the vanished medicine bottle.

"Listen, darling," said Frances when I asked her in some anxiety if she knew anything about its disappearance. "Listen very carefully, because I'm going to speak very carefully. You've mislaid that bottle, do you see? You thought you put it in that drawer, but you can't have done because it isn't there. You probably have a vague memory of moving it to a safer place, haven't you? Yes, I expect you have. But for the life of you, you can't remember where that place was. Very awkward and irritating, but on the whole perhaps rather a good thing; because you can't give it to the police now, although you want to."

"Frances," I said, "you're taking a very big responsibility."

"I'm not afraid of responsibilities."

"But what's the idea?" I asked doubtfully. "I don't

like it, you know. Why is it on the whole rather a good thing that I can't give that bottle to the police?"

"Well, you see, supposing there *is* arsenic in it——"

"We know there is," I interrupted. "The police have searched Oswald's Gable from roof to cellar. There's no arsenic anywhere else. It must be in that bottle."

"Exactly. And that means—well, what doesn't it mean? The end of Glen as a doctor. Perhaps they might even arrest him for manslaughter. I know Glen was incredibly foolish and careless and ought to be punished; but not that way. If that bottle ever turns up again, much later, I'm going to send it somewhere to be analysed myself; and I shall tell Glen what was in it. That will be quite enough punishment for him, to know he killed one of his greatest friends."

"Humph!" I said, still doubtfully. "But, my dear girl, it's not so simple as all that. Who's to say that he didn't put it there deliberately?"

Frances stared at me. "*What?*"

"I mean, as a blunder it's almost too much. Glen has a poison cupboard. I've seen it. Though it's true that, like any other doctor's poison cupboard I've ever seen, it's never locked and half the poisons aren't kept in it. But arsenic in an ordinary, mild indigestion mixture—no! As a mere mistake, the thing's incredible. You know the rumours that are going round the village. Glen hoped to step into John's shoes. He had his eye on Angela and her money as John's widow. What easier than to poison John and certify the death himself as from epidemic diarrhœa?"

Frances' eyes almost popped out of her head. "You —you *can't* believe what you're saying, Douglas."

"I don't, my dear," I assured her. "I know Glen, and I know that such a thing is impossible. But the police mightn't think it impossible. They might think it very logical. Or, if they didn't think that, what's to stop them believing that the bottle arrived at Oswald's Gable perfectly innocuous but that Angela herself stuffed it with arsenic from some secret store of her own? . . . In other words, we're up against big issues. Are we justified in interfering?"

Frances did not pause to think.

"Doubly! Trebly! Fifty-fold!" she exclaimed indignantly. "If it's even possible that such ridiculous conclusions might be drawn, we must stop them. I don't care if it is interfering with the police in the execution of their duties, or whatever the phrase is. Besides, it isn't. It's stopping them from rushing to silly conclusions. *We* know that can't be the truth, and that's all that matters. So remember, Douglas—you've forgotten where you hid that bottle. And you won't remember till I tell you to. Promise?"

Well, some husbands may condemn me, but not, I think, many. Frances has twice the head that I have, and I'm not ashamed to admit it—any more than Frances would be ashamed to admit that I have twice her physical strength. I promised. And I still believe I was right to do so.

2

Anneypenny was in the news now.

It was amusing, in a way, to us to see how the newspapers handled the situation. They knew all about the arsenic, of course, but not a hint of the word did they print. Instead they ran long stories about the post-mortem (to satisfy a grief-distracted widow), the dramatic semi-exhumation (ordered at the last minute by the same widow, kindly assisted by her helpful brother-in-law), and the insistence upon an analysis of the organs (still by that self-same widow). At the same time there were unexplained prophecies of an early inquest, explanations of just how wealthy the grief-stricken widow would now find herself and just how little difference the death would make financially to all members of the deceased's own family, and apparently pointless descriptions of John's habits, life and friends in Anneypenny, all sandwiched in between appreciations of his work and importance in the engineering world. Many of their readers must have been puzzled by what looked like an attempt to make a newspaper story out of just nothing at all; but we who knew realised how cunningly the ground was being prepared for what was evidently expected to be a sensation of the first magnitude.

As for ourselves, things were, rather against our expectations, quiet and comparatively normal for the next two days. The inquest was announced for the third day, and Frances and I duly received subpœnas to attend, and we were, of course, interviewed by the police.

This interview took place in the early afternoon after my somewhat eventful visit to Oswald's Gable. I was at work in the smallest apple orchard and had to be summoned indoors by a flustered but delighted maid. Frances, I learned, had already "been good enough to answer a few questions" from Superintendent Timms and Detective Inspector Carson, and I professed my willingness to follow suit.

There is no need to write out the interview in full. Both police officers were bland and courteous, though formal, the superintendent massively rotund, as suited his rank and responsibilities, the detective inspector tall and loosely built. I had not seen them in Angela's bedroom but found, rather to my surprise, that I knew both of them by sight, and they seemed to take it for granted that they knew me; so the atmosphere, if official, was friendly.

I was interested to see how like a detective story their questioning was. If there was a difference, it lay in the complete lack of subtlety. They questioned me closely about my visit to John on the day he was first taken ill, and I gave them a minute and careful account of everything I had seen, fixing the times (about which they were insistent) as closely as I could. They asked me what I knew of John's indigestion, and I told them what little I did know, adding for good measure how much more seriously John's doctor had viewed it than had the patient himself. They asked me if I knew of anyone who had a grudge against him, and I had to admit that I could think of no one; everybody had liked him and wished him well; I found it impossible to believe that anyone could deliberately have poisoned him; the thing must have been an accident.

"Maybe, sir, maybe," the superintendent answered non-committally.

It was then, at the end of the interview, that I imperilled the friendly atmosphere by presuming to offer advice.

"I hope, Superintendent," I ventured, diffidently enough, "that you won't concentrate too much on any single line to the possible exclusion of others. You know what I mean. There is violent prejudice in a certain quarter against one particular person. Those of us who know that person well feel that the suspicion is absurd: not merely because the lady is our friend, but because such a thing is entirely outside her character. You won't, of course, attach any importance to that as evidence, but I do hope you won't allow yourselves to be persuaded, or even tricked, into chasing a red herring."

"I think, Mr. Sewell," said the superintendent stiffly, "that you can safely leave it to the police what lines of enquiry they pursue."

"Oh, of course," I agreed hurriedly.

And that was that.

But my hope that the police might keep an open mind was not to be fulfilled. Frances went up to Oswald's Gable after tea to offer Angela a consoling word and was denied admittance to her bedroom. A large policeman (not our local friend) on duty in the passage outside informed her that the medical officer considered Mrs.

Waterhouse too ill to see anyone except her nurse and himself.

At that point Rona pushed her head out of the bedroom, saw Frances and took her downstairs to explain.

"They'd let Rona stay, in the end," Frances told me afterwards. "They didn't want to, but you know what Rona is when she's made up her mind; and after all, they'd no real excuse for turning her out. But they've made Glen give an undertaking not to attend Angela; the Torminster police doctor, Doctor Fitch, is going to look after her, and Rona has agreed to take instructions from him."

"They're keeping Glen away, are they?" I said gloomily. "That means they've heard those damned silly rumours in the village, I suppose. But what's happening? Have they arrested Angela?"

"No. As far as I can make out they'd like to, and they would have done if they could have found a single grain of arsenic in the house. But of course there isn't any, so they've got no evidence against her."

"Well, of course, they haven't, the idiots; because everyone except themselves and that fellow Cyril knows she didn't do it, so naturally there's no evidence against her," I said somewhat snappily, for I was still worried over the very vital evidence that we were withholding. "But if she's not under arrest, what right have they to say who may see her and who mayn't?"

"I don't know. But there's always a way for the police to do what they want, isn't there? I think she's under surveillance, or preventive detention, or something like that; anyhow, she's under it all right, and they won't let anyone see her but her solicitor and Rona, who's supposed to be nursing her."

"Well, it's a blessing she's got one ordinary contact with the outside world still. And for that matter she couldn't have a better. Rona won't stand any more nonsense than she can help. Any other news?"

"I don't think so. Oh yes, Rona said the police had taken samples from the drains and traps for analysis."

"A lot of use that will be. Oh, my goodness, Frances, I wish you'd never sneaked that bottle of medicine."

"Do you? I can't make up my mind whether I do or not. But I promise you one thing. If the police do go off their heads and arrest Angela, you shall have it back—and do what you like with it."

3

Excitedly as the whole of Anneypenny discussed the case during these two or three days before the inquest, opinion was, I think, almost unanimously in favour of Angela's innocence. There were, of course, those who remembered her brother, and opined that blood would out and you never could tell and all the rest of it, but of the large majority Mrs. Robert Perriton was a fair example.

Mrs. Perriton, elderly, poker-backed and suspected of dyeing her hair, lived with her prim little old husband in an attractive Queen Anne house with a few acres of park to it, out on the other side of the village. She was known as a fussy but kind-hearted person, and was generally regarded as our local busybody; that is to say, she ran the branch of the Girls' Friendly Society, the Village Institute and half-a-dozen other worthy activities, and was the recognised person for a girl to run to in time of trouble. I had always liked Mrs. Perriton, and so did Frances; but there were many who laughed at her as a typical old maid who had somehow got married by mistake.

On the afternoon after my interrogation by the police Mrs. Perriton presented herself at our house and, having known me since I weighed twelve pounds or less, made no bones about running me to earth in the corner of the old walled fruit garden where I was working.

I greeted her with muddy hands and clod-covered boots, and she waved such details aside with her umbrella.

"I knew you wouldn't come to tea with me if I asked you, Douglas," she said, showing her huge teeth in a horse-like grin, "so the mountain has come to Mahomet. No, never mind your mud, my dear boy, and go on with what you're doing. I can talk while you're working, and so can you. It's about this dreadful business at Oswald's Gable."

"If you've come to pump me, Mrs. Perriton," I grinned back, "I warn you that I don't know any more than you do."

"Nonsense! You know a great deal more. But I haven't come to pump you—though you can perhaps tell me that there's no truth in this ridiculous rumour one hears everywhere that they're going to arrest Angela Waterhouse?"

"I'm pretty sure they're not."

"But they'd like to if they could, eh?" Mrs. Perriton said shrewdly. "Preposterous! Angela Waterhouse hasn't got the guts to murder a fly. Why, she doesn't even hunt. You'd better tell the police that, by the way. Now if it was Rona Brougham . . ."

"*Rona?*" I echoed, astonished.

Mrs. Perriton laughed loudly. "Yes. Or Frances. Or you. Or Glen Brougham. Or a dozen others. Or myself, for that matter. Why, we've all got the courage, if we might not have the inclination. And we'll all come under suspicion sooner or later, mark my words."

I laughed. The idea of Mrs. Perriton under suspicion of murder seemed to me amusing.

Mrs. Perriton shook her head at me. "Yes, laugh if you will, my dear boy, but it's true. This is going to be a very horrible scandal; and anyone who knew that poor Mr. Waterhouse at all is going to have his or her name mentioned in a most unpleasant way, just as surely as half my girls are mentioning that man Freeford who had the bad luck to be dismissed from Mr. Waterhouse's employment just a week before he died."

"I didn't know John had dismissed anyone. Who was he? A labourer?"

"Yes, I think so. At any rate he had been engaged in helping Mr. Waterhouse with his building. But I'm afraid he's a bad lot. Things had disappeared before where he was employed, and you know what men are about their tools. I believe it was a favourite hammer, which Mr. Waterhouse found in Freeford's tool bag, that caused the trouble. Freeford, of course, swore he'd only borrowed it, but Mr. Waterhouse said he didn't want men who borrowed his tools. I'm afraid Freeford got very drunk at the Goat that same evening and said some exceedingly foolish things, which of course he would never have dreamed of when he was sober."

"This is all news to me," I said. "You seem to be very well up in the details, Mrs. Perriton."

"My girls tell me a great deal," replied Mrs. Perriton simply. "In fact they sometimes tell me a great deal too much, about things I would rather not know. . . . Still," she went on more briskly, "that is not what I want to talk to you about. It's Mitzi Bergmann."

"Mitzi?"

"Yes, she has to go back to Germany. You know what the police need. Are they likely to raise any objection?"

"When does she want to go?"

"At once. Today, if she could. Certainly tomorrow."

"But it's the inquest the day after tomorrow. She can't possibly leave before that. Hasn't she been subpoenæd?"

"Yes, that's just what I've been telling the silly child; but she only weeps and says she must go at once."

"Why must she go?"

"She says her parents need her."

"Are they ill?"

"Not that I know of. They simply need her, all of a sudden."

"Selfish little brat," I commented indignantly. "She doesn't like the scandal and wants to clear out—leaving Angela and Rona and everyone else in the lurch. Doesn't she realise that now of all times she's likely to be needed most?"

"I suggested something like that to her, but she only weeps louder and says she must go at once. I'm not altogether sure that it's only selfishness, Douglas."

"What do you mean?"

"I believe she's had orders," said Mrs. Perriton, looking like a mystery horse.

I leaned on my fork. "What orders?"

"We-ell . . ." Mrs. Perriton obviously prepared to make revelations. "I've been in close touch with the girl this last year or more. Perhaps she's told me rather more than she's told other people. She felt drawn to me, you see, because I used to know Germany so well myself, before the war. Anyhow, she told me some astonishing things. Did you know, for instance, that there is an organisation in London, working directly under the embassy, which keeps track of every single German citizen in this country?"

"I'd heard something like it."

"It's a Nazi organisation, of course. Mitzi is a Nazi, naturally. Well, she has to be," defended Mrs. Perriton quickly. "It's not worth any German's while not to be. And she has parents in Germany. They'd get at them. Anyhow, Mitzi *is* a Nazi; she's been through the Deutsches Mädel-Bund, or whatever it's called, and she has to take her orders from this organisation in London. And it's my belief they've *ordered* her back to Germany."

"But why should they?" I could not make head or tail of Mrs. Perriton's story, but I was convinced that she had something behind it. Mrs. Perriton may be a fussy old lady, but she is not a fool.

"Ah, that I don't know. But did you know Mitzi went up to London yesterday—without leave? She simply went. And yesterday evening she came round to our house with her eyes all red, saying she must go back to Germany at once. In fact if you ask me the girl's been very queer ever since John Waterhouse died."

"She's been upset, naturally," I suggested.

"Upset? Oh yes. Almost too much upset. But what with? Not only grief, I'd warrant; because while he was alive Mitzi didn't seem any too favourably impressed with Mr. Waterhouse."

"What?" I said, genuinely surprised. "Why, she was devoted to him. And I know he liked her. They used to tease each other all the time. I've often heard him ragging her about the Nazi system and so forth."

"A mistake." Mrs. Perriton shook her head. "A great mistake, to rag any German. The Germans have no sense of humour about themselves. It makes me doubt very much whether they can really come from the same stock as ourselves. I know that Mitzi felt Mr. Waterhouse's ragging very much. She could not bear that anyone shouldn't admire her beloved Germany, and she has a very simple way of getting over the defects of the Nazi system: she doesn't believe they exist. Show her the most sober and categorical account in a reputable newspaper of some case of persecution in Germany, and she'll say flatly: 'It isn't true.'"

I sighed. "Yes, that's part of the trouble. Still, what bearing has this on John's death?"

Mrs. Perriton looked grave. "I don't suppose it has any. But I don't think that child ought to be allowed to slip out of the country, as she undoubtedly intends to do, until the mystery of Mr. Waterhouse's death has been cleared up. After all, as one living in the house she must have some information of importance to give the police."

"But what do you want me to do, Mrs. Perriton?"

"I thought," said Mrs. Perriton naïvely, "that you

might like to drop a hint to the police to warn her that she mustn't run away."

"Oh!" I said blankly. "Is that what you thought?"

"Well, perhaps not *all* I thought." Mrs. Perriton laughed hugely but rather artificially. "You can try and guess the rest."

4

I did not drop a hint to the police. It was none of my business, and I was not going to be officious. And in consequence (at least, I suppose it was in consequence) Mitzi did go—the next afternoon, with nothing but a small attaché case in her hand and leaving all her belongings behind.

The newspapers made a sensation of it, of course. DISAPPEARANCE OF STAR WITNESS ON EVE OF INQUEST. NAZI FLEES TO NATIVE GERMANY, and all the rest of it. But that was nothing to the sensation caused in the village. With instant unanimity everyone jumped to the conclusion that Mitzi was the murderess, and had now fled the country in the approved way. And certainly the flight looked bad enough. What was the reason for it? That it must be a guilty one the village took for granted, and rumours of every fantastic description seemed to put themselves immediately and automatically into circulation. The least of these was that Mitzi having made her way out of the grounds of Oswald's Gable, had met a large black saloon car, obviously by pre-arrangement, with drawn blinds and a sinister Teuton at the wheel, and been instantly whisked into the unknown.

As a matter of fact this rumour was not without foundation. The police eventually traced Mitzi to Harwich and on board a boat for Rotterdam, and she undoubtedly was conveyed away from our neighbourhood in a car which she must have met at some fixed place by appointment; but where the car came from, whose it was and who drove it remained a mystery.

This touch of the genuine thriller naturally brought our excitement up to boiling point, as well as justifying the hints already thrown out by the newspapers; and it was to be expected that the inquest would prove a popular attraction as great as any cup tie.

The sensation of Mitzi's disappearance was, however, the only new event that happened during this period, and it added to rather than elucidated the general mystery of John's death.

One result on the ordinary person was that one felt that one had to discuss the case and go on discussing it. Frances and I talked about it for two solid hours after tea without arriving at any conclusion; for though we felt that we two alone knew the real truth about John's death, we could not make out how this new development concerning Mitzi fitted in. Then Frances had an idea.

"Go and ring up Glen and ask him to dinner," she said. "He's all alone, with Rona away. And he might have some news."

Glen, however, would not come to dinner, having a patient to see after surgery, but threw out a casual invitation to me to drop round during the evening and drink a mug of ale. I accepted with alacrity.

5

Visiting a doctor on a friendly instead of a professional basis is always a haphazard affair. Barely had I been furnished with a chair in Glen's sitting room and the promised mug of ale, when the usual interruption came and he was summoned from the room to see an untimely patient.

Returning in a couple of minutes, he dropped a pile of books on my knees with a grin.

"Here's something to keep you occupied. I shall be about twenty minutes."

I looked at the titles. They were Taylor's *Medical*

Jurisprudence, the *Pharmaceutical Codex* and a couple of other standard works on the use of drugs in medicine. I opened the first, looked up "arsenic" in the index, and was at once engrossed.

When Glen came back, half an hour later, I was able to feel that I now knew as much about arsenic as he did.

"A good deal more than I knew a fortnight ago," he commented drily when I remarked as much. "Poisons don't enter into the ordinary G.P.'s work, and one soon forgets what one had to mug up about them. That's why so many poisoners get away with it."

I referred to one of the books. "Well, you saw the post-mortem. Was there any fatty degeneration of the liver?"

He grinned. "Certainly not extreme, no."

"Was there any running of the eyes during life?"

"No, there was not. And no rash, no thickening of the skin of the palms and soles, no falling out of the hair, no shingles, pains in the limbs, or muscular weakness. If there had been, I might have stood a chance of diagnosing arsenical poisoning—though I doubt if I should have even then. Who would ever have connected it with old John?"

"In other words," I pursued, "it was a case of acute arsenical poisoning and not chronic?"

He nodded. "Without any doubt. I hope the other chaps are managing to ram that into the heads of the police. It makes all the difference."

"Of course it does," I agreed out of my new knowledge. "It fixes the time within pretty narrow limits when the dose must have been taken. Why? Have the police other views?"

Glen snorted. "They've been trying to work on the theory that John was poisoned by repeated small doses; and all those twinges of indigestion he had, like the one that evening when we were all dining there, were the results of new doses. It's that confounded Cyril's idea, and he's managed to persuade the police it's the right one. It fits in with the fool theory about Angela, you see."

"The police are still convinced it was Angela?"

"Up to now they are. Let's hope Scotland Yard will show them a little sense."

"Scotland Yard?" I echoed.

"Yes. That's not for publication, but I believe the Chief Constable's insisted on calling them in since Mitzi got away from under the noses of our chaps."

I whistled. "That sounds like business. Glen . . . do you still believe it was murder?"

Glen shrugged his shoulders. "What else could it have been? John wasn't the chap to suicide himself in any case, and certainly not without the usual note to the coroner."

"There's always accident," I said carefully. "By the way, what's your idea of the time when the fatal dose must have been swallowed?"

"Well, as near as one can judge, sometime in the middle of the morning. Between 11 A.M. and twelve probably covers it."

"Almost simultaneously with his taking the treble dose of your medicine," I said in a tone that I hoped sounded easy. "I suppose you didn't put any arsenic in that, by mistake for soda bicarb, did you?"

Glen laughed. "It's the sort of mistake any doctor might make, isn't it? But it's funny you should say that, because believe it or not but the police have got some sort of bee in their bonnets about that medicine. Apparently it was thrown away after John died, and they can't find it. Timms was here this morning, asking me all sorts of damn fool questions about where I kept my arsenic and so on. I'm afraid I put the old chap's back up by laughing at the idea."

"Very funny," I said, and reflected that I should be able to tell Frances that, whatever suspicions we might share, they certainly had never occurred to Glen himself. Indeed, so lightly had he taken my tentative hint that

I was almost convinced myself for the moment that the medicine must be as innocent as Glen obviously believed it to be.

Glen refilled our mugs with the excellent brown ale which he always kept in cask in his cellar.

"By the way," he said, "look out for some fun to-morrow."

I pricked up my ears. "At the inquest?"

"Yes. I understand the police have one or two things up their sleeves which are expected to cause some small stir."

"What things?"

"I've no idea. But as the road signs say, I have been warned."

CHAPTER VII

All About Arsenic

1

THE inquest was held in the village schoolroom. It opened at eleven o'clock, and before half-past nine a crowd had gathered round the building through which Frances and I and the other witnesses had to push our way by force. I believe not a few enterprising persons had actually run excursions from Torminster and other parts of the neighbourhood, and I heard afterwards that the trains from London had been unprecedentedly crowded.

The arrangements made inside by the police were primitive but adequate. A couple of tables and some half-dozen chairs at one end of the room were provided for the Coroner, the Chief Constable, Superintendent Timms, a certain Mr. Archibald Bellew who (as we learned in feverish whispers) was to watch the proceedings on behalf of Angela, another barrister who was to watch them for the Treasury, and Angela's solicitor. School forms along one side of the room accommodated us witnesses, and on the other side tables and more forms supplemented by some rough benches had been set out for the large number of journalists who were expected.

Rona, arriving just after ourselves, found a place next to Frances and informed her that she had succeeded in persuading or bullying a certificate from the doctor excusing Angela, who really was not fit to attend.

We then waited a quarter of an hour, feeling exactly like the urchins whose places we had usurped. During the interval Glen came in and dropped with a bored air into the seat next to me, and Harold took up a position beyond Rona.

Harold, of course, had gossip to whisper.

"I suppose you know," he informed us, "that they're going all out for a verdict against Angela?"

We intimated that we did not know.

"Oh yes," he asserted. "Then they'd have to arrest her, you see. That's why they didn't press for her attendance. They don't want her weeping in the witness-box and getting the sympathy of the jury. You see."

"How do you *know* all these things, Harold?" Frances demanded sceptically.

Harold looked mysterious. "You'll see," he said.

In due course the Coroner appeared, various conferences took place between the different officials, all looking most important, and eleven local farmers and other worthies were sworn in as a jury. I was glad to see a good friend of mine, one Thomas Cullom, of Handacott Farm, from whom I bought most of my manure, appointed foreman. Cullom was a sensible man and not likely to be too amenable to pressure—if indeed there was any truth in Harold's suggestion.

I was, in point of fact, not too happy about the Coroner, a Torminster solicitor named Rigwell: an honest and conscientious little man, no doubt, but, like too many coroners, impressed by his own importance.

Frances suddenly nudged me.

"Look," she whispered. "Along there, next to Mr. Waterhouse. I believe that must be Maurice."

I glanced along the bench on which we were sitting. Beyond our own little group there was a gap. Then, almost level with the Coroner's table, was a trio of men: Cyril Waterhouse, a dapper little man in a black coat and pepper-and-salt trousers with "solicitor" written all over him, and a young man, rather stout, with a pale, fleshy face and fair hair, who might have been any age between twenty and thirty. His likeness to both John and Cyril was unmistakable. I agreed with Frances that it must be Maurice.

"What do you think of him?" she asked.

"Not a very pleasing specimen," I whispered back.

"I think he looks a dreadful youth. A sort of caricature of John's bulk combined with Cyril's sharpness. No wonder John couldn't stand him." She turned to Rona. "Rona, is that Maurice?"

Rona glanced along the bench. "Yes," she said. "That's Maurice."

"Hush," I whispered.

The Coroner was beginning his address. In pleasantly informal tones he warned the jury to disregard everything they had heard outside the court and pay attention to the evidence only. Then Cyril Waterhouse was called and gave formal evidence of identification.

"Now let me see, Mr. Waterhouse," said the Coroner chattily. "I believe I am right in saying that you are primarily responsible for the fact that we are holding this enquiry at all today?"

"That is so," agreed Waterhouse firmly.

"You sent a telegram from London, immediately on learning of your brother's death, to the sexton here instructing him not to fill in the grave?"

"Yes. Notification of my brother's death did not reach me till after his funeral. I then sent the telegram."

"And you agreed with your sister-in-law, Mrs. Waterhouse, that a post-mortem was advisable?"

"I persuaded my sister-in-law that a post-mortem was advisable," Waterhouse corrected grimly.

"She did not want one?"

"At first, no. I persuaded her."

I groaned inwardly. Waterhouse was evidently determined to show no mercy.

"Now, so far as anyone knew at that time, your brother's death was a natural one. It had been certified as such, and I think no one suspected anything to the contrary. What reason had you for wishing a post-mortem?"

"I was not satisfied," Cyril replied crisply. "I knew

my brother. He was a very healthy man. His death did not strike me as a natural one."

"You felt that even in London, before you had so much as learned all the circumstances?"

"I did. I also formed the suspicion that things were being hushed up in some way."

"Hushed up?"

"Concealed from me."

"You therefore determined on an investigation?"

"That is so."

The Coroner then went on to bring out the circumstances in which the will had been found, the witness's astonishment on learning the size of the sum for which his brother had been insured, and the subsequent search carried out by him that same evening and subsequently. Waterhouse deposed that certain articles found during the search had been handed over by him to the police. The Coroner, I was thankful to notice, did not ask him his reason for making the search.

Then came the first sensation of the day, with an account by Waterhouse of how the parlourmaid had handed over to him a certain letter which Mrs. Waterhouse had given her to post, and how he had opened and read it, afterwards giving it to the police. The Coroner, who, after all, was quite a decent fellow, would, I think, have been glad to avoid reading out the letter in open court, but so much importance was evidently attached to it by the police that he had no option but to lay it before the jury. I watched the reporters' pencils racing as they kept pace with the hurried tone in which the Coroner got over a plainly distasteful task.

That concluded Waterhouse's evidence, but Mr. Bellew received permission to put a question.

"Mr. Waterhouse, you have told us that you carried out an intensive search throughout the whole house for arsenic. Did you in point of fact find any arsenic?"

"No."

"Nothing remotely resembling arsenic?"

"So far as I know, no."

"Nor any other kind of poison?"

"No."

"Thank you."

We resettled ourselves on the hard benches, glancing at each other surreptitiously. Waterhouse's evidence, in spite of the little cross-examination at the tail, had been about as damaging for Angela as the man had evidently wished to make it.

Rookeway, the surgeon, was the next witness, a dark, clean-shaven, self-possessed man who clearly had plenty of experience of coroners' quests behind him.

With an occasional question from the Coroner he described the post-mortem at which he had officiated, and the appearance of the body, which he called that of "a healthy, well-nourished man." There was no disease in any of the organs sufficient to account for death, the only unusual appearances being the slight reddening of the duodenum and, in a lesser degree, the jejunum. The witness added further details and referred to the good state of preservation of the body, and he was then asked point-blank by the coroner whether the appearances which he had described would be consistent with death from epidemic diarrhœa. Mr. Rookeway replied that they would be perfectly consistent. Pressed further, he stated that at the post-mortem examination there was nothing at all, except possibly the preservation of the body, to indicate that death had not occurred from epidemic diarrhœa.

"We know in fact that death was not due to that cause," the coroner remarked, "but in view of certain doubts which may be felt, I think we ought to clear this question up once and for all. So far as post-mortem appearances go, then, you tell us that there is practically nothing to distinguish epidemic diarrhœa from arsenical poisoning. Now what about symptoms during life? Can they be distinguished?"

"That depends on whether the arsenical poisoning is chronic or acute," Mr. Rookeway replied with an air of patient helpfulness. "That is to say, whether the poisoning has been carried out over a long period by means of small, non-fatal doses, having a cumulatively fatal effect, or by means of one large fatal dose. But I think my distinguished colleague, Sir Francis Harbottle, is better qualified to describe these symptoms to you than I am." .

The Coroner agreed, put a few more questions to the witness as to what post-mortem appearances might have been expected in the case of death from chronic arsenical poisoning, established the fact that these were not present in this instance, and called Sir Frances Harbottle.

"Good for the old boy," whispered Glen to me out of the side of his mouth. "He's going to let me down lightly."

I nodded, equally relieved. I had been afraid that the Coroner might have conceived it as part of his duty to deal severely with Glen over his error in diagnosis, but he was evidently going almost out of his way to exonerate him.

We leaned forward to get a good look at the famous analytical chemist who had come down to Anneypenny (as it almost seemed) to entertain us.

His evidence was short and very much to the point: he had found arsenic in all the organs and tissues submitted to him for analysis. The amount in the whole body he estimated at 1·43 grains. This meant that a much larger amount must have been swallowed. He gave it as his opinion that death had resulted from acute arsenical poisoning.

"Yes," nodded the Coroner. "Now will you tell us, Sir Francis, taking the usual symptoms of acute arsenical poisoning, and assuming that a doctor is called in to attend a patient whom he already has reason to believe dyspeptic, and assuming, of course, that the doctor has no suspicion of arsenical poisoning, would there be anything in the symptoms to suggest to him that it was arsenical poisoning and not epidemic diarrhœa?"

"Nothing at all," pronounced the witness. "The symptoms are practically identical. It is impossible to diagnose acute arsenical poisoning with any certainty. The only way, if suspicion has been aroused, is to send a sample from the eliminations for analysis."

"But in the ordinary way it is not likely that suspicion would be aroused?"

"No."

Glen nudged me. "Notable example of solidarity of the medical profession," he whispered; but I could see that he was pleased.

The Coroner's next questions were to ascertain the time which might be expected to elapse between the swallowing of the fatal dose and the appearance of the first symptoms. As to that, the witness would only give approximate figures. Nausea and some pain might be expected in anything between an hour or two hours, though it might be longer; vomiting would follow shortly afterwards; more pronounced symptoms would not appear for some hours after that. Death might ensue on the third day, but not earlier.

"I see. That sounds as if it would not be easy, even by working backwards, to fix the exact time of swallowing the dose?"

"It is impossible to fix the time exactly; the nearest one could get to it is with a half-hour's margin either way. That is, assuming that the time of the appearance of the first symptoms is known. If the patient did not mention these and one has to work back from the major symptoms, the margin of error, of course, is greater—at least an hour either way, giving a period of two hours in all."

The Coroner kept the great man another ten minutes, explaining the difference in symptoms between chronic and acute arsenical poisoning and such matters, and was able to establish beyond doubt that this could not have been a case of chronic poisoning and that in consequence the twinges from which John had suffered must have been due to indigestion alone and could not possibly have been caused by arsenic.

"Let's hope that knocks out friend Cyril's theory once and for all," muttered Glen to me.

Glen himself was the next witness.

The Coroner in a friendly way proceeded to take him through John's illness and the treatment he had prescribed. Glen admitted quite frankly that he had not at first regarded the case as a serious one; right up to the end he had not expected the patient to die, indeed had believed that his condition was improving; he had attributed death to syncope, or heart failure, following too great a strain. Epidemic diarrhœa had been fairly prevalent in the district that summer; it was sometimes ignorantly known as "English cholera," and was by no means always fatal; the witness had noticed no difference at all between the symptoms in the present case and those in the cases which he had been treating of epidemic diarrhœa. The treatment he had prescribed had been at first a combination of bismuth and morphia, the bismuth in ten-grain doses to stop the sickness and five-minim doses of morphia to soothe the pain. On the second day the violence of the symptoms had abated somewhat, and an effervescing mixture was in consequence prescribed consisting of citrate of potash and bicarbonate of soda. On the last day a bismuth-and-chalk mixture was administered. By that time the patient was in a decidedly weak state, but the witness had not considered his condition critical. On the last occasion when he saw him, the patient's temperature was 99°. It had been once nearly up to 101° but for the most part had been only just above normal. Death had ensued quickly, after a short coma.

"Thank you, Doctor Brougham," said the Coroner. "Yes, that is quite clear. And now we come to the time at which the poison must have been swallowed. You will understand, of course, how important it is for us to fix this within as narrow limits as possible. From your knowledge of the case, have you formed any opinion on this point?"

"It's difficult to say, of course, but my opinion is that the poison must have been swallowed sometime between 11 A.M. and midday on the day when the illness first occurred."

"On the third of September," nodded the coroner. "Yes. You can't put it within narrower limits than that?"

"No; and it's possible those may be too narrow."

"On what do you base those limits, Doctor Brougham?"

"On the times at which Mr. Waterhouse complained of the various symptoms, and the degree of their intensity."

"Quite so. Mr. Waterhouse gave you a full account of his symptoms? Perhaps you will tell us what he said?"

"He said he had a slight pain shortly before lunch and felt a disinclination to take any food. He did eat a moderate lunch, however, and felt no discomfort during the meal; but was sick about half an hour after it, with more severe pain in the stomach. The pain passed off but recurred at intervals during the afternoon. Just before teatime the symptoms became more pronounced, and of such violence as to alarm the household. I understand that Mr. Waterhouse himself did not wish to send for me, assuming that his illness was the same as that for which I had already begun to treat him, but Mrs. Waterhouse rang up my surgery. When she heard I was out, I believe she sent a message to Mrs. Sewell."

"Yes, yes. Now you say that you were already treating Mr. Waterhouse. What were you treating him for?"

"Gastric trouble. There had been a conversation a few days earlier in which Mr. Waterhouse had admitted to having some digestive trouble, and——"

"One minute. This conversation was a private one between you and Mr. Waterhouse?"

"No. It was after dinner one evening, and several people were present." Glen enumerated the party. "Mr. Waterhouse was a little reluctant to admit that there was anything wrong with his general health; he was very proud of it. I don't think he really believed in doctors, but the others pressed him to let me examine him, and in the end he agreed. We were all intimate friends, and the conversation was mostly a joking one."

"You had the opinion at that time that there was some digestive trouble?"

"I knew there was. I told him that evening that he probably had a gastric ulcer developing and ought to cut down his smoking and put himself on a diet."

"What was his reply to that?"

"He said he wouldn't take any medicine I sent him, and I think I told him that would be his responsibility. There was some mention of Christian Science. Mr. Waterhouse gave us to understand he didn't believe in medicine or drugs. He was maintaining that there was nothing really wrong with him. I told him he needed a holiday."

"In any case, as a result of that conversation you did in fact examine him?"

"Yes, a few days later. He was in pretty good condition for his age, and his heart seemed sound. I repeated my advice that he should give up smoking for three months, and told him I would make out a diet for him and send him round a bottle of medicine."

"Did he undertake to follow your advice?"

"Not he. He said he'd sooner have indigestion than go on a diet, and I needn't bother to make up any medicine for him because he'd only pour the filthy stuff down the sink."

The Coroner joined in the laughter which this answer produced.

"I told him I'd send round a nice-tasting medicine," Glen added, "and he'd have to pay for it whether he drank it or not. He said in that case perhaps he'd better drink it."

"In fact the whole thing was treated between you as a joke between old friends?"

"Yes."

"And you did send round a bottle of medicine?"

"The next morning, yes."

"That is, on the day he was taken ill. What did the medicine consist of?"

Glen explained that the medicine had been an ordinary sedative composed of bicarbonate of soda, bismuth oxicarbonate, mag. carb. pond., a trace of morphia, and aqua menth. pep., or in other words peppermint water.

"Did you make up this medicine yourself?" enquired the Coroner, so casually that I pricked up my ears.

"I did."

"That is your usual practice?"

"No, usually my sister does the dispensing for me. On this occasion she wanted to catch a train soon after breakfast, and as there were only three or four bottles of medicine to make up I told her I would do them."

"At what time did you make up this bottle?"

"Directly surgery was over, about ten o'clock."

"And the others at the same time?"

"Yes."

"They would have been made up, I understand, in accordance with the prescriptions which you enter in a book kept in the surgery for that purpose. Is that correct?"

"Perfectly. I have shown the police my prescription book, with the prescriptions entered for that day, including Mr. Waterhouse's."

"Quite so. You have had plenty of practice in dispensing medicines, Doctor Brougham?"

"Plenty."

"Of course. Still, there are one or two questions I must put to you in this connection, just as a matter of form. You have a supply of white arsenic in your surgery, I believe?"

"I have. The remains of an old lot belonging to my father. It hasn't been used for years."

"Where is that kept?"

"In the poison cupboard."

"Is the poison cupboard kept locked?"

"No."

"No?"

"No."

"But isn't it a regulation that the poison cupboard should be kept locked?"

"I think if you were to examine the poison cupboards of every doctor in this country at this moment, not one in a thousand would be locked."

"That seems to me a very sweeping statement," commented the coroner, not without severity, "and I sincerely hope it is not correct. At any rate you keep a poison book?"

"I do."

"Does the amount of arsenic which you now have in your surgery tally with the amount shown in the book?"

"No."

"No?"

"I seem to have half an ounce more than the book shows," Glen replied with an audible chuckle.

The Coroner did not smile. "How do you account for that?"

"I can't. Presumably a package of arsenic was added to the store at some time and not entered in the book, possibly by my father."

"When did you last check the arsenic entry?"

"I've never checked it before," Glen replied blandly. "I enter in the poison book any supplies I buy, and make a note when the supply is exhausted. I've never bought white arsenic nor used it, so there are no entries."

"Isn't that very haphazard?"

"I don't think so. I can hardly be expected to make an entry in the book every time I give a woman an injection of a hundredth of a grain of hyoscine, for instance. I'd be so busy making entries that I'd have no time to see any patients."

The friendliness of the Coroner's attitude had noticeably lessened. "Doctor Brougham," he said stiffly, "I am bound to consider the possibility that the arsenic which entered Mr. Waterhouse's body might have been somehow contained in the medicine which you dispensed and sent round to him. If the arrangements governing poisons in your surgery are as haphazard as you tell us, what precautions had you against such an error occurring?"

"Merely that neither my sister nor myself are congenital idiots," Glen replied with a slightly contemptuous smile, "and that it would be impossible to mistake a small jar in the poison cupboard for a large jar on the shelves at the other end of the surgery. The suggestion is absurd."

"I'm glad you're so sure," the Coroner replied drily. "Have you, as his medical attendant, any other theory as to how the arsenic may have been introduced into the body of the deceased?"

"None. That's the business of the police, not mine," Glen replied with airy composure. "I assume, though, that he took it in mistake for something else."

"Unfortunately there is no evidence on that point. Nevertheless what I am anxious to establish is that you are perfectly satisfied in your own mind that when that bottle of medicine left your surgery it could not by any possibility have contained arsenic—put in, let us say, in mistake for some other ingredient."

"I'm perfectly certain it didn't. It's out of the question."

"There was nothing in any of the prescriptions you made up that morning to cause you to get anything from the poison cupboard at all?"

"Nothing. I didn't go near it. I see you have my

prescription book there. You can see that the other prescriptions were just as innocuous as this one," Glen said with a little smile.

"Yes, yes. And so far as you can recall there was nothing in the slightest degree unusual in the making up of any of these prescriptions? I am sorry if I seem to be pressing you on this point, but you will understand that it is necessary to make as certain as is humanly possible."

"I quite understand," Glen said with a kindly air. "No, so far as I can recall there was nothing in the slightest degree unusual—except," he added with another little smile, "that the mag. carb. pond. jar was nearly empty, which was not like my sister's usual efficiency, and I had to refill it from the store cupboard."

"Ah!" The little coroner pounced on the point. "But I understand it was generally Miss Brougham who kept the jars full, not yourself. There is no possibility that you may have refilled the jar incorrectly?"

"From the poison cupboard instead of the store cupboard?" said Glen with an open grin. "No, I think not. If I had, half Anneypenny would have been dead by now. . . . Besides, I refilled it after I had made up this prescription, not before."

"I see. Then I think we may take it as fairly certain that when the bottle of medicine left your surgery, it contained nothing of a harmful nature. In point of fact, at what time did it leave?"

"The boy takes the bottles out for delivery as soon as they have been made up. On that day he would have taken out those four by about a quarter or twenty past ten."

"Yes, yes, I think there is some evidence that he delivered it at Mr. Waterhouse's door soon after half-past ten. The bottle was sealed?"

"I corked, wrapped and sealed it myself, and wrote Mr. Waterhouse's name on the wrapping paper."

"Exactly. Then if it arrived in that condition, it could obviously not have been tampered with on the way. . . . We shall perhaps be able to find out later," remarked the Coroner to the jury, "whether it was actually put into Mr. Waterhouse's hands in the same state. . . . Now I understand, Doctor Brougham, that since Mr. Waterhouse's death this bottle has not been seen. Have you any knowledge of what happened to it?"

"None. I can only tell you that it was not in his bedroom late on the evening of the third of September, because I looked round for it to give him a dose."

"Did you ask him what had become of it?"

"Yes, but only casually. He thought it was still in the room, but I couldn't find it."

"Very curious. Perhaps even significant. And certainly unfortunate. Very well, Doctor Brougham, I think that is all. Oh no. Did you ever discuss the question of the cremation of her husband's body with Mrs. Waterhouse?"

"I did."

"I believe she wished it to be cremated?"

"I don't think she minded either way. She asked me what I advised."

"And what did you advise?"

"I advised that it should be cremated, if this had been Mr. Waterhouse's own wish. However, in the end Mrs. Waterhouse decided against it."

"I see. Thank you, Doctor Brougham."

Glen strolled back to his seat.

"Thank God that's over," he muttered to me as he dropped back on to the hard bench.

Rona followed her brother to the witness stand.

Her evidence was on more stereotyped lines. She gave a brief account of John's illness and death, explained how it was that she came to be nursing him, went out of her way to emphasise the loving anxiety and distress of Angela whom she was now nursing in her turn, prostrate as she was over her husband's death (in actual fact I thought Rona rather overdid Angela's distress, in view of the letter which we had recently heard read out), and confirmed her brother's evidence concerning the surgery arrangements and how it had come about that he dispensed the bottle of medicine for Oswald's Gable instead of herself. Asked if she knew what had become of the bottle, she equally had no explanation for its disappearance and said she had not noticed it in the bedroom when she took charge there. I remarked that the Coroner asked her no questions about the rather drastic treatment which she had meted out to John before Glen arrived that evening, and deduced that she had not thought it necessary to say anything about that to the police. Privately I agreed with her. The police are apt to be fussy over such matters as the administration of hypodermic injections of morphia by unqualified persons; though no doubt they would have passed the stomach pump. Personally I would have felt less qualms at taking an injection from Rona than from many doctors; but if she wanted her unorthodoxy covered, I was quite prepared to help her do so.

Rona was able to assist to some extent in fixing the onset of John's illness by describing his condition when she arrived that evening. As she had come straight from the station and the five fifty-seven train from Torminster, the moment of her arrival could be fixed within a minute or two. This evidence went some way to confirm Glen's opinion that the fatal dose must have been swallowed in the middle of the morning.

The Coroner asked her one or two questions, framed so as to convey the impression that Angela had been anxious to have the body cremated but had been dissuaded. Rona, seizing on the innuendo rather than the actual question asked, took the opportunity to affirm bluntly that Angela had wished nothing of the sort; the question of cremation had only come up quite casually, and it was clear that Angela had not cared either way.

Rona had already been told she could stand down, when the Coroner called her back.

"Miss Brougham, did Mr. Waterhouse mention to you during the course of his illness that at some time in the middle of the morning of the third of September he swallowed, not a single dose of the medicine which your brother had sent him, but had drunk off half the contents of the bottle?"

"No," said Rona flatly.

She was dismissed and Glen recalled. The Coroner put exactly the same question to him.

"Yes," said Glen.

"Did he give any reason?"

"He said he had had an extra sharp attack of pain, and thought the medicine might relieve it."

"The bottle was clearly labelled with the correct instructions?"

"Oh yes: one tablespoonful to be taken every four hours."

"What did you say to Mr. Waterhouse when you learned what he had done?"

"I told him he was a darned fool and that it was lucky there was nothing in the medicine that could hurt him."

"You were not alarmed?"

"Certainly not. It could not have harmed him."

"That's all, thank you, Doctor Brougham."

A frightened small boy then deposed that he had delivered a wrapped bottle of medicine at Oswald's Gable at some time before eleven o'clock on the morning of the third of September, and opined that the time must have been nearer half-past ten than eleven.

Then came the moment to which I had not been looking forward in the least.

"Let me see. . . . Ah yes," said the coroner. "Mr. Douglas Sewell, please."

CHAPTER VIII

International Interlude

1

MY ordeal was, however, not to be just yet. Before I had reached the stand a feverish whispering had broken out among the great ones congregated round the Coroner's table, one of them leaned forward and whispered to the Coroner, and the result was an adjournment for lunch.

With the stiff faces of those who are unaccustomed to being stared at in public, we pushed our way through the crowd and made for home. Harold had to go the other way, but Glen and Rona walked with us as far as our turning.

"Well, my friend," remarked Rona when we were clear of the throng, "that was all very instructive. What do you think of British justice now?"

"British justice?"

"They're trying to pin this thing on an innocent woman."

"Oh, I see. Yes, I gather they're trying to convey to the jury that Angela put the poison in the medicine after it arrived at the house."

"Precisely. The only question is whether they'll succeed. What do you think of the chances, Glen?"

"Personally," said Glen, "I don't think they'll get the verdict they want. There are some good old scouts on the jury who liked John and wouldn't want to see his wife accused of his murder—whether they believe she did it or not. But I wouldn't like to bet on it."

"It depends on the other evidence—yours and Frances', for instance, Douglas."

"Rona," said Frances, "didn't John really ever say anything to you about having drunk off half the bottle?"

"Oh yes," said Rona calmly. "But I don't draw the

line at a bit of perjury to prevent a ghastly miscarriage of justice."

"I don't agree," Glen said rather defensively. "Best thing is to tell the truth and let them make what they can of it."

"I wonder," said Frances, and I knew she was thinking of the medicine bottle.

I said suddenly to Rona:

"You're quite certain Angela didn't do it. Well, I suppose we all are. But if she didn't, who did?"

"That's for the police to find out—if they can," said Rona. "Personally I'm not going to advance any theories, name any names, or indulge in any scandal. Once that sort of thing starts, there's no saying where it won't stop."

"My dear girl," said her brother, "do you imagine it hasn't started already?"

We had reached our turning, and stood for a moment at the corner.

"In any case," said Frances, "it's a question that will have to be answered. Or won't it?"

"I don't know." Rona looked troubled. "Don't you think the probability is that there's a good deal behind all this that we know nothing about?"

"Come on," said her brother. "I want my lunch."

After all, my ordeal was not a bad one.

Frances had somehow got separated from me as we re-entered the court; and before the proceedings began I saw her surrounded by a group which included Superintendent Timms, the Inspector, the Coroner, a tall, soldierly-looking man whom I recognised as the Chief Constable of the county, not long appointed, and various other officials. They seemed to be talking excitedly to her, and she to them, but I had no idea what it was all about. She took her place beside me just before I was called to the stand, looking very mysterious and important, but shook her head firmly to my whispered request for information.

Even to me, nervous as I was, the Coroner's questioning seemed almost perfunctory. I was asked to describe John's condition when I went to Oswald's Gable that evening, which I did to the best of my ability; and some questions were put to me concerning the conversation in the drawing room on the night we had all dined there. On this point I was able to confirm Glen's evidence, but to add little to it. I also confirmed Cyril Waterhouse's account of the finding of the will, and to this I managed to add a word or two indicating Angela's apparent indifference to its contents. And that was all. Not a word was put to me about the medicine bottle—to my great relief.

I returned to my seat, and Frances' name was called.

"Wish me luck," she whispered with a somewhat wry little smile as she went.

I followed her with my eyes. She looked very pretty, I thought, in her neat tweeds and a jaunty little hat with a tiny feather in it; but I could see she was nervous.

"Mrs. Sewell," the coroner addressed her in a tone of stern displeasure, "you have just made a communication of remarkable importance to the police. I must ask you to repeat it to the jury. Tell us, please, what happened before you returned home after being summoned by Mrs. Waterhouse after tea on the afternoon of the third of September."

I held my breath.

"On receiving Mrs. Waterhouse's message," Frances spoke out bravely, "my husband and I went at once to Oswald's Gable. He joined Mr. Waterhouse in the library, while I went upstairs to comfort Mrs. Waterhouse, who was much upset over her husband's sudden illness. I stayed with her till my husband sent for me to telephone to Doctor Brougham, which I did. When Miss Brougham arrived I went back to Mrs. Waterhouse and stayed with her except for short intervals till we left. Just before we left I went upstairs to say good-night to Mr. Waterhouse and say I hoped he would soon be better. I asked him if he had no idea what had made him ill, and he said he hadn't. He added jokingly that he thought it must have been the medicine Doctor Brougham had sent round, and said something about the remedy being worse than the disease. Mr. Waterhouse only said that jokingly, but I wondered whether there might be something in it; because, although Doctor Brougham is a very clever doctor, I knew he did not usually do his own dispensing, and I thought that he might have made some mistake, or mixed up the jars or something. So just in case anything like that had happened, I thought it would be a good thing to take it away from Mr. Waterhouse; and . . . well, I did. I didn't say anything to Doctor Brougham about having taken it, because I thought he would be hurt at the suggestion that there could be anything wrong with the medicine."

Frances stopped speaking, a little breathless but quite composed.

There was dead silence in the court-room. It was one of the worst moments of my life; but there was nothing I could do.

"Let us get this quite straight," said the Coroner. "You removed a bottle of medicine from Mr. Waterhouse's bedroom on the evening when he was first taken ill, the third of September, at approximately 9.10 P.M.; you kept that bottle in your possession without telling anyone that you had it, until you brought it with you here this afternoon; and you then handed it over in my presence to Superintendent Timms. Is that correct?"

"Perfectly correct."

"Superintendent, just show her the bottle, please. . . . Mrs. Sewell, you identify this bottle as the one you removed from Mr. Waterhouse's bedroom?"

"If it's the one I just gave the Superintendent, I do."

"Have you tampered with it in any way while it has been in your possession?"

"Certainly not."

"Not removed any of the contents? It's in exactly the same state as when you took possession of it?"

"Exactly the same."

The interrogation was broken off while the officials conferred again. There was some byplay with the bottle, which the Superintendent was holding very carefully in his handkerchief, and finally I could see him pouring some of its contents into a smaller bottle, which someone seemed to have brought for the purpose. This smaller bottle was then handed to Sir Francis Harbottle, who hurried out of court with it.

"Good God!" I heard Glen mutter with deep feeling while these operations were in progress. "She's a nice one, your wife is."

I had nothing to answer.

"He's going off to analyse it straight away," Harold whispered excitedly to Rona as the famous chemist disappeared through the door. He leaned across me. "What's the betting there's arsenic in it, Glen?"

"Ah, blah!" said Glen.

The Coroner was returning to business.

"And now, Mrs. Sewell," he said, "I must ask you to explain the reason for this extraordinary action. Withholding evidence is a serious matter. Very serious. What is your explanation?"

Frances smiled sweetly. "I'm so very sorry. I had no idea I was withholding evidence. As a matter of fact I'd forgotten all about the bottle in the upset and confusion over Mr. Waterhouse's death. Then when I heard you asking about it this morning, I remembered I still had it and thought the police might like it, so I brought it with me this afternoon and gave it to the Superintendent."

"Humph!" The Coroner stroked his chin and gazed

fixedly at her. As Frances showed no signs of wilting, he gave it up. "Well, I won't say anything more about the matter here, though no doubt you will be hearing something from other quarters. Now let me see . . ."

The rest of Frances' evidence was a distinct anti-climax. She merely had to corroborate what Glen and I had already told about the after-dinner conversation and the little attack of indigestion on John's part which had led up to it; but since it had now been so definitely stated that the poisoning must have been acute and not chronic, I could not see why any further importance need be attached to that episode.

The eyes of everyone in the room followed her back to her seat. I did my best to look as if I thought that nothing of importance had occurred, but I don't suppose anyone looked at me in any case. In fact I was so busy looking unconcerned that I quite failed to realise that Harold was not called next, as might have been expected.

"Eileen Pritchard," summoned the coroner.

A faint jog from Frances' elbow was followed by the whispered words: "Tell you about it afterwards." I nodded slightly and fixed my attention with a great show of interest on Angela's parlourmaid, almost unrecognisable in a neatly cut coat and skirt and smart hat which even I instantly recognised as something in which I had not long ago seen Angela herself.

Pritchard gave her evidence with an air of self-righteous importance. When the Coroner questioned her about the search of the house which she had helped Cyril Waterhouse to carry out, she gave us to understand that it had not been a matter of mere obedience to orders but the co-operation of two upright persons against an evildoer: for that Pritchard considered her mistress to be an evildoer was to be heard between every two words she uttered. I could have cheerfully smacked the girl for the smugness with which she identified each bottle and jar that was held up before her, and named the places from which they had been taken.

As for the intercepted letter, Pritchard plainly expected the thanks not merely of the court but of every decent person for her action. I was glad to notice that the Coroner dealt with her in a severely impersonal way, with no hint either of praise or blame.

Toward the end of her evidence Pritchard broke fresh ground.

It was important in a case of this nature, the Coroner had remarked, to try to trace the movements of the deceased as closely as possible before he was taken ill. He therefore put to the parlourmaid a series of questions designed to show just what John had done that morning ever since he got up. From Pritchard's replies a fairly clear idea could be gained, though, as the Coroner was the first to comment, there were gaps.

He had come down to breakfast as usual, then, at half-past eight and had it, again as usual, alone with Mitzi Bergmann. Angela always breakfasted in bed. Pritchard had served porridge, kippers, and eggs and bacon, with the ordinary coffee, toast and marmalade. So far as she saw from the state of the dishes afterwards, John had eaten a normal breakfast: that is to say, a fairly large one. Not having been in the room, she had no idea whether John and Mitzi had talked, but she thought it was Mr. Waterhouse's habit to read the newspaper at breakfast and not say much.

At about half-past nine, after his usual matutinal visit to his wife, Pritchard had seen him from her pantry cross the stable yard, presumably to visit the building operations which were taking place near there. Three men were employed on the building, a mason and two labourers. She had not seen Mr. Waterhouse come back into the house, but it had not been a nice sort of day, and he might have come back at any time. In any case, when the parcel post came not long after ten (pressed, she thought it would be about ten minutes past) and she took a package which had come by it into the library, Mr. Waterhouse was in there, reading his newspaper by the fire.

The Coroner made a pause here to ask a few questions about this package. In answer Pritchard described it as not very big and not very small. Pinned down, she thought it would be about eight inches long by three or four wide and deep.

"Well, I dare say you could have got a medicine bottle into it," she explained, evidently choosing the first example that came into her mind. (I glanced surreptitiously at Frances and saw that she was having the grace to blush.)

Pritchard did not wait while the package was unwrapped, and she had no idea what it contained. The wrapper had been in the wastepaper basket the next morning, but it had gone with all the other rubbish into the refuse destructor, and she had not had the curiosity to examine it—why should she? The Coroner did his best to prod her memory, and she gave a tentative opinion that the name and address had been written in ink and not typed as if it had come from a shop, and though neat enough the package had not that air of having been born a package and nothing else which a shop's packer is able to produce at will and no amateur can ever achieve.

"Well, probably it's of no importance," said the Coroner comfortably, having made quite certain that his witness could not even make a guess at what the package might have contained and had seen no object lying about later which might have come out of it. "But we have to consider everything."

After the incident of the package Pritchard had not seen her employer again until half-past twelve and had the idea that he had been out off and on during the morning. He had, however, certainly been in part of the time, for the bottle of medicine, which she had put on the hall table after taking it in from Dr. Brougham's boy at some time round about twenty minutes to eleven, had disappeared from it before half-past. She could not say at what time it had been taken from the hall, or by whom, but she did notice when passing through at about half-past eleven that the bottle had gone. Why had she not taken it into the library, like the postal package, seeing that it was addressed to Mr. Waterhouse? Because, explained Pritchard with an air of finality, she always took in things that came by post in the proper way, but other things she put on the hall table. She did not add why postal material was thus singled out for special treatment but clearly considered it proper that it should be so.

At half-past twelve, then, she had answered a ring from the library, and Mr. Waterhouse had asked her to bring him a glass of cider. How had Mr. Waterhouse appeared? Very queer. In what way queer? Well . . . *queer*—looked as if he had a pain—very quiet and subdued, sitting all huddled up in his chair. The Coroner, shrewdly suspecting that a too-vivid imagination was being called into play, ascertained that Mr. Waterhouse had made no reference to feeling queer and had said nothing beyond the request for the cider, and then gave up that line of enquiry.

Pritchard had next seen him when she served lunch. She admitted with reluctance that he seemed to have eaten a fairly normal meal. Miss Bergmann and Mrs. Waterhouse were both present at lunch, no one else. She had not seen Mr. Waterhouse again until she was called in to help Miss Brougham with him that evening. She had served tea as usual in the drawing room but had not seen Mr. Waterhouse there, and she had noticed afterwards that only two out of the three cups had been used.

That concluded her evidence.

The Coroner then adjusted his spectacles and looked exceedingly severe.

"It is much to be regretted," he said after a premonitory clearing of the throat, "that another witness who might have given valuable evidence concerning the deceased's movements on this day has seen fit to absent herself. I refer to Fräulein Bergmann. I understand that a subpœna was served upon her in the proper way, and I must take this opportunity to say that it is a very serious matter to fail to put in an appearance when one has been called as a witness, to this or any other court. I hope the authorities will deal suitably with this young woman should she ever set foot in this country again."

We all looked very solemn while we wondered what treatment could suitably meet such an offence: from the Coroner's tone, hanging seemed the least penalty Mitzi might expect.

Superintendent Timms leaned forward and whispered to the Coroner, who suddenly became human again with a jerk.

"Dear me, a most important question that I quite forgot to put to the last witness, yes. Miss—er—yes, Pritchard, will you take the stand again, please."

The question was whether, during the meals she had served that day, Pritchard had noticed if Mr. Waterhouse had been the only person to partake of any dish. Pritchard had not exactly noticed that but thought not, on the grounds that she would have certainly noticed if it had been so. Nor any drink? Yes, Mr. Waterhouse had been the only person to drink cider at lunch.

"Yes, and there is that glass he had in the library, at about half-past twelve. Let me see, Superintendent, I believe Sir Francis has—— Very well, Miss Pritchard, that is all, thank you. Yes, Superintendent . . ." The Coroner had a short whispered conversation with the police officials.

The Waterhouses' cook was the next witness: or rather, the late cook, for it soon appeared that the lady had been under notice to leave when John was first taken ill, and had in point of fact left the next day, causing Mitzi to scour Torminster in vain for a successor until Rona, with an aplomb that any other woman must almost reverence, had rung up a friend of hers in the neighbourhood who was leaving in a week's time to winter abroad and had calmly borrowed her cook then and there, under the plea of extreme urgency and serious illness. This story, the full details of which I did not hear until after the court had adjourned, was complete news to me, so modest over her achievement had Rona been.

The woman, who gave her name as Maria Pfeiffer and her nationality as Austrian, was an enormous creature, almost qualified to deputise for the fat lady in a penny show; never have I seen such a broad expanse of back view as she waddled to the stand.

"You were cook to Mrs. Waterhouse?" asked the Coroner after the preliminaries had been settled.

"I am perfect cook," responded the witness with a beaming smile.

"I beg your pardon?"

"I am perfect cook. Vairy good. Wiener Schnitzel—Apfel Torte—Bratkartoffeln—ah!" She kissed her pudgy fingers.

"Yes, yes. Er—you understand English?"

"I spik perfect. I am perfect cook," agreed the lady, who seemed to want to bring the latter point home.

"Yes." The Coroner looked a trifle harassed. "Now tell us, please. You were acting as cook to Mrs. Waterhouse at the time Mr. Waterhouse was taken ill?"

A frown appeared on the rubicund, full-moon face. "I not make him ill. I am perfect cook."

"No, no, of course not. Er—you were under notice to go at the time?"

"Notice? What is that, pliz?"

"You had been dismissed? You were leaving?"

"Of course I leave," agreed the cook indignantly. "I no stay in Chew house."

"Chew?" The Coroner looked helplessly at his attendant officials, who looked helplessly back at him. "Chew?"

"Mitzi Bergmann. She is Chew. I am Nazi," announced the witness proudly. "I Austrian Nazi."

"Yes, yes. But that has nothing to do with us. Did you——"

"Pritchard, she Chew also. I not stay with Chews."

"I'm quite sure Miss Pritchard is nothing of the sort," retorted the Coroner testily. "In any case, it does not matter now if she is. Will you kindly answer my question: you were under notice to go at the time Mr. Waterhouse was taken ill?"

"I tell Madam I not stay with Chews," responded the witness proudly. "I poosh her out of kitchen. I perfect cook." She looked round for applause.

The Coroner gave up that line and tried another. "Now listen carefully, please. Are you quite sure that on the day Mr. Waterhouse was taken ill nothing improper—that is to say, nothing that should not have been there—could have got into the food that you sent into the dining room?"

The witness appeared to consider this. Then she replied again with a beaming smile: "I cook vairy good. I perfect cook. Wiener Schnitzel—Apfel Torte—Bratkartoffeln—ah!"

The Coroner wiped his forehead.

"You see to the dishes that come out from the dining room?"

"Oah yaas."

"Could you tell from the appearance whether any dish had been partaken of by one person only?"

"One person onlee?" The witness pondered. Then she brightened. "I one person onlee. I eat all that from dining room comes. Ja wohl. Ich esse alles was aus Speisezimmer zurück kommt. Ich esse viel," she added with pride. "Sehr viel. Kolossal! Grossartig! Ach!"

The Coroner gave it up. "I think," he explained to the jury, "that the witness is telling us that she finishes anything that comes out from the dining room. That answers the question I put to her, and shows that nothing harmful—that is to say, of course, arsenic—could have inadvertently found its way into the food on the day Mr. Waterhouse was taken ill." He had one more try. "Do you remember whether you finished the dishes on the day Mr. Waterhouse was taken ill?" he asked the witness loudly.

She beamed on him. "I eat all," she said simply. "I perfect cook."

"That will do," said the Coroner.

Glen jogged my elbow. "Interesting case of arrested development," he murmured. "I should say she stopped short at the age of eight. But it might have been seven."

Frances jogged my other elbow. "What lies!" she whispered indignantly. "She couldn't cook a thing. Angela had awful trouble with her."

"Doesn't matter," I whispered back. "She ate."

"From the look of her," whispered Frances, "she'd eat the cat's dinner."

"She probably did," whispered Glen across me.

I caught the disapproving eye of Superintendent Timms, and guiltily hushed them.

There was some whispering going on among the officials round the Coroner, and I saw the latter nod to Mr. Bellew, who rose.

"One moment, please," said Mr. Bellew pleasantly to the witness, who had been about to leave the stand. "Can you tell me if Mrs. Waterhouse was in the kitchen the morning Mr. Waterhouse was taken ill—that is, the day before you left?"

"Bitte?" The cook looked puzzled.

"With the Court's permission, I'll repeat the question in German," said Mr. Bellew affably, and did so.

A flood of German answered him. Mr. Bellew put another question in the same language. Another flood greeted it.

"Come, come, Mr. Bellew," said the Coroner testily, "this is most irregular. We should have a properly qualified interpreter."

"I'll repeat the substance of the witness's remarks in the form of a question to her," soothed Mr. Bellew. He did not add that anyone could play old Harry with the rules of evidence in a mere Coroner's court, but his gentle smile implied it.

"Am I to understand that this is what you have been telling me?" he went on to the witness. "That on the morning Mr. Waterhouse was taken ill Mrs. Waterhouse came into the kitchen and herself prepared a . . . I'm sorry, my German isn't good enough for that. Can you tell us in English what Mrs. Waterhouse made?"

"A limonspong," replied the witness promptly.

"A . . . a . . . ?"

"A lemon sponge," supplied Rona in a clear voice.

"Ja wohl," nodded the witness vehemently. "A limonspong. Gewiss. I spik perfect English."

"Yes, a lemon sponge. For whom did you think she was making it?"

"She make for herself, *natürlich*."

"You understood her to be making it for herself. Now tell us, Maria: did you like Mrs. Waterhouse? Did you find her a *liebe Dame*?"

"Gar nicht!" shouted the witness, flushing to the point of apoplexy. "She not good lady. She bad lady."

"And why did you think Mrs. Waterhouse a bad lady?" asked Mr. Bellew blandly.

"She say I not can to cook. I! She say I must go. I poosh her out of kitchen. She is Chew. I perfect cook."

"That is all, thank you," observed Mr. Bellew gratefully to the Coroner.

But that gentleman had not received a legal training for nothing.

"Did you eat the remains of the lemon sponge when it came out of the dining room?" he asked the witness, slowly and distinctly.

"I eat?" repeated the witness with a virtuous air. "No, no. I not eat what should be for the night dinner.

Pritchard, she eat it. Pritchard vairy greedy, like all Chews."

The Coroner waved her away.

"I suppose we had better have Miss Pritchard back, since the point has been raised, though I really don't think it has any importance. Miss Pritchard! Ah, there you are. Yes, take the stand again, please. Miss Pritchard, you served a lemon sponge for lunch on the day in question?"

"I did," said Pritchard, breathing rapidly.

"Did any of it go out?"

"Pretty well all of it went out, sir."

"Ah! And did you finish it, in the kitchen?"

"Not me. It's a lie, sir. Maria, she ate the lot. She was like that. Eat us all out of house and home, she would. I never seen anyone so greedy in *my* life. And it's a lie to call me a Jew. I——"

"Miss Pritchard," interposed Mr. Bellew deftly, having received the Coroner's permission during these heated remarks. "Miss Pritchard, can you tell us who had any of the lemon sponge in the dining room?"

"Only Mr. Waterhouse, sir. It was his favourite dish. He always used to say no one could make it like Mrs. Waterhouse. But she never touched it. Didn't care for it herself."

"Miss Bergmann had none?"

"No, she left the table early. I remember now. It was something she had to do for Mrs. Waterhouse."

"But I thought you told the Coroner just now that there was no dish partaken of by one person alone."

"I—I forgot about the lemon sponge, sir," stammered the girl. "I forgot Miss Bergmann wasn't there when I served it."

"But you remember now?"

Mr. Bellew sat down with a significant look at the Coroner, who avoided it.

"Clarence Ventnor," he called.

Mr. Ventnor, a dapper, dry little stick of a man, agreed that he was the late Mr. John Waterhouse's legal representative and gave a business address in Bedford Row. He then proceeded, in a perfectly undramatic manner, to produce a dramatic moment even more surprising than that with which Frances had already startled us.

"Mr. Ventnor," the Coroner asked, "would you describe your late client as a wealthy man?"

Mr. Ventnor stroked his chin.

"At the time of his death," he replied precisely, "certainly not. He had been a wealthy man, but for the last few years he had been drawing on his capital freely—I might even say recklessly. At the time of his death he had very few investments left. He was, in fact, a comparatively poor man."

This bombshell, which left us all breathless with astonishment, appeared not to startle the Coroner.

"Poor enough at any rate," he pursued, "to keep up the heavy premiums on his life insurance policy only with difficulty?"

"So poor," corrected Mr. Ventnor, "as not to be able to keep them up at all."

We looked at each other uneasily. The inference was quite painfully obvious. What else, I wondered, had Mr. Ventnor to divulge?

CHAPTER IX

Scotland Yard Is Not So Dumb

1

THE Coroner continued placidly with his questions: so placidly that I knew he was acting, and indeed his occasional surreptitious glances at the busy Press tables gave him away.

"Do you know why Mr. Waterhouse had been drawing on his capital to this extent?"

"He had expensive hobbies and liked to gratify them. Mr. Waterhouse," added the solicitor with disapproval, "seemed incapable of distinguishing between capital and income. I considered it my duty to remonstrate with him over the way in which he drew on his capital for current expenses, but his reply was always the same: that he would be able to make more money when necessary. In the meantime, he pointed out, his wife was amply covered in the event of his death by his life insurance policy."

"But not if he were unable to keep up the premiums," commented the Coroner. "But we shall come to that in a minute. Did you agree that Mr. Waterhouse could make more money when needed?"

"I consider it doubtful whether anyone can make money at will," replied Mr. Ventnor drily. "In the case of Mr. Waterhouse it is my opinion that toward the end he had lost even the will."

"Can you explain that, please?"

"Certainly. I saw Mr. Waterhouse a fortnight before his death, in my office. He seemed in low spirits and told me he wished to make an alteration in his testamentary dispositions. I understood that it was as a result of a communication made to him by his wife."

"He asked you to draw up a new will? What were his instructions?"

"He informed me that he intended to cut down the

amount of his life insurance. He had maintained a policy to bring in the very large sum of one hundred thousand pounds at death, in order that his wife should be left with an income approximately equivalent to the annual sum which they had been enjoying together, and thus suffer no diminution of the standard of her living by his death. Mr. Waterhouse intended to cut this down to one tenth of the amount. This sum was to be left to Mrs. Waterhouse outright; there were no stipulations about remarriage."

"Did Mr. Waterhouse give you any idea whether he had divulged this change of intention to any other person?"

"He did not. I have no ideas on the question."

"It would, however, not be too much to say that his death happened very opportunely for the principal beneficiary under his existing will?"

"I agree."

We had been listening with all our ears. When Mr. Bellew rose, there was not a sound to be heard.

"When was this new will to be signed, Mr. Ventnor?"

"I can't say. I had not completed the draft. Other questions might have arisen. Perhaps a fortnight, perhaps a month."

"Mr. Waterhouse never gave you the slightest idea that he had told his wife about this new will and the change in his life insurance?"

"He did not."

"As a matter of fact I believe the present policy has some months yet to run?"

"It expires on the twenty-third of May next."

"Exactly. You agreed with the suggestion, Mr. Ventnor, that Mr. Waterhouse's death happened very opportunely for the principal beneficiary under his old will—that is to say, without mincing matters, his wife. Did Mr. Waterhouse say anything to you about the possibility of his wife's marrying again, should she become free either through divorce or any other way?"

"He did."

"He appeared to you to expect such a thing?"

"One might put it as strongly as that, yes."

"But under his existing will if Mrs. Waterhouse remarries, she loses half her legacy of the insurance money?"

"That is so."

"That half goes, I believe, to Mr. Maurice Waterhouse. So would it not be equally fair to say that Mr. Waterhouse's death happened just as fortuitously for the secondary beneficiary under the old will, who would not have appeared in the new will at all, as it did for the principal beneficiary?"

"Undoubtedly that is so," agreed Mr. Ventnor courteously.

Mr. Bellew sat down; the Coroner nodded Mr. Ventnor away.

"The court will now adjourn," he said. "I am sorry we have not been able to conclude the proceedings in one day, but in the circumstances that has been impossible. We will meet again tomorrow morning, at ten-thirty sharp. All witnesses will please attend at that hour."

We bustled out of the little school-room in a bunch.

"The nasty work's begun," observed Glen to me—not, I am afraid, without relish.

"I noticed that the Coroner seemed to bend a formidable eye on that young man sitting on the bench behind us, when he said that bit about witnesses tomorrow morning," remarked Frances on my other side. "There he is—the young man, I mean: just ahead. Who is he? Do you know, Rona?"

"Yes," said Rona. "That is Philip Strangman."

2

"Well," said Glen, "that appears to sum the case up to date."

We had persuaded the Broughams to come back to a late tea with us; and since it was a Wednesday, and Glen had no surgery on that day, they were able to linger; though Rona had given Angela a promise that she would return to Oswald's Gable for dinner. I, at any rate, felt that it was almost a physical necessity to go over the evidence we had heard with other people whose understanding was possibly subtler than mine, and find out if they had read anything more into it than I had—though goodness knows I had read enough.

"Sums up the case?" I repeated.

"Yes." Glen lounged back in his chair and stretched his feet out to the fire. Needless to say he had occupied without hesitation the most comfortable chair in the room (mine). The women were seated on the couch opposite the fire, as is their incomprehensible way; a couch has always seemed to me quite the most uncomfortable of all seating arrangements, and why women prefer them to the soothing embrace of a well-designed armchair is a problem I have never been able to solve.

Frances had snatched a minute while taking her hat off upstairs to explain to me her action over the medicine bottle.

"Well, it's no good pretending," she said with an unwontedly shamefaced smile. "When I heard the Coroner asking all those questions about it, I got frightened. I didn't want to drag you into it, darling, so I told them you knew nothing about it. Glen really decided me, before lunch, when he said the best thing is to tell the truth and let them make what they like of it. After all, it was only him I was trying to shield, and if he feels that way, why shouldn't I?"

"I'm sure it was the best thing to do," I told her. "And damned sporting of you to shield me, too. I wouldn't have let you if I'd known."

Frances kissed me. "I knew you wouldn't, you silly old man. That's why I didn't let you know. Now let's go down and hear what Glen has to say about it."

Glen had a good deal to say, and he said it pithily. He

was not in the least grateful to Frances for trying to protect him, being convinced there was nothing to protect, rated her for suspecting him of being such a rotten doctor as to mix up arsenic with soda bicarbonate, and pointed out that she had done him only harm instead of good because while the bottle was still absent people had been able to suspect him. He told her that she was an interfering little busybody and what she needed was to be put across some grown-up person's knee and given six of the best with a hairbrush, to teach her to mind her own business. Frances expressed due contrition; admitted that she needed six of the best but wasn't going to take them from him, while I had not the moral stamina required by a successful wife-beater; and begged that the incident might now be considered closed. Glen agreed, with the reservation of the right to cite it in evidence against her should she ever be guilty of officiousness again; and the conversation then became more serious.

"I mean it sums up the case against Angela," Glen continued now. "And a pretty poor case it is. I don't see how the police can arrest her, unless this jury brings in murder against her; and they're not going to do that."

"You think not?" said Rona. "They might. You know what juries are."

"I know what Cullom is," retorted Glen. "And Hay, and Colwill, and Turner, and Oke, and all the rest of them. Not they. They've got more sense."

"Well, I hope you're right." said Rona.

"Why, look what's happening already," Glen amplified. "Dirt flying everywhere. Young Maurice Waterhouse shown to have a motive, that fellow Bellew suggesting the cook shoved arsenic in the limonspong."

"I shouldn't be at all surprised," put in Frances. "According to Angela the woman's quite mad, and hasn't the first idea about cooking."

"The country's flooded with Austrian cooks who haven't the first idea about cooking," Rona agreed gloomily. "Any Austrian who wants a nice trip to England, with three times as much to eat as she gets in her native country and four times as high wages, has only to call herself a cook and she can get into this country without question. There's an agency that specialises in getting over women like that and foisting them on unfortunate employers here at preposterous wages under the pretence that they're trained cooks. Why our Ministry of Labour doesn't insist on some kind of professional qualification I can't understand. I know of one case——"

"Now then, no politics," interrupted Glen. "Keep the party peaceful."

"It's not a case of politics. It's economics."

"All the worse," retorted Glen. "So you think it's another case of Eliza Fenning, do you, Frances?"

"Eliza Fenning?"

"Another cook, who was convicted of trying to polish off a whole family with arsenic. As a matter of fact she didn't even try, but they hanged her all right."

"No," I said. "It was Angela this woman had her grudge against. If you're right about the arrested mental development, she wouldn't have tried to kill John. And you heard her admit she thought Angela had been making the limonspong for herself alone. If it was she at all, she aimed at Angela and hit John."

Rona looked at me. "That's a very shrewd observation, my friend."

I began to feel a little pleased with myself.

"Not so shrewd," Glen hastened to deflate me. "That limonspong was finished up in the kitchen by Pritchard and Maria."

"But they both denied it," I protested feebly.

"Ah, blah," said Glen. "Give me another cup of tea, Frances."

Rona helped herself with an absent air from the plate of cakes I was holding out to her.

"Need it have been murder at all?" she said quietly.

"Oh," Frances cried impulsively, "I do hope it wasn't."

"There's no evidence that it was," I pointed out.

"And none that it wasn't. And not much either way," Glen observed. "Or too much. As for the Coroner trying to pin me down to a time for swallowing the stuff, it can't be done. There's evidence that John had a pain before lunch. But he'd been having pains for the last month. We don't know whether that one was natural or arsenical. And consequently we don't know whether he had the stuff before lunch or at it. It can't have been later, but between ourselves it might have been any time between 9 A.M. and one-thirty—that is, from the beginning of breakfast to the end of lunch."

"What about the mysterious package that came by the parcel post?" asked Frances.

"Samples of winter suitings," said Glen contemptuously.

"Samples of *what*?"

"Or wallboards, if you like. Or some patent new cement. Or asbestos batons. That's most likely. Why, the man must have been getting dozens of parcels of samples, every day."

Glen broke off to light a cigarette, which he waved at us largely.

"Look here, it's like this. Some fellow dies—any fellow, anywhere. If you ferret round enough, you'll find two or three people who are not sorry he's dead. It doesn't matter who you hit on. Take a point in anyone's life, any point, and you'll get the same result. And of course you'll get things, too, like a cook under notice, a parcel of samples by the morning post, a glass of cider when no one else in the house had a glass of cider, and so on and so forth. That's just ordinary life. But assume murder, and these things take on a totally different complexion. The people who for one reason or another aren't sorry the man's dead then have a *motive* for killing him; the parcel of samples (which John probably threw in the fire) becomes a sinister package, the cook puts arsenic in the limonspong, and the parlourmaid puts poison in the porridge."

"Well?" asked Frances.

"Well, my point is, it's all nonsense. Suppose John had swallowed arsenic by mistake and we all knew it, suppose he'd left a letter behind him to say he'd committed suicide: well, all these things would fall into their proper perspective—trifles, with no importance to them at all. And that's just what I maintain they are."

"And John's death?" asked Rona quietly.

"Either murder by some person or persons as yet unknown, for a reason that we have no idea of; or else accidental. Probably the latter, knowing John as we all do. Certainly not murder by Angela. Probably not suicide, but in view of what we heard this morning that can't be ruled out. In any case I believe you hit it on the head at lunch-time, Rona: there's a lot behind this death of John's that as yet we know nothing about. We may never know it. Probably we shan't."

"I don't like not knowing things," Frances complained.

Rona looked at her in her level, rather disconcerting way.

"I prefer that sometimes to knowing them," she said.

3

Harold was right, as usual: Scotland Yard had been called in. Two of them came to see me not ten minutes after Glen and Rona had left, and with only a bare quarter of an hour before dinner-time. Under pretence of summoning Frances, who was upstairs changing her frock, I sent a hurried message out to the kitchen to hold dinner back indefinitely. Scotland Yard or no Scotland Yard, domestic details come first.

The two men introduced themselves with the utmost courtesy. They gave me their names, but of course I never gathered them; I did realise, however, that one was a detective chief inspector and the other a detective sergeant.

They were quite unlike what I should have expected from Scotland Yard, and still more unlike the local police officers. The chief inspector was round-faced and gave an impression of tubbiness, though presumably his height must have conformed with official requirements. The sergeant was tall and slender and rather elegant. Both spoke in cultivated voices, but with a manner in which blandness seemed to have been carried too far, almost to the point of obsequiousness. Quite five minutes were wasted in their apologies for troubling me and my protestations that it was no trouble. Would they like to see my wife? Well, if it really wouldn't be too much inconvenience, they would be grateful for the opportunity. Would they like to see her alone, or with me? That was just as I, and she, preferred. Would they have a glass of sherry? Why, that was exceedingly kind, almost too kind of me, but they found it better not to drink on duty. But I was just going to have a glass of sherry myself, and it was awkward to drink alone. Oh well, in that case they would come to the rescue—but only just a drain in the bottom of the glass, really. Ha-ha. Yes, yes. Dear, dear.

Having been regaling myself lately with a selection of American detective stories from Evesham's library in Torminster, I marvelled. The bullying, hectoring, loud-mouthed, exceedingly unpleasant detective of American fiction would have considered these men almost imbecile in their softness; yet presumably they got results.

The interview lasted half an hour and was conducted in the same charming spirit throughout. Frances joined us in ten minutes or so, and the proceedings were more in the nature of an informal chat than a police interrogation. In point of fact Frances and I did chat, quite garrulously. A question from one or other of our visitors would produce not merely an answer, but a confirmation, an allusion, an anecdote, all manner of divergencies.

I think that secretly Frances and I felt that the two men, so far from being frightening, were so pleasant, and so much at sea, and so rather helpless, that we became doubly talkative in a kind of subconscious effort to help them out.

We chatted, therefore, of Angela (and the officers appeared quite to share our conviction that, whatever had happened, Angela was not guilty), of the conversation once more the last evening we had dined there (and the officers quite agreed that, since the poisoning had been proved to be acute and not chronic, John's spasms on that and similar occasions had no importance), of Glen as man and doctor (and the officers almost outdid us in their admiration of Glen in both capacities), of village life (and the officers, who surprisingly both turned out to come from rural homes, each regretted their change to urban surroundings), and of twenty other things. Only when they had already risen to go did the detective inspector, in the most courteous way possible, explode a small bombshell under my feet and with it blow up all my pitying assumptions of their helplessness and inefficiency.

"There's only one thing I don't understand," he said in an even more apologetic tone than before, "but no doubt you can explain it. I should have thought you would have mentioned to the local police officers the fact that Mr. Waterhouse was here on the morning of his death. We have to try to trace all his movements that morning, you know."

I stared at the man. "*Here*?" I repeated incredulously.

"Why, yes," apologised the chief inspector. He consulted a little red notebook. "He was in this house roughly between 11.20 and 11.45 A.M. He came by way of the meadow that divides his land from yours, and your pear orchard. Some nice trees you have there, too, sir, if I may say so."

"But—but I have no idea of this," I expostulated. "Are you sure?"

"Oh yes." The chief inspector was gently reproachful. "I think there can be no doubt about it."

"Did he see me?" asked Frances suddenly.

"Our information is that he did, madam. You received him, I believe, in this room. He had a glass of sherry with you, did he not?"

"Yes, he did. I remember now. At least I suppose it was that day. But it was such an ordinary thing for Mr. Waterhouse to stroll round here, especially in the mornings, that I'd forgotten all about it. Yes . . . that would have been the last time . . . Yes, it must have been that day. He came to see you about some winter wash for his fruit trees, Douglas," Frances added, turning to me. "At least that was the excuse. Really, he wanted to tell me about his pains and drink a glass of sherry."

"Yes, he'd been making some experiments in fruit-tree washes, in the intervals of building," I said mechanically. "He was always saying the standard washes were no good for the type of bug his trees bred. John had an experimental mind." I was talking quite at random, for the sake of talking. It was not like Frances to have forgotten such an important detail as that John had been actually in our house, to say nothing of having had a drink there, between the very hours which Glen had fixed as the probably fatal period. On the other hand it was inconceivable that she had deliberately concealed the fact.

"You didn't see Mr. Waterhouse that morning, then, sir?"

"No," I said slowly. "I remember the morning well. It was a wretched one, and I had to be out in the rain all the time."

"Yes, that fixes it," Frances said quickly. "John said he hadn't seen you on the way over, and it was too wet to go looking for you. He'd talk to you about the wash another time."

"I see," said the chief inspector. "Mr. Waterhouse's visit seemed to you quite unimportant, then, madam?"

"Oh, quite. He would come over like that two or three times a week."

"And he said nothing significant about his aches and pains? I think you said he discussed them?"

"Oh, nothing: except that he let me understand that he was rather more worried about his indigestion than he would have liked everyone to know. I think he used to tell me, or rather hint, things like that, because he knew I didn't talk. He just said he was really rather glad that we'd bullied him into consulting Glen professionally, and he supposed he'd have to go on a diet and all the rest of it like any other middle-aged crock. I laughed and told him he was just as vain about his health as a woman about her looks."

"I see. Well, there doesn't seem to be much in that, does there? It's very good of you and Mr. Sewell to have answered our questions so frankly. I'm afraid we've repaid you rather ill by keeping you from your dinner, so we won't detain you any longer."

I accompanied the officers out into the hall, and there was the usual pause by the front door.

"Expensive sort of hobby, Mr. Waterhouse's," remarked the chief inspector casually.

"You mean building? Yes, very," I agreed, my hand on the latch.

"A bit of a weakness of mine, if only I could afford it. What I should like to build would be one of those real old houses, with secret cupboards and concealed staircases and priest holes and all the rest. That must be real good fun, planning a place like that."

"Yes," I said perfunctorily, "I expect they got some fun out of it."

"Was that how it took Mr. Waterhouse, I wonder?"

"Not that I know of," I said in some surprise. "Why?"

"Oh, I was only trying to get some idea of his mind. But perhaps it takes a twisted one like mine to have a weakness for secret hiding places, ha-ha. Not that they wouldn't be useful, for storing valuables in when one was going away. I should have thought, from what I can gather of him, that might have appealed to Mr. Waterhouse."

"Well, he hardly ever went away."

"To stay away, you mean, sir? But I suppose he was in to Torminster often enough?"

"Oh yes. I think he used to run in there fairly often, in his car. He had a weakness for the cinema, I know."

"Did he indeed? Well, it all helps to make a picture. Good night then, sir, and thank you again."

I went back to the drawing room and poured myself out another glass of sherry.

"Well, I seem to have put my foot in it again," Frances said cheerfully. "Poor John! The last time he came, too. And I never thought about it again. Do you think they'll arrest me and not Angela after all?"

"I shouldn't be surprised," I said. "In any case I don't think I should do it again if I were you. But what I want to know is, how the deuce did those two know John had been here when I didn't even know it myself?"

"They're not so soft as they look," said Frances. "I began by feeling rather sorry for them. Now . . . I don't know . . . I think I'm a little frightened."

4

At a quarter to ten that evening the telephone bell rang. I answered it.

"Hullo!" said a voice. "That you, Douglas? Alec here. Are you and Frances alone?"

"Yes," I said wonderingly. "Why?"

"Could you give me a bed tonight?"

"Of course. Where are you?"

"Speaking from Torminster. Sorry, and all that, but it's a bit urgent. All right, I'll be with you in half an hour."

I went back to the sitting-room.

"Alec's just rung up from Torminster," I told Frances in the slightly guilty tone of every husband when one of his own relatives is to be entertained. A wife takes for granted that hers have a prior claim. "He wants a bed tonight. I said we could give him one."

"Well, really." Frances rose. "It's a little late, isn't it?"

"He said it was urgent."

"The maids will have gone to bed. All right. I shall have to see to it myself. The room isn't aired, but I can't help that."

"Of course not," I soothed. "He won't mind. What on earth can he want to see me about?"

"I should ask him," said Frances, and made her exit. The best of women are apt to turn a little acid before the unexpected and untimely guest. They seem to think that guests, even male guests, expect so much more than they do. I was quite sure Alec would not notice whether his bed was aired or not. So long as he had something to sleep on, and bacon and eggs for breakfast, he would be perfectly content.

Alec Jeans, I should explain, is a cousin of mine and an excellent fellow. He retired from the Indian army with the rank of major two or three years ago, found leisure very heavy on his hands, and in consequence managed to land some kind of a job at the War Office which occupies him adequately except when he wants to get away for a bit of shooting or fishing.

He drove up to the front door just half an hour later. I helped him put his car away in the garage, watched him instinctively stoop as usual as he came in at the front door, for he is an extremely tall man and many bumped foreheads have made him wary even of doors with six inches clearance for him, and took him into the sitting-room.

From Frances' greeting no one could have suspected her views as implied, but nobly not expressed, half an hour earlier. As a matter of fact Frances has rather a weak spot for Alec.

"Well, what brings you to these parts?" I asked when we were furnished with drinks and settled in our chairs.

"Oh, nothing much. Just mooching round the country, you know. Hope I didn't put you out, by the way, dropping in at this hour?"

"Not a bit," Frances said sweetly. "I like informality. It's unexpected, and that's always welcome in a humdrum life."

I said nothing. Alex had accompanied his explanation with an almost imperceptible wink at me. I interpreted this as a request to ask no questions, so asked none.

I had been right. Not till Frances had gone to bed and left us to ourselves did Alec say a word that was not frivolous. Then he grinned at me.

"Good for you. Not that Frances isn't safe as houses, but what the mind doesn't know the imagination can't worry over."

"It is something urgent, then?" I said.

"Well, yes, in a way. Look here, mind if I keep you up a bit late tonight?"

"Not in the least. What about?"

"You knew this chap Waterhouse pretty well, didn't you?"

"Very well."

"I thought so. In fact that's why I'm here. I want you to tell me everything about him that you can. And that's official."

"Official?" I repeated stupidly.

"That's right. I'm hot from headquarters. I told them one of the blokes in the case was a cousin of mine, and they sent me down right away."

"Headquarters? Do you mean Scotland Yard?"

"No, no. The War House."

"But what have they got to do with Waterhouse?"

"Well, strictly between ourselves, quite a bit. Waterhouse was doing a job of work for us, and the theory is that he got bumped off as a result. But it seems so darned unlikely that we can't believe it. I've been sent down to try to find out what I can."

A light slowly dawned on me. "Oh! You're Military Intelligence, of course. Yes, I believe John told me he was in the branch for a short time at the end of the war. But what's all this? Do you mean he was doing spy work of some sort?"

"No, no," said Alec disgustedly. "None of your cheap thrillers. He was just doing a bit of routine organisation work in this district. Nothing out of the ordinary. Dozens of chaps who were in the branch during the war still lend a hand. You'd be surprised if I told you some of their names. And in addition this chap Waterhouse had sent in a few darned useful reports when he was working out East. But nothing that anyone would want to bump him off for. Still, he had a German in the house, hadn't he? Girl called Bergmann?"

"Yes. But it's impossible that she could have had anything to do with his death. A most inoffensive, harmless, amiable creature."

"Is that so? Well, you may like to know that your inoffensive, amiable creature was smuggled out of this country by German agency, and semi-official at that; and what's more, they were in a deuce of a stew to get her out."

"But why?"

"That's what we want to know. You've no idea?"

"None. But that she didn't poison John I'm convinced."

"Um! This wife, now. Any chance of her having done it?"

"None," I said emphatically.

"Then who did? What's the local theory? What's your own idea?"

"There is no local theory. We're all flummoxed. My own idea is that he took the stuff himself, by accident; but don't ask me how, because I can't imagine."

"You may not be so far wrong, at that," said Alec

drily. "What about this girl of his in Torminster? Know anything about her?"

"What girl in Torminster?"

"You didn't know he kept a girl in Torminster? Good Lord, what's happened to the nose for scandal in rural England? I thought everyone here would know about her. Still, I believe she's harmless enough; or so Scotland Yard seems to think."

"They'd got on to her so soon?"

"Oh yes. Smart chaps, Wentworth and Daggers. By the way, it was sporting of that old chap Ventnor not to mention the legacy to her."

"There's a legacy? Yes, there would be. You could trust John to do the right thing."

"So I gather. In fact he did the right thing sometimes in a pretty big way."

Something in Alec's tone caught my attention. "What do you mean by that?" I asked.

He shook his head. "Not at liberty to say. But don't worry. You'll hear tomorrow."

"It's the resumed inquest tomorrow."

"It's the inquest I'm talking about. Don't drop a hint to anyone, Douglas," Alec grinned suddenly, "but there's going to be a shock or two tomorrow; and the biggest shock of all is coming to . . ."

"Whom?" I asked apprehensively.

"The Coroner," said Alec.

CHAPTER X

Shocks for the Coroner

1

I GOT to bed late that night. Alec kept me up talking till nearly 2 A.M.; and by the time we had finished he must have obtained a fairly clear picture of Waterhouse and his household. But beyond the interesting item that John had been engaged in some kind of mild work for the Intelligence Department, I received no information in return.

When we took our seats in court again on the next morning, therefore, I was feeling distinctly heavy in the head; and it was only hearing my own name loudly repeated that brought me to my senses. Startled, I jumped to my feet.

"Ah yes," the Coroner said to me. "Mr. Sewell, will you take the stand again, please. I think there are one or two points which you may be able to clear up for us while we are waiting for the report on the contents of the medicine. Yes." He rapidly turned over some papers in front of him.

Not any too happily, I made my way to the stand, wondering what was in store for me now.

"Let me see," said the Coroner pleasantly enough. "I think you told us you were a fruit farmer, Mr. Sewell. You make use of a number of different kinds of spray for your trees, of course?"

"I do."

"In some of these sprays, is arsenic employed?"

"Yes," I agreed, outwardly (I hoped) calm but inwardly a little apprehensive.

"You have arsenic in your possession, then?"

"Yes, but . . ."

"Well?"

"Not solid arsenic," I explained. "I mean, I don't make up my washes myself. I buy them ready mixed. That is to say, they contain other ingredients besides arsenic."

"Oh, quite so. What other ingredients?"

"Well, lime," I said, trying hard to remember what were the components of the ordinary arsenical washes. "And sulphur. And perhaps copper in some form or another."

"Nevertheless, these washes are highly poisonous?"

"Oh, certainly."

"And the poisonous agent would be the arsenic?"

"I suppose so. Yes."

"Had Mr. Waterhouse been carrying out any experiments with fruit-tree washes?"

"I believe he had. He had spoken to me about it. But . . ."

"Yes?"

"I don't know whether he had been experimenting with arsenical washes. I had gathered that it was the ordinary tar-oil distillate washes, for winter spraying."

"But it might have been arsenic, so far as you knew?"

"It might have been," I conceded.

"One other question, Mr. Sewell. Have you checked your supply of arsenical washes lately? That is, since you learned that Mr. Waterhouse had met his death from arsenical poisoning?"

"No."

"No?"

"I never connected the two ideas. In any case it would have been quite useless."

"How is that?"

"These washes are contained in large five-gallon drums. I have a fair idea of the amount left over when the spraying is finished but certainly not to within a dozen fatal doses."

"You mean the fatal dose would be very small in size?"

"I imagine so."

"Even the dregs left in an apparently empty drum might constitute a fatal dose?"

"Probably."

"What happens to your empty drums, Mr. Sewell?"

"Various things. Sometimes the tops are cut off and they are used as containers, sometimes they are thrown on the rubbish heap and left to rust."

"You take no special precautions with those which have contained arsenic?"

"No."

The Coroner sighed, as if wondering why the whole population of Anneypenny had not got itself poisoned before now with such carelessness about, and dismissed me.

Alec, who was sitting next to me, muttered something facetious as I sat down, and I grinned feebly.

The evidence of two men employed by Waterhouse on his building operations followed mine. These testified to having seen him at certain times during the fatal morning, and one of them explained for me the mysterious knowledge of the Scotland Yard men by adding that he had noticed Mr. Waterhouse disappearing, through the field which bordered on my pear orchard, at about a quarter past eleven.

The Coroner then put on an ultra-severe expression and announced that he believed Mrs. Sewell was in possession of certain important information which she had not divulged to the court yesterday.

Frances, recalled, agreed that Mr. Waterhouse had visited her on that morning, apologised for having forgotten the incident which she saw now ought to have been volunteered to the police, and recounted again what had happened. She spoke calmly and clearly, with all proper respect to the court, and gradually the Coroner's severity diminished. I thought he had finished with her when I saw a new arrival among the notabilities clustered round his table lean forward and begin to whisper to him.

Automatically I looked enquiringly at Harold, two or three places away.

Harold instantly obliged. "Represents the insurance company," he whispered. "They'll be wanting a verdict of suicide, naturally. Then they wouldn't be liable. I expect this chap wants the Coroner to bring out the possibility a bit more."

Alec nudged me. "Who's the know-all?"

I smiled at the comment on Harold's slightly self-important air, and mentioned his name.

Alec nodded. "Oh yes. I've heard of him." He turned his head and looked at Harold carefully.

The whispering at the Coroner's table ceased.

"Mrs. Sewell," said the Coroner impressively, "for all we know you may have been the last, or very nearly the last, person to have seen Mr. Waterhouse before he swallowed the fatal dose of arsenic, by some agency which we are here to determine. It is necessary for us to consider the possibility, among others, that Mr. Waterhouse died by his own hand; and therefore any evidence which you can give concerning his state of mind when he was with you is of great importance. Kindly tell us exactly how he seemed to you in this respect."

"Well, I don't know," Frances considered. "He seemed perfectly ordinary."

"Not dejected at all? From what you have just told us, did he not seem to you rather worried about his health?"

"Not worried, no. Perhaps he wasn't quite so cheerful as usual, but I certainly wouldn't have called him dejected."

"Would the word 'depressed' describe him?"

"Yes, I think it would."

"He said nothing to you about his matrimonial—h'm —embarrassments?"

"Not a word. I was taken completely by surprise yesterday."

"You had heard no hint of them from any other source?"

"None."

"Would it be putting it too high to say that you were Mrs. Waterhouse's closest confidante in Anneypenny?"

"I suppose I may have been, in Anneypenny. But certainly not outside it. Mrs. Waterhouse had her circle of closest friends elsewhere."

"Yes, yes. Quite so. Well, Mrs. Sewell, it is my duty to ask you this question: does anything in Mr. Waterhouse's manner that morning suggest itself to you now, in the light of later events, as indicating that he might have been intending to take his own life?"

"Nothing at all," affirmed Frances with emphasis.

The Coroner looked enquiringly at the insurance company's representative, who promptly jumped up.

"But he was depressed?"

"Oh yes, a little. Like we all get sometimes."

"We have already heard evidence that he was much depressed over the revelation made to him by his wife; had he seemed to you, during the last few weeks of his life, to be altogether less cheerful than formerly?"

Frances considered this. "Yes, I think on the whole he had been."

She was allowed to go.

The police evidence followed, in its usual stereotyped form. That is to say, the Superintendent described how he had been called in to the case, gave a very sketchy outline of the investigations he had made, enumerated the various scent bottles, medicine bottles, jars and tins which Cyril Waterhouse had handed over to him from Angela's bedroom and bathroom, and admitted that in spite of careful enquiries at all chemists' in our own and surrounding counties, no purchase of arsenic by either Mr. or Mrs. Waterhouse had been traced. Apart from this, neither police official added anything to our knowledge.

When that had been disposed of, I saw the Coroner looking at his watch.

"He's wondering when the analyst is going to turn up," Harold told us.

There was a short consultation with the Superintendent and the Home Office representative, and then the Coroner proceeded to read out a statement which had been taken on oath from Angela.

It was in the usual stilted phraseology, and I could not detect a single sentence which Angela might have spoken spontaneously. From its guarded tone I gathered that her solicitor had been present: an impression which Rona confirmed for me.

Briefly, Angela denied all knowledge of her husband's death, denied that she had ever purchased or obtained arsenic by any other means, and denied any knowledge of the intended alteration in the will. She knew her husband had been suffering from indigestion recently, but had not considered it serious; she knew nothing of the package which had arrived for him by post on the fatal morning. She had not urged that his body should be cremated, merely suggested it as she had understood that it was his own wish. She had informed him recently that she wished to be released from their marriage, and had told him frankly that he had cause for divorce. He had taken the information quite calmly, and she had received the impression that he would be just as pleased to end the marriage as herself: there was no longer any question of love, but both expected to remain good friends. He had made enquiries about her future financial provision, and on learning that it would not be particularly sound had offered a most generous allowance. She had gathered the idea that he too would probably marry again, though he had not definitely said this. In any case all had been most amicably arranged, and she was quite certain that it had been a relief rather than a cause for distress to her husband.

It was a good statement, from Angela's point of view, for it showed that she had no cause at all to wish her husband out of the way; though this, of course, depended entirely on the truth of her assertion that she knew nothing of his failing finances, nor of the altered will. There was nothing to disprove her contention of ignorance; though there was equally nothing to prove it.

The Coroner read it drily, and without comment.

The next witness was the young man, Philip Strangman.

A buzz of excitement went round the court as he took the stand. Here, we felt, was recompense for our own tribulations. The moment was undeniably dramatic.

Strangman was a black-avised young man, with what appeared to be a fixed scowl. He glowered at us and he glowered at the Coroner. One could see, in the impression he conveyed of sulky strength, how much he would have appealed to a neurotic like Angela.

The Coroner, full of the moral righteousness of his kind, glowered back.

"I will come to the point at once, Mr. Strangman. Is it correct that you and Mrs. Waterhouse were contemplating marriage, in the event of her being able to free herself from her marriage to Mr. Waterhouse?"

"It is," replied Strangman loudly.

"The fact that she was already married did not deter you?"

"It did not."

"You have perhaps little respect for the marriage tie?"

"When it is an unhappy one, I have none."

"H'm!" The Coroner stroked his chin. "You had the impression that Mrs. Waterhouse's marriage was an unhappy one?"

"I know it was."

"She told you so, perhaps?"

"She had no need to tell me anything. Anyone could see her marriage was a failure."

"Nevertheless she did tell you so too? Come, sir, I am asking you."

"She told me nothing definite," muttered the witness angrily.

"But you discussed her married life between you?"

"We may have done."

"And you showed sympathy with her unhappiness?"

"Naturally."

"You blamed Mr. Waterhouse?"

"I never met the man," returned the witness contemptuously.

"Young ass, young ass," murmured Alec at my side.

"I am not asking whether you ever met him," said the Coroner sternly. "I am asking if you considered Mr. Waterhouse responsible for his wife's unhappiness. Kindly answer the question."

"Of course he was responsible, insofar as he should never have married her. Otherwise I believe he tried to do his best."

"Did you feel any grudge against him for having made his wife unhappy by marrying her?"

"I don't know what you mean by 'grudge.'"

"I think you do, Mr. Strangman; and I see you are not willing to answer the question with a plain yes or no."

"Then you're wrong," said the witness rudely. "I'm quite willing to answer it, with a plain no!"

"I see. You heard Mrs. Waterhouse's statement read out just now. Do you agree with what she says concerning your joint plans?"

"Entirely."

"You and she had already stayed together in a hotel, as man and wife?"

"You know we had."

"The fact that she was another man's wife did not perturb you?"

"I refuse to answer that," retorted the witness loudly. "I'll answer only questions of fact. This isn't a court of morals."

"Kindly allow me to conduct the proceedings in my own court as I see fit," returned the Coroner, flushing with anger. "I take note of your refusal, and any conclusions which the jury may draw from it will be justified. Have you any objection, then, to telling us whether the *fact* of the disparity between your and Mrs. Waterhouse's ages did not weigh with you at all in the matter of this contemplated marriage?"

"There wasn't so much disparity as you seem to think," replied Strangman sulkily.

"Are you not a medical student?"

"One could become a medical student at your age, if one liked. That means nothing."

The Coroner was controlling himself with difficulty.

"How old are you?" he snapped.

"Twenty-eight."

"Then you had a career before you decided to practise medicine?"

"No."

"You are telling us that you have been a medical student all this time and have not yet succeeded in qualifying?"

"I am telling you nothing of the sort. You asked me if I had had a career before deciding to practise. I had not. The word 'career' denotes some sort of success. I had a succession of unsuccessful jobs. Then I inherited a small legacy and decided to lay it out in qualifying as a medical man. That is my history." Strangman spoke with a small, scornful smile. In proportion as he had succeeded in rousing the Coroner to wrath, the more had his own calmness grown. He struck me as a most irritating young man.

"I see. I see. Now as a medical student you no doubt have—— What is it? What is it?" broke off the Coroner testily.

A uniformed policeman, trying to engage his attention, was offering him what looked like a letter.

The Coroner snatched it and threw it on the table in front of him. "That sort of thing can wait."

"It's marked 'Very Urgent,' sir," I heard the policeman say in a low voice.

The Coroner made the noise usually spelt as "Tchah!" and turned back to his witness.

But another interruption came. Just before the policeman made his unwelcomed advance, I had seen Sir Francis Harbottle edge into court. Superintendent Timms had at once jumped up and hurried over to meet him, and the two now made their way to the Coroner's table. There was a short confabulation, and the Coroner waved Strangman off the stand. His place was at once taken there by the analyst.

"I am sure you are a very busy man," observed the Coroner to him in honeyed tones, no doubt for our benefit, "and we will therefore take your evidence at once, Sir Francis. Now I understand . . . yes, yes . . . you have made tests on certain samples supplied to you by the police here, which I believe were taken from some of the drains and traps at Oswald's Gable. Yes, here they are. Quite." He nodded toward an orderly row of jars which the Superintendent was engaged in laying out from a case which Sir Francis had brought with him. "Is that so?"

"It is."

"And have your tests shown any result?"

"In the samples labelled A, B, C, D, E, G, H, I, J and K," replied the analyst in a gentle voice, "I obtained nothing which might not have been expected to be present. In the sample labelled F I established the presence of minute traces of arsenic."

"Ah!" The Coroner did not disguise his interest, shared indeed by all of us. "The sample labelled F. Yes, let me see . . . That came from . . . yes, the bathroom basin . . . the bathroom, that is, shared by Mr. and Mrs. Waterhouse. Is that so, Superintendent? Yes. . . . Now, when you say 'minute' traces, Sir Francis, you mean, I take it, that there was not a measurable quantity of arsenic?"

"That is so. There was just enough to cloud the mirror in Marsh's test, but no more. That meant a very small quantity indeed."

SHOCKS FOR THE CORONER

"Quite so. But there can be no doubt at all that arsenic was present? The test is infallible?"

"Oh, quite."

"Yes. Now let me see. The jury must understand this exactly. No arsenic was found in . . . yes, in the trap from the basin in Mrs. Waterhouse's bedroom, the bath, the bidet in the bathroom, the W.C. next to the bathroom, the pantry sink, the scullery sink, the bath and basin on the second floor, the . . . yes, yes, well, I needn't go into all that. The point is that traces of arsenic were found only in the trap of the basin in the bathroom used, I think we may presume, exclusively by Mr. and Mrs. Waterhouse. . . . Now would you expect to find such traces in the ordinary way, Sir Francis, in the trap of any bathroom basin?"

"I should not."

"Their presence would surprise you?"

"Decidedly."

"H'm! The bathroom basin, yes. There seem to be a number of basins. Have you the plan there, Superintendent? Oh yes, I see it. There are basins in both bedrooms as well as the bathroom. No doubt the one in the bathroom would not be used so much, especially in the case of illness. . . . Supposing a concoction containing arsenic to have been poured into a basin in normal use, Sir Francis, how long would you expect traces of arsenic to remain in the trap?"

"Not very long. It would depend to some extent whether there was any turgid matter already in the trap. If that were the case, and the basin was not used for some hours after the arsenical compound had been poured away in it, one might expect the arsenic to impregnate the turgid matter and therefore remain considerably longer. If the trap were clean, a few more sluicings would wash all traces of the arsenic away."

"I quite understand. You have examined the matter from the trap. Would you describe it as turgid?"

"Yes, distinctly."

"Did its condition suggest to you that the basin had not been used very often?"

"I formed that opinion, yes."

"Did any other conclusions present themselves to you? Did you, for instance, form any conclusion from the mere presence of arsenic in the trap?"

"I don't quite understand."

"Well, did it suggest to you that the arsenic was probably swallowed by the deceased inside or outside the house?"

"That is perhaps a little outside my sphere, but the conclusion would be that it was swallowed inside the house, certainly."

"Perhaps I should have prefaced the question with another, to bring it more into your sphere. Were you able to form any opinion as to whether the arsenic in the trap was a part of the patient's eliminations, or whether it came from some other source such as the vehicle of administration?"

"I cannot pronounce definitely on that. I found no evidence of elimination, but that is by no means conclusive."

"Did you find traces of any other drugs in the residue?"

"No, none."

"But is that equally not conclusive that they could not have been there originally?"

"Exactly. Arsenic is a heavy substance. It would tend to sink further, and therefore remain longer, than other more soluble drugs."

"But taking it on a broad basis, your opinion is that the presence of arsenic in the trap, although with the qualifications you have mentioned, would appear to indicate that the fatal dose was swallowed inside and not outside the house?"

"For what it is worth, that is my opinion."

"And that would mean that this arsenic would be the surplus poured away after the administration?"

"In that event, yes."

"Quite so," agreed the Coroner, and directed a significant glance toward the jury. If, as Harold had affirmed, the authorities really wished to obtain a verdict against Angela, the analyst's evidence had certainly helped them.

"And now," said the Coroner, "we come to the medicine bottle."

A little flutter went round the court. I felt my heart give a funny little jump, and then there was a horrible void. As one does at such moments of intense dread, I concentrated my energies on looking outwardly impassive.

"You have now been able to make a test of the contents of the bottle, Sir Francis?"

"I have."

"What did you find?"

"I established the presence of sodium bicarbonate, bismuth oxicarbonate, magnesium carbonate pond., and a faint trace of morphia."

Sir Francis ended his sentence and looked blandly at the Coroner. There was dead silence in the little courtroom.

"Did you," said the Coroner, "find any arsenic present?"

Sir Francis, who could not have been unaware of the sensation of which he was the centre, appeared quite unconscious of it.

"No," he said. "None."

A curious little sighing breath went round the court.

"Arsenic was not present even in minute traces?" persisted the Coroner.

"There was no arsenic present at all."

"The medicine in fact contained nothing but the ingredients which we have already heard enumerated in the prescription?"

"That is so."

An irrepressible buzz broke out. I heard various, characteristic comments from those immediately surrounding me.

"Oh, thank goodness," Frances murmured.

"Well, I knew that already," Glen muttered in a tone of disgust. I really believe Glen had been the only completely indifferent person in court.

"That's a nasty smack for them," was Harold's observation.

I said nothing. Rona, equally characteristically, said nothing; but I noticed that she exchanged a small smile with her brother.

The Coroner was plainly disconcerted—so disconcerted, in fact, that he did not at once attempt to quell the buzz of comment and speculation. It was plain that the authorities had confidently counted on arsenic being found in the medicine. Evidently the test had been concluded only just in time to allow Sir Francis to reach the court, without having warned the police of his negative result.

There was another of the whispered conferences with which we were becoming so familiar. The Coroner seemed to realise that Sir Francis Harbottle was still on the witness stand, and looked at him in a puzzled way before saying:

"Oh—er—thank you, Sir Francis. I think that is all. You have nothing more to tell us? No. Then we won't keep you any longer."

I noticed with surprise that Alec had slipped away from his seat, had drawn Superintendent Timms out of the conference, and was speaking to him earnestly. The Superintendent looked even more astonished for a moment than I felt; he listened, nodded and went back to the Coroner. Alec returned to his seat beside me.

"What on earth . . . ?" I was beginning, when he hushed me, with a significant look towards the Coroner.

I saw that gentleman listen with an appearance of testiness to the Superintendent's whisper, and then take up and open the letter which all this time had been lying on the table in front of him. As he read it I saw his expression become fixed in almost incredulous amazement. He stared at it for some moments, then excitedly called the attention of the others to it. There was a positive hum from the little group. Evidently something quite unexpected had happened, and we were all agog to know what it was.

At last the Coroner waved the others back, and cleared his throat. The court instantly became silent.

"Gentlemen," said the Coroner, addressing the jury, "I have just received the most remarkable communication—a veritable voice from the tomb. It is a letter, addressed to me here, in this court, and I am assured that it was unmistakably written by the hand of Mr. John Waterhouse himself. I will read it to you at once."

CHAPTER XI

Secret Cupboards and Secret Ladies

1

"THE letter," continued the Coroner somewhat dubiously, appears to have been posted in London yesterday evening. London, S.W.—that is to say, the south-western district, though I really don't know what conclusions we may draw from that. Here are its contents.

"TO THE CORONER,
"*The Courthouse,*
"*Anneypenny, Dorset.*

"SIR: *The fact that this letter has been delivered to you indicates that an enquiry has been instituted into the cause of my death. To avert any possible misconception over this matter is the purpose of this letter.*

"*Dr. Brougham has told me that I am suffering from summer diarrhœa. That is not the case. I am suffering from arsenical poisoning. I could have enlightened Dr. Brougham, but after thinking the matter over fully I have decided not to do so, for reasons which appear to me adequate. In any case he could not help me; I know as much, and perhaps more, about arsenical poisoning and the treatment for it, and can do all that is necessary or useful. I do not at the moment expect to die: but if this letter is ever posted, it will mean that I was wrong.*

"*First I must say that the whole thing is entirely my own foolish fault. I have been experimenting lately with certain arsenical and other compounds as a means of destroying fruit-tree pests. My experiments have been made not on whole trees, in the form of washes, but on individual specimens of the pests at my desk. I have been keeping the various compounds, in bottles and jars, in a secret cupboard which I made in my library when I was carrying out some repairs there. Usually I return the poisons to that cupboard as soon as I have finished with them, but by an unfortunate mischance I must have carried a small bottle of arsenic in solution upstairs to my bathroom when I went up one day last week (I cannot remember which) to wash my hands. I do not know whether I put the bottle absent-mindedly into the cupboard myself, or whether I left it out and it was put in there later by a maid; but it certainly arrived there.*

"*Yesterday morning I had two or three sharp attacks of indigestion. I drank a large dose from a bottle of medicine which Dr. Brougham had sent round, hoping it would relieve me, but if anything it made me worse. I then remembered that I had in my possession an herbal infusion which had been given to me by a native in India; I had a short bout of indigestion when I was in that country, and I remembered that a dose or two of this infusion had relieved it very much. I thought I would try it again. The bathroom is not well lighted, and the medicine cupboard is in a rather dark corner. I remembered the bottle quite well: it was dark brown in colour. I saw a dark brown bottle in the cupboard, rather dusty, and assumed that it was the one. I was in considerable pain at the time, and did not examine the bottle as closely as I should have done before taking a dose of it. I realised, however, that the stuff tasted bitter and quite unlike my recollection of it, and I assumed that it had gone bad and poured the rest of it away down the basin. My subsequent illness I attributed to the gastric symptoms from which I had understood from Dr. Brougham that I am suffering. It was not till today that I began to realise what must have happened. I have visited the library and found that the bottle of arsenic is not in the secret cupboard, which seems proof of what I have done. I retrieved the empty bottle from the bathroom, where I had left it, and put it in the cupboard. The police can find it there. It has not been rinsed, and if it shows traces of arsenic this will be proof positive, since, if I were now present in your court, sir, I could swear that that is the bottle from which I drank.*

"*I have decided to say nothing about this arsenic to Dr. Brougham or to anyone else, for these reasons. I do not expect to die; and if I recover, I should regret having made an unnecessary fuss. If I do die, I have no doubt that Dr. Brougham will take it for granted that my death is due to the gastric trouble which he has diagnosed and will therefore issue a certificate in the usual way and no question will be raised. If, on the other hand, I divulge the presence of arsenic, and death, if it occurs, is known to be due to arsenical poisoning, the company with which my life is insured would be morally compelled to investigate the possibility of suicide.*

"*How could it be proved that I did not commit suicide? My life is insured for a very large sum. My finances, it will certainly be shown, are none too sound. I should not be there to explain that I was on the point of accepting an extremely lucrative offer in Indo-China to re-establish them, or that I had said nothing about this offer to anyone else, in accordance with my usual habit, in case the thing fell through at the last moment. No, the argument of my insurance company would be that I had purposely over-insured my life, with the deliberate intention of committing suicide when I could no longer pay the premiums; and I am not sure that a jury would not agree with them. In that case my wife would get practically nothing. I shall therefore keep the whole business to myself, in the confident expectation that there will be no need to have done anything else.*

"*That, sir, is the explanation of why you are now holding an inquest on me, and I shall be mightily obliged if you will read this statement of mine to the jury, if you are sitting with one: if not, I ask that it shall be read in open court.*

"*Yours very truly,*
"JOHN WATERHOUSE."

It may be imagined what effect the reading of this document had upon all of us, to say nothing of the jury. Speaking for myself, I can say that I was filled with an

SECRET CUPBOARDS AND SECRET LADIES

enormous relief, mingled with a curious feeling of disappointment; that the latter was unworthy I must admit, but I must equally confess to it. And what is more, I would swear that it was shared by everyone in the room. Much though we might deplore it, we could not help the feeling that somehow we had been cheated.

The Coroner, too, seemed to resent the lost opportunities of drama.

"As I said," he continued in a disapproving voice, "this letter appears to have been posted in London yesterday. How this could have occurred is not clear. I take it that the deceased sent the document under cover to a friend, with instructions to post it in certain circumstances. I have received no indication that the person who posted it is willing to come forward and assist justice, but I sincerely hope that he, or she, will realise that it is a bounden duty to do so. In the meantime——" He broke off to confer once more with those around him.

"In the meantime," he concluded, "the police will wish to make certain investigations. There is a postscriptum, which I have not thought necessary to read to you, giving exact indications where this—h'm!—secret cupboard is to be found. Also no doubt the police will wish to test the letter for fingerprints. I need scarcely remind you that we can take nothing for granted. The court is therefore adjourned until . . . yes, until today week. Everyone will attend then at the same time as this morning."

Hubbub, until then with difficulty restrained, at once broke out. It was amid a veritable surge of excitement that we struggled out of court. Everywhere people were giving their impressions of this new development to other persons who were less willing to receive than to give their own; reporters were elbowing sober citizens out of their way in frantic efforts to reach telephones before anyone else; the crowd outside was eagerly questioning everyone within reach.

"You'll lunch with us, of course," I said to Alec as we fought our way through the door, bearing Frances like some precious casket of jewels between us.

"No lunch for me today, my son," Alec grinned back. "Nor for you either—unless you'd rather not come to Oswald's Gable and have a look-see for that secret cupboard."

"You're going to do that without the police?" I asked.

"With the police," Alec corrected. "The Scotland Yard minions are waiting for us there at this minute. And so is a worthy architect, whom I had the foresight to appoint to meet me there at just about this time."

I looked at him. "You seem to have known a lot about what was in that letter of John's."

Alec cast a wary glance at Frances' back, now a safe distance ahead of us.

"Naturally," he said. "After all, I posted it."

2

Somehow we made our excuses to Frances, having seen her to our own door and exchanged with her expressions of relief that the bogey of the medicine bottle had, after all, proved to be but a bogey. Luckily Frances' mind seemed so occupied with this that we were able to evade any questions as to our immediate intentions—which I gathered Alec would not have been disposed to answer.

"Well, sorry to miss the sherry and all that, but I have to push off now," he said casually enough. "Little job of work, and I've pulled in Douglas to help me."

Frances looked at him vaguely from the doorway.

"Sherry? What sherry?"

"Oh, I don't know. Any sherry. The sherry you drink with your friends."

"Frances doesn't drink anything," I put in fatuously. "Surely you knew I had a teetotal wife, Alec."

"Oh yes, of course," Alec mumbled, abashed as one is on forgetting an ethical foible on the part of another. "Sorry, Frances. Well, come on, Douglas."

"We'll be back as soon as possible; keep us something to eat," I said to Frances, and she nodded acquiescence. Fortunately Frances never had been a woman to ask unwanted questions. Inclined to cherish her own reserves, she respected those of others without feeling it necessary to suspect them.

On the short way to the Waterhouse home I succeeded in getting the facts from Alec.

Briefly, Waterhouse's letter to the Coroner had reached the chief of the War Office Department, in which Alec was working, by post on the previous morning. It had been enclosed in an official letter to that same chief, envelope and letter both in Waterhouse's own writing, which had been posted in Torminster on the previous day. The chief, knowing that Alec had relatives in that part of the country and was more or less familiar with the lie of the land, had sent for him and given his instructions.

The covering letter Alec had not seen. It had been of a confidential nature, but Alec had gathered that Waterhouse, while not exactly denying the truth of what he had written for the Coroner's benefit, had hinted somewhat broadly that he himself was not altogether satisfied that the whole truth lay in the explanation as put forward to the Court; he had hinted, too, less broadly, that his poisoning might not inconceivably be a result of the activities which he had been undertaking on behalf of the department. This sounded quite incredible, but some indications had come his way that certain foreign agents regarded his work as a great deal more important than it really was. And he had added, Alec knew for a fact, a warning to the effect that Mitzi Bergmann had been meddling with his papers, and though he had no definite evidence against her, she had better be deported.

This letter, combined with the fact of Mitzi's hurried

removal from the country, had thrown the chief into something like panic. Alec had instructions to see the Scotland Yard men, call the pursuit off, somehow induce the Coroner to make sure that a verdict was returned in accordance with Waterhouse's official explanation, and above all make sure that no breath of a whisper got about concerning Waterhouse's connection with the department.

"I saw the Scotland Yard fellers in Torminster yesterday," Alec concluded. "No trouble there. I told them what Waterhouse had written to the Coroner, and explained more or less how I came to know, and luckily they were ready to accept it as the truth. We couldn't investigate till the letter had been delivered, of course, and I'd arranged with the post office to have it sent along so as to reach the Coroner in the middle of the proceedings. It looked better, and gave him time to get all his witnesses called and done with first. So we fixed to meet at the house, with the architect, at lunch-time today. The local men will be along, too, no doubt, so we ought to have a merry party."

Not that the party was merry. On the contrary, it was somewhat tense. The local police were half disgruntled at being cheated of their mystery murder and half thrilled at being caught up into issues so far outside their own experience. The two Scotland Yard men, gentle and genial as ever, seemed totally unexcited.

The help of the architect was not needed to locate the secret cupboard, for Waterhouse's instructions had been precise. It was, in fact, no more than a hinged piece of the skirting board in the library, which, when released by a secret bolt operated through a small hole in the flooring a couple of feet away, lifted up to disclose a cavity in the wall some two and a half feet long by a foot or more deep.

There were bottles there, right enough. The task was to find the right one. For the little cavity was crowded with bottles, small and large, white, blue, black, brown

SECRET CUPBOARDS AND SECRET LADIES

and green. At the sight even the detective inspector was moved to exclaim, in a respectful way, that the gentleman seemed to have collected enough poisons to wipe out half Dorsetshire. This was not, however, strictly accurate, for a closer examination revealed that most of the bottles contained stuff of the type which is fairly harmless when taken in small quantities and only noxious in inordinate doses.

I took Alec aside, smitten by a sudden inspiration. "Do you know what all that is?" I said to him. "I'd bet anything you like it's stuff that Waterhouse has removed from his wife from time to time. She's a fixed hypochondriac, you know, and enjoys nothing better than dosing herself with a new drug. By the look of that cupboard Waterhouse kept a stricter eye on her hobby than one would have expected, and just quietly took away from her anything he didn't approve of. It would be like him, too."

"Well, well," said Alec. "What things a feller will build a secret cupboard for."

(I may add that this inspiration of mine probably hit on the truth; for I managed to extract later from Angela the information that she had often missed bottles of medicine, tablets and the like, and could not imagine what had happened to them. It had been most mystifying and irksome, she added.)

While the examination of the bottles was in progress, with the architect wandering round and about the library, tapping the walls and plying a two-foot rule as if in hopes of discovering another hidey-hole, we had been joined by Sir Francis Harbottle himself, who in a diffident way which I found most attractive presented himself and asked if he could be of any help.

His offer was promptly accepted, and the result was speedy. In less than five minutes of sniffing and tasting he fixed upon a certain empty bottle.

"This contained arsenic," he said simply. "There are

more than a few drops still left at the bottom. Besides, you can see the deposit quite distinctly. I'll make an official analysis, of course; but I can tell you at once, gentlemen, with complete certainty, that there has been a strong solution of arsenic in this bottle." He held it up to the light and gazed at it earnestly. "Not very much. Perhaps not more than an inch. But quite definitely arsenic."

We all looked at each other.

"Well," said Superintendent Timms somewhat heavily, "that seems to clinch it."

No one contradicted him.

In point of fact no one had a chance, for a sharp yelp from our roaming architect attracted all attention to him.

"I say," he exclaimed, "I think I've found another cupboard."

We hurried over to him.

He seemed alarmed by our eagerness. "It may be nothing at all," he retracted hastily.

"Well, what is it?" asked Alec reasonably enough.

"I *think*," said the architect cautiously, "there may be one here." He was standing by the chimney breast, which projected some way into the room, leaving a long alcove on either side. At a spot about a foot above the mantelpiece on one side of the chimney projection the architect was tapping gently.

"The chimney would be drawn in here, you see," he explained. "There would be a hollow in any case behind this panelling, but from the sound . . ." He fiddled with the beading that bordered the panels. "Ah!" A whole panel swung out, and we all crowded round. Inside was a cupboard about nine inches deep and reaching to the ceiling, fitted with shelves and full of packages neatly tied up with white tape.

"Letters!" observed the Superintendent with satisfaction, taking out one of the packets and turning it over curiously.

With composure Alec removed it from him. "I think," he said firmly, "that with your permission, gentlemen, I had better take charge of these. Anything in your line will, of course, be handed over to you, but I can see at a glance that most of these concern us."

The Superintendent looked disappointed but did not venture to oppose the proposal. The Scotland Yard men nodded gravely.

Casually Alec dropped the package which he had taken from the Superintendent into his pocket and shut the cupboard door.

"I'll seal this," he said, and did so. "This room had better be locked. And in view of these two discoveries, no doubt you'll arrange to have the whole house thoroughly vetted. In fact Mr. Stares could begin the job at once."

There was a murmur of assent, and Alec nodded to me.

"We may as well get along then," he said.

We made our farewells and left.

"You expected another cupboard," I said as soon as we were in the drive. "That's why you brought the architect."

"Something like that," he agreed.

"And those letters didn't concern your department at all. They were letters from women."

He glanced at me. "Not so slow as you look, are you, Douglas?"

"Even I could see that. Good Lord, I should never have thought that John . . . Did you *know* he was that way?"

"We know a good deal about our own chaps," Alec replied cautiously. "But so far as our work was concerned, he was perfectly safe."

"So you forestalled the police and laid a claim to his very private correspondence. Why?"

"Bung the lot in the fire. Much better. No need to take up unnecessary scandal. No need to let the police in on a lot of personal secrets either."

"No," I said. "I'm grateful, Alec."

"Eh?"

"But I think you'd better hand over to me that packet you've got in your pocket."

"Eh?"

"I recognised the writing. Funny the Superintendent should have hit on that particular package, wasn't it?"

"I don't understand," said Alec.

"Oh yes, you do," I told him. "To put it plainly, I'd like to give them back to Frances. She may be worried over what's happened to them."

Alec handed me the package.

3

I gave the letters back to Frances after lunch. Alec had disappeared, a little precipitately. No doubt he feared a domestic upheaval; though with Frances and myself there was small danger of anything like that.

"These were found, with other packets of letters, in a secret cupboard in John's library," I told her. "No one has seen them, and I haven't undone the tape. I don't want to know anything about them."

She looked at the package curiously. "Fancy his keeping these!" She smiled. "How absurd of him."

"It's always absurd to keep letters," I said.

She looked at me quickly. "Douglas . . . you didn't think there was anything *wrong*, did you?"

"No," I said.

"They're just friendly notes, and . . ." She ruffled hastily through the bundle. "Yes, here's one postmarked Kirby Moorside. And one from Venice. And . . . oh, I remember writing this one, at a café in Territet. Darling old idiot he was to keep them. You know, I was always sorry for John."

"Were you?"

"Yes. I suppose it wasn't really Angela's fault, but

... well, what is the perfect wife? Thirty per cent. companion, thirty per cent. housewife, thirty per cent. mistress, and—what's that make?—oh yes, ten per cent. charming individual, I suppose. And Angela wasn't any of them. As a wife Angela was a hundred per cent. failure. I knew John went with other women."

"Did you?"

"He told me. In fact he asked if I thought it was a rotten trick on Angela. I said it wasn't: if Angela couldn't, or wouldn't, do her proper job, she could have no complaints. Poor old John! He took things a bit heavily, you know. We used to discuss ethics for hours. In fact I believe I deputised for the thirty per cent. companion part of Angela. Mitzi did most of the housewifery. As for these, poor old darling," Frances added, holding out the package to me, "you can read every word of them."

"Of course not," I said. "Naturally I believe you, absolutely."

In any case Frances might have known that I would not read the letters.

We never referred to them again.

4

It is strange, almost terrifying, how different each one of us is from our friends' conception of us. What is one to make of the charming stranger one has just met? Of one thing we may be certain: he is totally unlike the idea we formed of him—ludicrously unlike. Under that genial exterior is he a mean-spirited, vicious brute? What is his secret weakness? For, depend upon it, he has one, if not a dozen. What is his private hell?

I was beginning to learn more about John after his death than I had ever known during his life. Who would have imagined that bluff, paternal old dabbler in concrete and mortar was a shrewd agent of the Military Intelligence, a secret womaniser who kept a paid girl in Torminster?

What extraordinary episodes might not lurk in the past of such a man? And had the past ever risen up to take its revenge in the present?

It was the thought of that girl in Torminster that worried me. Heaven knows I am no Puritan, and it was not with the moral aspect that I was concerned. I just could not see John with a girl at all, let alone a paid one. What manner of woman was she? Was there real affection between them? Did she make up in some way for Angela's deficiencies? Normally I am not a curious man, but these questions irked me, for I had been fond of John myself once. In any case, excuse it or not, before Alec left Anneypenny that day I had got from him the girl's name and address, and the next time I was in Torminster, two days later, I called upon her.

What I hoped to gain I do not know. It was really no more than a rather impertinent inquisitiveness that took me to her door. But I have been glad since that I yielded to it.

Torminster is not a modern town, but already it has been invaded by a few tall, red brick blocks of flats. It was in one of these, on the Anneypenny side of the town, that Miss Lily Upcott lived. I rang the bell, noted the well-polished brass of the letter box and handle, and waited. The door was opened almost at once.

"Miss Upcott?" I said.

"That's right," was the cheerful response. "Want to see me? Come inside."

I followed her into the little sitting-room, made even smaller than it need have been by a superfluity of furniture but undeniably cosy. We sat down, and I had a good look at my hostess.

She was a large, tall, bonnily built woman, with one of those broad faces with prominent cheekbones that betoken at the same time a lowly origin and a good nature. She was older than I had expected: I put her age at twenty-nine or thirty.

"Well?" she said with an easy smile. "Is it business or a friendly call?" I must not give a false impression of her. There was no invitation in her smile. It was one of frank friendliness and nothing more.

"The latter," I said. "I've come really about—John."

The smile was wiped off her face. Her look became definitely hostile.

"What's that got to do with you?" she demanded. "If you're one of them Nosy Parkers of reporters, you can clear out now." She looked quite capable of throwing me out, too.

"No, no," I said hastily. "Nothing like that. It's simply that John was—well, I suppose in a way he was my closest friend. I just thought I'd call to make sure that you were quite all right and had—er—everything you needed."

Her face cleared instantly. The Cockney accent, which had become more pronounced with her anger, grew less noticeable again.

"Oh, I see. Nice of you. John told you about us, then? Well, he wouldn't have done that if he hadn't known he could trust you, so I can too."

She beamed at me. I felt a little mean over the deception, but did not contradict her assumption.

"Certainly you can trust me."

She leaned back in her chair and stretched her strong, magnificent body, smiling at me with an easy camaraderie which I liked. In five seconds, it seemed, she had adopted me as an old friend. It struck me that she was a born adopter. Some women are. She had probably adopted John.

"Let's talk about him," she said. "I've been fair starved for someone to tell me the news. Poisoned! Well, fancy that. Whoever could have wanted to poison John? Real upset I was when I heard about it. I was ever so fond of John."

That means, I thought, that you weren't in love with him. He certainly wasn't in love with you. That would have allowed you to respect and feel affection for each other in a perfectly calm way, without all those complications which love, that curse of mankind, must inevitably introduce: an ideal relationship.

We talked for a time of John's death, and I told her so much of its inner history as I judged it good for her to know. Then she began to reminisce about him, and I was content to listen.

"The police!" she exclaimed with great scorn, in answer to some casual remark of mine. "Oh yes, they've been here. But I didn't tell them anything. Not likely! I didn't even tell them I'd been in service at Oswald's Gable. Let them find it all out for themselves if they want to know."

"Indeed? I didn't know that either."

"Oh, didn't John tell you? Why, that's how I first knew him. Ever so sorry for him I was, too, with that good-for-nothing wife of his, always pretending to be ill and no more wrong with her than you or me. Oh yes, I saw through her all right. That's why she gave me my notice. Couldn't bear anyone to see through her, she couldn't. Upon my word, I wouldn't be surprised if she didn't poison him after all."

"Oh no; that's quite out of the question. . . . Er—John used to visit you here often?"

"He usually dropped in when he was in Torminster. Generally of a Thursday, and any other day convenient. He knew he'd always find me in of an afternoon."

"Why Thursdays, particularly?" I asked idly.

"That was the day I made my caramels," smiled the girl, not without pride. "Every Thursday morning, regular as clockwork. You wouldn't believe how John used to like them. I made them specially for him, of course. Used to take away a boxful every week, he did, and if he didn't come in of a Thursday afternoon I'd post him some, just so as he wouldn't be without. Regular sweet tooth he had. They're good, too, though I say it as shouldn't. Here, I've still got some left, though I haven't had the heart to make any more, not since . . . Oh well, it's no good crying, is it? Here, try one." While speaking she had jumped up, knocked over a small table, wiped her eyes, blown her nose, extracted a tin box from a drawer and was now offering me the contents.

I took one of the large, sugary lumps with appropriate thanks. It was certainly very good, for those who like such things: and I'll admit it was a surprise to me to learn that John did.

While I was still engaged in manœuvring it round my mouth, trying to find a place where it would fit, there was a ring at the bell. Up jumped the lady again, and bounced out to the front door, leaving the door of the room ajar. I could not help reflecting that she must have made a somewhat dynamic parlourmaid.

From where I was sitting I could see her talking at the door to a short, rather pimply young man. The talk was in the nature of an altercation. The young man seemed to want to come in, and Lily would not let him. She dealt with him firmly but very kindly, and from the sulky expression on the young man's face I gathered that he was used to being dealt with thus and knew that protest was useless. Finally the door was shut upon him, and Lily returned to me.

"That was Bert," she announced cheerfully.

"Bert?"

"That's right. We're getting married now. I wouldn't marry him before because it wouldn't have been fair to John. John needed me more. Bert's young and he could wait, and so I told him many a time when he was pestering me to give up John."

"Did John know about Bert?" I asked with secret amusement at this curious romance.

"Oh no. Not likely. It would have spoiled things for

him. John was so generous. He'd have wanted me to marry and settle down while I had the chance. It would have made him miserable to know I was keeping Bert off for his sake. Not but what the legacy won't come in useful now. John always said I ought to use it to get married on, and that's just what I'm going to do."

"You knew about the legacy, then?"

"Oh yes. That was part of the arrangement John made. Very generous, he was, and told me from the beginning he would make provision for me after he was gone. Oh dear: I can't hardly believe it even now. I miss him ever so."

"You've still got Bert," I ventured to point out.

"That's different. Not but what Bert isn't a nice young chap, and doing well at his job, too. Assistant to Lorder's, he is—you know, the big chemists in the High Street—and expects to be manager before he's done. Oh yes, regular ambitious, Bert is, and properly set on getting on. It's his afternoon off today; that's why he came round; to take me to the pictures."

"You shouldn't have sent him away, if it was on my account. I have to be off in a few minutes myself."

"Not till you've had a cup of tea," exclaimed Lily, jumping up once more. "Besides, I haven't talked nearly enough about John. Poor old John! And I hadn't seen him, not for a whole week before he was taken bad. Now you just sit there and look at the paper, and I'll have tea in a jiffy."

I sat.

When I finally left, an hour later, I carried away the impression of a singularly honest, good-natured, sincere soul. John had chosen wisely.

So, for that matter, had Bert.

CHAPTER XII

Revelation to a Fruit Farmer

1

THE case was over, the mystery at an end.

"Accidental death." Most disappointing to all the sensation-seekers in the daily press. The newspapers, knowing their public, dropped the thing like an unclean rag: their implied disgust was obvious. The report of the short proceedings which concluded the adjourned inquest was relegated to a very back page.

As a news item they deserved little more. Alec had evidently done his job well. The Coroner, with an air of childlike innocence, called his evidence. The statement made in Mr. Waterhouse's letter had been fully confirmed. A brown bottle, containing the remains of a strong solution of arsenic, had been found where he had written that it was; the bottle had been tested for fingerprints and shown those of Mr. Waterhouse alone; the police were satisfied, the Coroner was satisfied, everyone was satisfied. Accidental death.

The Coroner was not absolutely correct. Everyone was not satisfied. It is to be doubted, for instance, whether the insurance company was satisfied; but if not, it could no longer do anything about it. Cyril Waterhouse was definitely dissatisfied; but he too could do nothing. (Nothing had been said to him of the secret issues involved, which were indeed known in Anneypenny to me alone, and I, of course, was bound to secrecy.) He departed with his son, only just managing to restrain, behind thinly compressed lips, his obvious conviction that his sister-in-law was a murderess who had succeeded in bamboozling the law, the police and everyone except himself. I think none of us were sorry to see the last of the man.

Not even Cyril had been able to ignore his brother's

letter to the coroner; but he had fitted it ingeniously into his theory of Angela's guilt by supposing that John had written it to shield his wife, after discovering that Angela had poisoned him. According to Harold, this view was also held in amateur criminological circles in London; but it was certainly not current in Anneypenny. Not one of us had ever seriously believed that Angela could be guilty, and most of us were content to accept John's letter as literal fact; though I, knowing too much, could not be so easily satisfied.

There were others, knowing ones, who opined that John really had committed suicide after all, and his letter was a brilliant and successful effort to cover the fact. These people gave as his motive the discovery of Angela's infidelity. The fact that Angela and John, though fond enough of each other in a way, were certainly not in love was not allowed to weigh.

On the whole, however, there was singularly little talk, and within a week of the verdict the whole affair had passed more or less into history. Angela, making, exactly as Glen had foretold, a miraculous recovery, rose from her bed and departed unobtrusively for the South of France; and we all took it comfortably for granted that her black-avised lover was to join her there; though in point of fact, as I heard later, he did nothing of the sort, remaining more sensibly in London to work for his finals.

In our own little circle the topic of John's death became more or less taboo, and even Harold was induced to conform to the decencies in this respect. But one evening, when I happened to be alone with Glen, Frances having run Rona into Torminster to see a film, I raised the subject. I did so deliberately. Glen's attitude had puzzled me ever since we had heard John's letter read out in court. I could not make out whether he accepted John's explanation or not, and I rather wanted to know.

Glen will fence, if allowed, for hours; but he will usually

respond to a straight question. When we had our pipes well alight, and no word had been spoken for at least five minutes, I put the straight question to him.

"Glen," I said, "do you believe that letter of John's contained the truth about his death?"

Glen looked at me. "Yes," he said after a pause. "I suppose I do. At any rate it covers the facts. I shouldn't have thought him capable of such a gross bit of carelessness, but I've come to the conclusion John wasn't altogether the man we thought him."

"He certainly wasn't," I agreed. "But in what particular way?"

"Oh, almost any way you like. In fact anything we believed him to be, he was probably the opposite."

"That's pitching it rather strong," I demurred. "At any rate he was a good old sort."

"Oh yes. One of the best. To us."

"To us?"

"We never came up against him. I doubt if John was quite such a good sort to those who did."

"He always used to say he was incapable of ruthlessness."

Glen nodded. "Exactly. And we believed him. Haven't you ever noticed how much we take for granted that what a person says about himself is true? John was very fond of disclaiming certain qualities. Result, we automatically disclaimed them for him too. Mostly, I should say, we were wrong."

"John probably believed he was speaking the truth."

"Maybe. But few of us like speaking the exact truth about ourselves, except the mental exhibitionists."

"Well," I said a little irrelevantly, "I'm glad it wasn't murder."

"Um," said Glen.

There was another silence, which I broke.

"You were right about Angela, Glen. And I suppose this sudden improvement in health will be maintained?"

"Oh yes. Unless the next husband discovers a cure for cancer or does anything else calculated to attract admiring attention."

"I've never asked Rona. Did she have a terrible time with Angela that fortnight she was there?"

Glen grinned. "Pretty poor, I believe. But there were compensations."

"Angela keeps a comfortable house at any rate," I ruminated. "Queer about servants, isn't it? Angela can't have been a good mistress, but those self-centred, selfish, exacting women always seem to get good service; while really model employers, like Frances and me, who try to do the best we can for our maids and treat them with every possible consideration, get let down right and left."

"It's the slave mentality," Glen answered carelessly. "They like being treated rough. Be kind to them, and they despise you. That girl of Angela's—what was her name?—would never have stayed with Frances or Rona. She hated Angela, of course, but she respected her devastating selfishness and felt somehow morally compelled to work for it."

I laughed. "Pritchard, yes. An unpleasant type. Funny you should mention her. I had rather an amusing encounter with her this morning."

"Eh? I thought she'd been sacked—and left, according to Rona, in floods of penitent tears."

"Yes. She was coming back to get some of her things."

I told Glen of the incident.

I had been going down our lane to the village that morning when I passed a neatly dressed girl who looked somehow familiar. The girl smiled and said good morning, and I, feeling I ought to know her, stopped and asked vaguely how she was. She replied that she was quite well and asked politely after Mrs. Sewell. It was not till she volunteered the information that she was going into a new place in Torminster on Monday, and had come back to get some things she had left behind, that I recognised Pritchard.

At that I made to pass on, but the girl detained me.

"Oh, sir, perhaps you could give me some advice. There's something been worrying me, and I don't know what I ought to do about it."

I promised her my advice for what it was worth.

"It's about that cider, sir. You remember I said in my evidence that I took Mr. Waterhouse a glass of cider in to the library at about half-past twelve. Well, I've remembered since it must have been nearer twelve than half-past, because I know Mrs. Waterhouse wasn't in the kitchen when I fetched it, and she'd been there before making the lemon sponge; and I know she wasn't there when the baker called, which he does round about twelve every day, because that Maria asked me how many loaves——"

"Well," I said, cutting short this breathlessly delivered rigmarole, "what's the trouble in any case, Pritchard?"

"Why, sir, do you think I ought to go to the police and tell them I've thought about it and believe I must have made a mistake about the time I took in the cider? I wouldn't like to have to tell them I made another mistake, seeing I made one in my evidence already; but if you think it's important, sir . . ."

"I can't see that it's of the faintest importance," I told her, a little impatiently, for I was in a hurry. "The whole affair's over and settled; and in any case what would a few minutes matter one way or another?"

"Oh, thank you, sir. Then I won't bother about it. That's a weight off my mind."

I extricated myself from her unnecessary gratitude and went on my way.

"It all rather bears out what you were saying," I told Glen. "I was a bit fierce on one occasion with the girl, so it's to me she comes for advice and then overdoes the gratitude."

Glen was grinning again, broadly. "No doubt. But it's darned lucky for Angela she did make that mistake over the time."

"For Angela? Why?"

"You asked just now if Rona had a bad time with Angela. She did. It took all her efforts to dissuade Angela from throwing herself on the police and confessing to the murder of her husband, through that same glass of cider."

"*What?*"

"Well, perhaps you'd better keep this under your hat," said Glen, still grinning, "but there was a bit of a muddle over that glass of cider. Actually it was Angela's glass. She drinks a glass of cider every morning, because someone once told her cider was good for the kidneys. Professes to loathe the stuff, of course, but nobly sacrifices herself for her kidneys. John used to have a glass, too, round about eleven, and he generally drew them both and gave Angela hers. Well, apparently he did so as usual that morning, and it must have been before he strolled over to your place. Have you ever seen a woman with a glass of something she doesn't like? She'll carry it all round the place with her before she drinks it instead of getting it over quick and nasty like a man. Angela seems to have been accompanied by that glass of cider most of the morning. She had it with her in the drawing room when she wrote a letter; she had it with her in the kitchen when she was making that famous limonspong (the only dish, I gather, that Angela is able to make with her own white hands, and goodness knows how she can make that); and she carried it with her, so far as Rona could make out, into the larder to show it the limonspong being put on the shelf to set. But there she left it and, like Angela, forgot all about it.

"Then along comes Pritchard, with a haughty request to Maria for a glass of cider for the master. The cider barrel was kept in the larder, you see. Probably you know the place; it's the old dairy of the house and big enough for half-a-dozen larders. Pritchard wasn't allowed in the larder by Maria; so it was Maria who had to draw the cider when it was wanted. And naturally, being a thoroughly lazy slut and seeing a glass standing there already, she picked it up and gave it to Pritchard. John, of course, had no idea he was drinking stuff that had been drawn over an hour earlier, and history stops short of recording whether he found it a trifle flat."

"But what's all this got to do with Angela murdering him?" I asked, bewildered.

"Why, you see, Angela had dissolved in it some tabloid or other of her own. Killing two birds with one stone: the cider for the kidneys, and the tabloid for some other portion of her perfectly sound anatomy. When John was taken bad she instantly jumped to the conclusion that it was her stuff that had done it: for by that time she knew about the cider, having gone to look for it just before lunch and learning from Maria that it had gone into the library. It was a new concoction that she hadn't sampled before, and she still blames John's death on it, the ridiculous woman. However, I will say she made the greatest amends in her power. She threw all the rest of the tabloids down the W.C. That must have caused her a wrench."

"Then you don't know what it was?"

"Oh yes, I do. It was something young Strangman had made up for her. For the nerves. I've forgotten the details, but the stuff was perfectly harmless. Aloes and soap, probably. No, don't you see? It's all a case of wish fulfilment. John was in the limelight, through having died. When we thought he'd been murdered he was still more in the limelight, poor chap. There was only one way Angela could turn the limes on to herself and away from him, and that was by being put on trial for his murder. Consciously she professed to dread such a ghastly idea, but all the time her subconscious was egging her on to try to get into that dock."

"Good heavens," I said inadequately.

"Oh, it's not so rare as all that. In fact I believe it's the case with the majority of detected murderers. Certainly most of them thoroughly enjoy their trials. To be the centre of all that attention and the cause of all that fuss flatters their egoism no end. And what could be more attractive than to receive the attention and cause the fuss, and yet not have to do the unpleasant deed?"

"Then it's lucky Rona did manage to dissuade her," I said drily, "for I doubt very much whether our local police would have grasped the psychological complexities involved."

We pondered the strange ways of the human mind for a few minutes in silence, with the help of a mouthful of beer.

"Did John know there was nothing organically wrong with Angela?" I asked. "It was a complete surprise to me."

"I don't know," Glen said slowly. "I think on the whole that he believed she really was an invalid. We're all fairly suggestible, you see, and Angela certainly was a first-class suggester."

"On the other hand, that secret cupboard of his was half full of patent medicines and pills and things which I'm pretty sure he must have unobtrusively removed from Angela's possession."

"Oh yes, he thought she drugged herself far too freely, as of course she did. He spoke to me about it more than once, and asked if something couldn't be done on the lines of treatment for a real drug taker: you know, keeping the shot the same size to look at, but gradually diminishing the drug content. In fact," added Glen with a chuckle, "I believe he may have tried his hand at something of the kind himself, because he borrowed an old pill-making machine of mine not long ago, as *he* said, to put up in handy form some foul-tasting Eastern preparation he had by him which was supposed to give one a distaste for smoking. That was after I'd warned him that he must cut down his smoking really seriously. He didn't let on, and I didn't ask him, but I somehow had the idea at the time that he intended to knock out a few plain chalk tablets to substitute for Angela's usual muck. Anyhow, I just casually mentioned that plain chalk tablets were procurable from any of the big drug houses, and he jumped at the notion: just the thing, he said. Lucky I did, too, because he reported afterwards that he couldn't make the machine work—some vital part broken or something. I hadn't used it for ages."

"Yes," I said, "but what I don't understand is why Angela should have imagined that a perfectly harmless tablet could change itself into arsenic as soon as it got into the cider."

Glen laughed shortly. "Then you don't know much about egocentrics, my lad. They can imagine anything they darned well like—and persuade 'emselves it's true, too. Little anomalies like that wouldn't worry Angela. She wanted subconsciously to have fed John arsenic; the fact that she'd only fed him aloes and soap and limonspong didn't matter a bit; to suit her purpose (and mind you, everything exists only to suit an egocentric's purpose, laws of nature and all) the aloes and soap must possess the peculiar property of generating arsenic on contact with cider. My dear old chap, there's no difficulty about that; none at all."

I felt lazily combative. "Well, why shouldn't something and something else generate arsenic? What *is* arsenic? What does it come from? How do they get it? What do you know about it?"

"Arsenic is a metal," said Glen austerely.

"No doubt, but I suppose even metals come from somewhere. Can't anything *make* arsenic? One hears of arsenical wallpapers, arsenic in cooking utensils, arsenic in beer barrels. There seems to be a good deal of arsenic about the place in a small way. Where does it come from? What causes it?"

"Good Lord, I don't know. I'm no chemist. Here, if you really want to know, have a look through these, and let me read the paper in peace." Glen got up, collected three or four books from a window seat and dumped them in my lap. They were the same ones that he had shown me before. Probably they had been lying on the window seat ever since. The Broughams' is one of those comfortable houses where everything does not have to be tidied away out of reach the instant one has finished with it, or even before.

I turned through the pages, but there was little or no information on the thoroughly fundamental questions I had posed; the books, which were medical ones, were concerned only with the causes of arsenical poisoning, its symptoms and its treatment, with all of which I was becoming quite familiar. That is always the trouble with technical books, for the layman; they never begin early enough. I still do not know what arsenic is or where it comes from or anything about it except that it is a metal, which means little or nothing to me.

I pushed the books aside and looked at Glen, sprawled in his chair, all arms and long legs. Something put into my mind the village rumours coupling his name with Angela's. There could never have been a rumour with less foundation. Apart altogether from the existence of Philip Strangman, of whom, of course, Glen had never heard and when he did took him with complete calm, Glen seemed to have no feeling for Angela as a person beyond a mild dislike or at most a pitying contempt; though as a case he seemed to have found her a peach. No, there was nothing along that line.

Queer about John's arsenical washes. Why had I had the idea that he was experimenting only with the tar distillates? He could not have told me so, of course; there would have been no point; on the other hand, he had certainly said nothing about arsenic.

A pity (my mind flitted on) that no other secret cupboards

had been discovered. Those two were so interesting that goodness knew what might not have been concealed in a third. Some other totally unexpected aspect of John's unexpected hidden life.

What kind of a man had John really been? Glen was as puzzled as I was. But in my opinion he went too far in making out that John had been the exact opposite of everything he had suggested himself to us as being. He was a kindly, good-natured man, that at least was certain. His treatment of Angela alone showed that. It would take a kindly, good-natured man to put up with Angela in marriage for so many years, and then see to it that she came in for a fortune afterwards.

How unfairly as well as unevenly wealth is distributed, I mused. In all her life Angela had never done a thing to deserve a penny from anyone, while there were excellent and conscientious gentlefolk in the district—I could name a dozen at least—who hardly knew how to make both ends meet. The deliberate destruction of a type, and a fine type, too, with all its faults, by the politicians to gain the votes of urban mobs is a tragedy when one is living in the middle of it.

But about John . . . what did I really think?

It will be seen that I was meditating very much at haphazard, certainly with no idea of worrying to the roots of the problem of John's death. Indeed I was hardly conscious that it still was a problem to me. The revelation, when it came, was therefore all the more of a shock.

Idly I allowed to skim across the surface of my mind the various events, rumours and surprises of the last five or six weeks. It was the middle of November now; John had died early in September. Equally idly, I reviewed the course of this same evening and the different items of information which I had gleaned or of which I had been reminded.

Suddenly a chord of memory vibrated, most disconcertingly . . . a voice . . . something said, which had been called to my notice again tonight . . .

I sat up, thinking hard.

If it was true, if I was right, it could only mean . . .

But it was true. I was right. There was no possible doubt about that. Then . . .

I began to trace the thing out, step by step. Yes, each bit fell into place. The jigsaw was complete. It only remained to compare it with the picture on the box.

I sank back into my chair, feeling quite overwhelmed by the revelation which had come to me. I could only regard it as a revelation, though the vision was logical enough.

I must have made some exclamation, for Glen put down his paper and looked at me.

"Hullo," he said, "what's the matter with you? Seen a ghost or something? You're as white as a sheet."

"A ghost?" I said with a silly little laugh. "No, I don't think *that* ghost wanted to be seen. . . . What? No, I'm all right, thanks. Just a bit of—of indigestion."

I wonder what Glen would have done then if I had said: "The fact is I've just hit on the truth about John's death. I know how he died, why he died, how the arsenic got into him, what was the purpose of that letter to the coroner, and just how much truth there was in the letter and how little, and why. In fact I know all. And I wonder what I'd better do about it."

Instead I said:

"I think I'll go home."

At this point in the narrative all the evidence has been put before the reader, who is in exactly the position of Douglas Sewell. Readers of this book may like to amuse themselves by pausing at this point and endeavouring to answer the following questions:

1. *Who (or what) was responsible for John Waterhouse's death?*

2. *How did the arsenic find its way into John Waterhouse's body, and why? Give a concise outline of the story behind his death.*

3. *List as many deductions as you can draw from Douglas Sewell's narrative, and the clues to them.*

4. *Do you think there is a Dominant Clue in this story? If so, what is it?*

CHAPTER XIII

Unrepentant Sinner

1

THE next morning I was still wondering what to do about it.

To Frances, of course, I had said not a word. It was in any case not the kind of thing one wanted to talk about. But after an almost sleepless night, during which I had gone over my arguments again and again, I was even more convinced that my inspiration had been right and that I (and presumably I alone) knew the real truth about John's death. Moreover, now that my mind had begun to work along these lines, a dozen little points had recalled themselves to my memory, insignificant in themselves, no doubt, but making a formidable sum. Indeed when one added these to the one outstanding fact which had presented itself to me the previous evening in the light of a revelation, it was difficult to see how the truth had escaped so long.

One thing at least I could do, by way of eliminating a certain possibility; for naturally, during the night, in my reluctance to accept what was now obvious, I had cast about for alternatives.

The masons and labourers who had been employed by John were still at their work at Oswald's Gable, finishing off the job on which John had last been engaged. I strolled over to have a word with them immediately after breakfast.

"Mr. Green," I said when the morning's greetings had been exchanged and the weather prospects duly discussed. "Mr. Green, I want to ask you rather a curious question. Did Mr. Waterhouse ever give any of you caramels?"

Mr. Green pushed back his cap and grinned. "Well, it's funny you should ask that, sir, because he did. Many a time."

"Did he give you any the last day you saw him?"

"Well, sir," said Mr. Green, "it's funny you should ask me that, because he did. Three parts of a boxful."

"Not a whole boxful?"

"Well, I wouldn't say as it mightn't have been a whole boxful, because the top was stuffed with paper; but when you took the paper out there wasn't more than three parts of a boxful."

"Was it the sort of box you'd get in a shop?"

"Well, sir," said Mr. Green, "it's funny you should ask me that, because it wasn't. It was a cigarette box. One of them that holds a hundred."

"Did Mr. Waterhouse ever say why he gave you caramels?"

"Oh yes. He said his sister sent them to him, but he and Mrs. Waterhouse didn't like sweets, and he knew I'd a couple of youngsters at home—well, getting on for eighteen the eldest is now—and he thought they might like them. Very thoughtful gentleman, Mr. Waterhouse always was. We shall miss him properly in this village, sir."

So that was that, and the problem of the mysterious postal package solved at all events.

I was not a little pleased with my astuteness, following the conviction that John really could not have had a secret passion for caramels.

As for the main matter, it was not until after tea that I made up my mind what to do.

In Anneypenny whenever anyone had a trouble, a problem or a doubt, there was one person to whom it was invariably taken: Rona. From Rona one could expect calm, intelligent and sympathetic discussion and, in nine cases out of ten, a resolution of the doubt, a solution to the problem or a lightening of the trouble. To Rona accordingly I resolved to take my present worry.

And I had remembered, too, during the night, more than one little incident which had somehow suggested to me even at the time that she suspected, or perhaps even knew, more about John's death than the rest of us: a suggestion which, in the odd way that minds have, mine at the time had refused to accept, though afterwards it was ready to present me with the fully fledged conviction. Some kind of inhibition, I suppose, automatically rejecting the unwelcome guest.

I knew when I could be sure of catching Rona alone: between six and seven when Glen was in his surgery.

At two minutes past six, therefore, I was ringing the Broughams' doorbell—the one rather pointedly marked "Visitors."

2

Rona's finely drawn eyebrows rose.

"You . . . *what* did you say, Douglas?"

"I know the truth about John's death," I repeated. "And so, Rona," I added firmly, "do you."

After all, I have known Rona all my life. We are in a position to speak frankly.

Rona looked at me steadily. "What makes you think that, my friend?"

"A dozen things. I've known it all along, really, but my mind wouldn't realise it."

"Well?" said Rona after a pause. "Then what is the truth about John's death, which you know and I know?"

I contemplated the end of my cigarette. "He was killed," I said, "by a caramel impregnated with arsenic, sent him by the girl he kept in Torminster. She's a good sort. She didn't know what she was doing. The arsenic was introduced by a young man who wants to marry her, a chemist's assistant with easy access to arsenic or any other poison. She wouldn't marry him while John was alive. Moreover, John left her a substantial legacy. He had told her of it, and no doubt she would have discussed it with the young man. That would have weighed with him, you can see. He would have had no difficulty in introducing the arsenic into the caramel mixture. She made it at a fixed time every week. He had only to call on her in her flat, make a pretext to get her out of the room, or even only turn her back, and drop the arsenic into the mixture. So very simple, isn't it?"

Rona was staring at me. "And you believe that's how John was killed?"

"No, Rona," I smiled. "I don't. I was only pretending. Actually he was killed (wasn't he?) by Angela and Philip Strangman; though it's a doubt how far Angela really knew what she was doing when she dropped that tablet Strangman gave her into the cider. She had a grand story to account for it—how she meant to drink the cider herself and all the rest of it. And in the absence of any further tablets, what's to prove that this wasn't a perfectly innocent one? It was a good idea to say she'd thrown the rest of them away. What do you think, Rona? Was Angela Strangman's accomplice, or only his tool? You were with her. You had an opportunity of judging. Were those hysterical self-accusations afterwards genuine or faked?"

"You're imagining things, my friend," Rona said grimly. "Rather dangerously. I should stick to fruit farming if I were you. Angela's as innocent as you are. And so is Philip Strangman."

"I know." I smiled again. "I just wanted you to tell me so. But you do know the truth, Rona; and I know why you've kept silent about it. It was for John's own sake."

"Indeed?" Rona spoke quite impassively.

"Yes. We all liked John, and it would be rotten to have him branded as a murderer. No wonder he wrote that letter to the War Office to explain everything away."

"Aren't you forgetting," Rona said kindly, "that it was John himself who was murdered?"

"Oh no. Because it was John who murdered himself

—by accident, so to speak. That is, when his plan to murder Angela misfired. What a bit of poetic justice, eh?"

"You must know," said Rona steadily, "that you're just talking nonsense, Douglas."

"Am I?" I retorted. "No, we must face the truth, Rona—as you've been facing it all this time. There can't be any doubt about it. John had arsenic in his possession. The empty bottle in the secret cupboard proves it. That's Point No. 1. Then John had borrowed a pill-making machine from Glen. He returned it, saying that he couldn't make it work. Fancy! John Waterhouse, the world-famous engineer, couldn't make a paltry pill-making machine work! Is that likely? I ask you. Point No. 2. Those are very suggestive, but Point No. 3 must surely be conclusive. It is this. During the period when John must have swallowed that arsenic there were only three known vehicles: Glen's medicine, since proved innocent, Frances' sherry, equally innocent, and his own cider. That means the arsenic *must* have been in the cider. Well, if Angela didn't put it there, who did? The cook? Pritchard? Hardly. But who drew the cider? John did. For whom? For Angela. . . . My dear Rona, you can't defend him. It's obvious."

Rona was breathing a little more quickly. "No, Douglas. You're wrong. There's a mistake somewhere. John—John wasn't like that. I can't let you say he was."

"Are you sure there's a mistake?" I pursued. "And what would the inference be if there was? You surely can't believe Frances put arsenic in the sherry?"

"No, no, of course not."

"You think perhaps she might have had some kind of a motive?"

There was no mistaking Rona's astonishment. "Motive? What motive could Frances possibly have?"

"Exactly," I agreed. "None. So what remains? You may be thinking there was a fourth possible vehicle:

the caramels which came by post that morning. But I've already found out that John gave them to one of the men working at Oswald's Gable. It's too much to believe that he could have eaten just one or two himself first, and by incredibly bad luck hit on the poisoned ones. No, it wasn't the caramels. And it wasn't the sherry. And we know it wasn't the medicine, don't we? So if it wasn't the cider, what was it?"

"But John's letter!" Rona cried. "You're forgetting everything. John explained it all."

"Yes," I said. "And you know as well as I do, Rona, that there wasn't a word of truth in the whole story he told."

"But . . . but John couldn't invent a story like that."

"No," I said. "*He* couldn't. And that's a clue in itself. Don't you agree?"

"I don't know what you mean," Rona said, quite feebly.

"Oh yes, you do." I looked at her straight. "No, Rona: none of those theories is the right one, because all of them leave out of account one vital factor—*the* vital factor, one might say, in the whole problem. That factor is known only to you and me, Rona, and to one other person who, a thousand to one, will never realise its significance—just as I didn't myself till yesterday evening."

"And what is this vital factor?" Rona asked, quietly enough but with a faint hostility.

"The fact that you knew that John was suffering from arsenical poisoning the moment you heard he had been taken ill, before you'd even seen him."

There was a silence.

"I knew . . . *what*?" said Rona.

"Yes. Don't fence, Rona. The items you enumerated to your maid on the telephone were the ordinary antidotes for arsenical poisoning; the treatment you carried out on John afterwards, before Glen took charge, was the proper treatment for arsenical poisoning. You knew John had taken arsenic, days, almost weeks before arsenic was ever mentioned."

Rona looked at me steadily.

"Well?" she said.

I was relieved that she had not denied it. Rona was always straightforward.

"Well, I've been asking myself ever since last evening, naturally, what that meant. John had hinted to you that he was going to commit suicide with arsenic, and you had disbelieved him at the time, to find later that he had really meant it? No. You had supplied John with arsenic for his tree-washing experiments and instantly divined that he must have swallowed some accidentally? I don't think so. Even that John had planned to murder Angela, as I said just now, with arsenic unwittingly supplied by you, and you saw the whole plan in a flash there at the front door, realised that it had gone wrong and instinctively knew what had happened? Not very likely. No. There's only one feasible explanation of your knowledge. You knew that it was intended to use the arsenic criminally. In other words, Rona, you and John conspired together to poison Angela; you supplied the arsenic, and you knew when the attempt was to be made; that's why you went to Torminster that day. You came back with that excuse about the gramophone records to call at the house and hear how things had gone. When you heard that it was John who was so ill, and no word was said about Angela, you knew that things must have gone wrong and you telephoned at once for the antidote. That's the truth, isn't it, Rona? You and John planned murder together?"

"It is not the truth," Rona said.

"But how can you deny it? Everything hangs together."

"It is not the truth." Rona was breathing a little quickly, though she appeared otherwise unmoved; but a little more warmth came into her voice as she went on. "You knew John. He was incapable of anything like that. John was . . . was . . ." She choked suddenly.

"I know he was incapable of it," I said as gently as I could. "So that leaves only one possibility, and that's the truth. Of course I knew it was the truth. I just wanted to hear you exculpate John with your own lips, realising what it meant. That was plucky of you, Rona, at all events. But you've been plucky all along. You needed pluck, too, when your plan went so disastrously wrong. I think you've found that a worse punishment than the official one, haven't you?"

Rona had pulled herself together. Imperturbably she looked me in the eye and said:

"I think you'd better tell me just what's in your mind, my friend."

"I think I'd better, too, and I can tell you in half-a-dozen words. It was you who poisoned John."

Not a muscle of Rona's face moved.

"You can have no proof of such a remarkable accusation."

"Oh yes, I have," I retorted. "I've plenty of proof. But if you mean 'evidence,' no, I admit I haven't. Proof and evidence aren't by any means the same thing."

"Then let me hear your proofs."

I lit another cigarette. It was an extraordinary situation, I suppose, but I knew Rona so well that it was not so impossible as it might have been with a stranger.

"Well," I began, and I remember my voice was quite conversational. "Well, it all goes back to that conversation you, John, Harold and I had that evening at the Waterhouses'. I wonder if you remember the details? I can recall quite a number of the things that were said, and most illuminating they look now. For instance, do you remember giving your views on the elimination of the community's drones? 'Why keep them alive?' you said. Then, a little later, John paid you a compliment, and you blushed with pleasure like a young girl. I noticed it particularly. Rona, that gave you away. I realised that evening that you must be in love with John, though I didn't attach any great importance to it.

"But that puzzled me yesterday. You see, as soon as I realised that it was the antidote to arsenic that you had told the maid to bring round, I knew it must have been you who poisoned John—deliberately or by mistake. At first I thought you must have done it somehow by mistake, though I couldn't see how that could have happened. Then I wondered if you had done it deliberately. Did you consider John had become one of the world's drones and so ought to be eliminated? But that seemed fantastic. Besides, I couldn't get over the fact that you were in love with him. People do kill when they're in love, but there seemed no possible motive here. You weren't the kind to say, 'If I can't have him, no one shall.' So I came back to the idea that though you must have been responsible for John's death in some way or other, it must have been an accident. But how? And what sort of accident could make you responsible? Only one thing was clear: that you couldn't have deliberately intended to kill John. If there was anyone who needed killing from your point of view, it was surely Angela.

"And then, Rona, I remembered a remark you made to me once when I said something about a possibility that someone had aimed at Angela and hit John. I forget the details, but you looked at me and said: 'That was a very shrewd remark, my friend.' As soon as I remembered that, and the significance of your tone, I wondered if that was what had really happened. It would have been like you, too, to salute the truth as it came, irrespective of the circumstances. And I saw at once that this theory accounted for everything.

"Let's go back to that evening at the Waterhouses'. You had said that in your opinion the drones ought to be eliminated. And what's more, you meant it. Other people may say that kind of thing for effect, but you never speak for effect, Rona. It's one of the things I've always admired about you. You didn't actually say that you were prepared to eliminate them with your own hands, but you sincerely believed that the useless members of the community ought to be put quietly out of the way. Even John believed you meant it. 'You Communists are so ruthless,' he said, and added that he wasn't ruthless himself. It's true that he wasn't so ruthless as you, Rona. Anyhow, the point is: who could be a more useless member of the community than Angela?

"So we have your head as well as your heart approving of Angela's extermination.

"I think probably you've been in love with John for some years, Rona. That may be why you've never married. (I'm sorry to have to mention this sort of thing, but it's all part of the case against you.) And just as you disapproved of Angela with your heart as well as your head, so you loved John with your head as well as your heart. Your head, for instance, must have told you that here was a man you could respect as well as love. A man with a big past behind him and a still bigger future in front—if he cared to make it. You're an intelligent woman, Rona. You knew well enough that if John was to play the part in the world that was possible for him, he needed a woman like you behind him: someone to share his enthusiasms and egg him on to bigger and bigger things. What couldn't he have achieved, with you? And what couldn't you have achieved through him? That would justify a good deal.

"Angela, on the other hand, was exactly the wrong wife for him. Not only was she useless to him, but she was a positive drag. He was stifled by her; she had sucked him of all enterprise and vitality; it was her influence that kept him wasting himself in a place like Anneypenny. You remember he told us that evening that he had settled down for good? And later he mentioned some big job he had just turned down, near Angkor. We all cried out on him; and no wonder. A job like that was just what his soul needed. Like all of us, you must have put his refusal down to Angela's account. I wonder if it was that very evening that you decided to rid the world, and John, of Angela? I shouldn't be surprised, because some of the conversation afterwards may have suggested to you a way.

"That kept me awake most of last night, Rona, trying to puzzle out how the devil you did it.

"You see, so far as we know (and we must take it as the fact), barring the meals of breakfast and lunch, there were only those three possible vehicles for the arsenic: the cider, the sherry and the medicine. And, unless either John or Angela was planning to poison the other, all the three seem equally innocent. Well, there may be two conclusions to be drawn. Either the arsenic was contained in some other vehicle of which we know nothing, or else one of those three wasn't so innocent as it seemed.

"What do we need, to fit the theory of your guilt? A, some vehicle, obviously, to which you had access; and B, one which was never intended for John at all but for Angela. Well, the medicine was the only one of the three to which you had access. Could that have been the vehicle after all, in spite of its having been analysed and found innocent, and in spite of its having been medicine for John and not for Angela?

"I puzzled a lot over that medicine, Rona. And in the end I found the answer.

"It was that same conversation at the Waterhouses' that put me on the track. You remember how we discussed John's indigestion. It was getting worse, but John's attitude to medicine and doctors seemed unchanged. He was an obstinate old devil, was John; and when he swore he wouldn't swallow a drop of Glen's medicine, we all took it for granted he meant what he said. There was some mention of Christian Science, too, I think; John was supposed to have leanings toward it, and you encouraged them. So much for John. But Angela! Now there was someone who wouldn't let a bottle of medicine lie idle.

Angela could surely be relied on to dose herself with any therapeutic drug that came into the house. And no doubt you noticed that as soon as John produced indigestion of his own, Angela's indigestion became instantly worse. If John refused to take his medicine, Angela would simply grab it. And from John's attitude it was a pretty safe bet that any medicine which went into that house, no matter to whom it was addressed, would be eventually swallowed by Angela, and by Angela alone. That was the bet, and you went banco on it.

"Glen probably confirmed your conviction that it couldn't go wrong. After he'd examined John did he tell you that John had said he'd pour any medicine that was sent round for him down the sink?"

Rona nodded.

"Did he add that John afterwards gave a sort of half-hearted hint that he might take a dose or two after all?"

"No," Rona said curtly. "Glen never expected John to drink the medicine. He only sent it round as a matter of form."

"Exactly. And that's how I reached the conclusion that the medicine was the vehicle for the poison. But it was a long time before I saw how it was done. Apart from the analysis, you didn't even dispense it. Glen made it up. And I'm quite sure Glen wasn't in league with you; it's quite out of character for one thing, and in any case there's no evidence. So somehow or other you must have induced Glen to make up a bottle of medicine containing arsenic. That was infernally clever of you, Rona.

"I saw in the end how you managed it. Two little facts, each a tiny bit out of keeping with your nature, gave me the clues. In the first place you went to Torminster that day and left Glen to make up the medicines. Now that isn't like you, Rona. I was a little surprised when I heard it. Because if you wanted to take a day off in Torminster, one would expect you of all people to make sure that it was not at the expense of extra work for anyone else. You would have got up twenty minutes earlier and made up those three or four bottles. Or you'd have made them up the evening before. But you wouldn't have left them for Glen.

"The second item is still more unlike you—so unlike you, in fact, that Glen himself commented on it in his evidence at the inquest. The mag. pond. jar was nearly empty. 'Not like my sister's usual efficiency,' said Glen. But he was wrong. Because when you do a thing like that—or rather, leave it undone—one may be sure you have a reason. And the only possible deductions to be drawn from those two facts are that you went into Torminster that morning for the deliberate purpose of *not* making up the medicines, and that the almost empty mag. pond. jar was part of your plan. In other words, Torminster was your alibi.

"Once I got as far as that, the thing began to take shape. It didn't take me long to see the point of the mag. pond. Glen, you may remember, specifically said that John's was the only prescription that morning requiring mag. pond. He also told us that all prescriptions were entered in a book. Add to this that 'pond.' means heavy, and that arsenic, too, is a heavy powder, and the thing becomes obvious.

"You already had the idea of substituting arsenic for some other drug of similar appearance if the prescription gave you a chance. You saw from the book that it did. You emptied the mag. pond. jar and substituted just enough arsenic for that one prescription, in case there was any further call for mag. pond. before you got home again, knowing that Glen would refill the jar: as in point of fact he did. And there was the lethal medicine, made up in all good faith by an innocent party with an unimpeachable alibi for you.

"And so we come to the next problem: how was it that when Frances took the bottle away from John's room, there was no arsenic in the medicine?

"Well, that wasn't very difficult. I thought carefully over the course of events that evening between your arrival and our departure, and it wasn't long before I remembered that you had a good half-hour in John's bedroom alone with him. In that half-hour you had ample opportunity to substitute for the poisoned bottle the innocent one which you had been carrying about Torminster all day with you for that purpose—having first surreptitiously poured away down one of the basins the exact amount from the innocent bottle that was missing from the poisoned bottle. Isn't that what happened?"

"You can hardly expect me to confirm what you're saying," Rona retorted with a faint smile.

"It doesn't matter. I know it's what happened, because there's no other explanation that will fit the facts. Except for me, you see, you were the only person to be alone with John and the medicine bottle during that period; and as we've already exonerated Angela and the rest of the household, we needn't worry over any opportunities they had."

"Have we already exonerated the rest of the household?" Rona said combatively. "What about Mitzi?"

"Poor Mitzi! I'm sure she was egged on, most unsuitably, to tamper with John's papers; and I'm sure she was hurried out of the country by a nervous Embassy; but I can't see one single iota of evidence to connect her with John's death. Can you?"

"No," said Rona.

"And how would she have got hold of arsenic? It would be fantastic to suppose that she was supplied with it officially, to rid the German government of John. No. In the whole case, Rona, there's only one person (in addition to Glen) with access to an *unchecked* supply of arsenic, and that's you. Is that why you used it, by the way? Or was it because the symptoms would tally with Angela's supposed complaints?"

"You're asking me leading questions, aren't you, my friend?"

"I'd like you to answer that one, because arsenic is a cruel weapon, and though I'm sure you're ruthless, Rona, I shouldn't have expected you to be cruel."

"Cruelty, kindness," Rona replied scornfully. "One would naturally be as humane as one could be, but there's only one thing that dictates action, and that's necessity."

"You mean you considered arsenic a necessity in this case for an undetected murder."

"You can put it that way, if it please you," Rona said indifferently. "The form of words doesn't matter very much; words are often inadequate."

I passed over without comment Rona's tacit admission of guilt, pleased though I was. Not that I had not been sure of my deductions, but it was satisfactory to have them confirmed. It was like Rona, too, not to boggle once things had come to a showdown.

"Yes," I said reflectively. "I remember your saying once, when we were discussing whether it could be murder, 'Murder—or criminal carelessness.' Of course I didn't realise then that you were speaking so bitterly of yourself. Frances nearly hit the nail on the head once, too, when she suggested that it might have been an accident but on somebody else's part, not John's. Queer, how near we got to the truth at times, and yet how far off we were. . . . You must have had a dreadful time, Rona," I added suddenly. I suppose it was illogical, but for the moment I felt even more sorry for Rona than for John.

She waved the remark aside.

"And how, my friend, do you account for that letter John wrote?" she asked, for all the world as if she were testing a case I was bringing against some stranger. "For write it he did, I can assure you of that."

"Well," I said slowly, "I can only suppose that you gave him some sort of half explanation which made him anxious to shield you. I don't imagine you found it necessary to tell him that you had been trying to poison his wife. Upset as you must have been, you would still keep your head. I should think you probably made up some tale of a disastrous mistake, for which you were responsible: something about having filled up some jar from the wrong stock. Anyhow, you certainly told him that it was arsenical poisoning he was suffering from, or he couldn't have written as much in the letter. I remember you said to me outside his bedroom door that first evening that it *might* be damnably serious. That not only indicates that you knew more about John's illness even then than the rest of us, but sounds as if you weren't by any means certain that it was going to be fatal. Perhaps you expected him to recover, and made him expect the same. From what I can gather of arsenical poisoning, death always seems unlikely; the process is so long, and all the time the patient seems to be getting better. As for the letter, you and John no doubt concocted it together, but I should put the draft down to you; it reads almost like an essay, not a bit the sort of phraseology one would expect from a man not used to expressing himself on paper."

"You know, Douglas," Rona said, "I've been underestimating you all these years." She spoke with a kind of surprise which showed me that my observations on the letter could not have been far short of the mark.

"You didn't really expect John to die," I went on. "And even when he did, the last thing you expected was an enquiry, considering Glen's certainty that death was due to epidemic diarrhœa. It really was very bad luck that Cyril's suspicions should have been aroused, out of no more than pique that Angela hadn't notified him properly of the death. Still, if the worst came to the worst you had the letter, and to do you justice, Rona, you would have used more than the letter if Angela had been arrested; I'm sure of that. But I think you didn't know whether to use the letter or not. I remember some questions, rather hesitant for you, that you put to Glen and me on the first day of the inquest; the letter had been posted to the War Office by then, of course, but you wanted to assure yourself that you had been right to post it. I take it that you were in Torminster on the day before the inquest? Well, it's so obvious that I haven't bothered even to enquire."

"I was, my friend," Rona said imperturbably.

"You know, it's odd that the Coroner didn't ask you about the letter. You were nursing John. If anyone might have been expected to know about the letter, it was you. But no one seems to have thought of you. By the way, it was you, of course, who planted all the evidence which the letter mentioned: the bottle with traces of arsenic in the secret cupboard and traces of arsenic in the bathroom basin—with John's approval, of course. And no doubt you chose the bathroom basin because it wasn't used much, with a basin in each of the bedrooms; the arsenic would stay there longer. John can't have expected to die. Right up to the end he must have been confident. I expect he took the concocting of the letter as a huge joke. He would have had complete faith in you to give him the proper treatment for arsenical poisoning; and, knowing John, I shouldn't be surprised if he wasn't laughing up his pyjama sleeve all the time at Glen for being so wrong in his diagnosis."

"As I said just now, Douglas, I've underestimated you," Rona said with a half-smile. "I should certainly never have given you credit for so much constructive imagination. I really feel it's due to you to tell you that you've been right, I think, on every single point."

"Oh well, after all, there were plenty of indications, if only one grasped their significance," I said, unable to help feeling flattered. The situation really was quite absurd. "Even you gave yourself away once or twice, Rona, you know, when you were off your guard. You were so very much upset over John's death, and you showed it far more than one would have expected from your normal control over your feelings. That convinced me that you were in love with John; and later I realised that self-blame accounted for your breaking down on Frances' shoulder. You know, Frances said right from the beginning that you knew something was wrong; I remembered that when I was trying to puzzle out whether it was really you who had done it. Frances is pretty acute, you know.

"Then another thing that gave you away was the way you blazed out at Glen when he mentioned that day at tea that there was nothing wrong with Angela at all. That wasn't a bit like you, Rona. I was surprised at the time. But of course he'd given you a shock—a much bigger shock that any of us suspected. For it must have been quite a shock, after you'd based your whole plan on the certainty that Glen would give a certificate without question if Angela were to fade quietly out, to learn that he would have done nothing of the sort. Naturally you felt for the moment as if he had been deceiving you most unfairly."

I paused.

"Is that all?" Rona asked quietly.

"Oh, I expect there are other points, but that's enough for the moment." I shook my head. "Rona, Rona, murder's a risky business. And the more elaborate the plan, the greater the risk. But I believe yours would have succeeded if only, by some fatal chance, a worse spasm of pain than usual hadn't driven John to try the medicine for relief. Otherwise it might well have reached Angela, just as you calculated."

Rona looked at me. "And what, my friend, do you propose to do about all this?"

"To do?" I repeated, taken for the moment aback. "Well, I suppose I shall have to . . . to . . ."

"Well?"

"That is, of course you'll give yourself up. It's pretty rotten, I know, but you've no alternative."

Rona smiled scornfully. "Come, Douglas, I wasn't at a public school, you know."

"Eh?"

"Your code of ethics isn't mine. In other words I certainly have an alternative. I shall do nothing at all; and if you approach the authorities with the story you've just told me, I shall deny every word of it. I shall deny that it was the antidotes for arsenic that I rang up for; what Alice wrote down at this end of the telephone has already been destroyed, and she certainly won't remember; I shall deny every other fact for which you can't produce corroborative evidence."

"But . . . you can't do that, Rona. I mean, they *are* facts."

"Possibly. But how are you going to prove them? How are you going to prove, for instance, that it was I who 'planted' the arsenic in the secret cupboard? Inference is one thing, my friend, proof another."

"But, dash it all, you've admitted it."

"Between ourselves, and for this one occasion only, perhaps. But really, Douglas: you've been exceedingly intelligent so far; don't spoil it all now. What may convince in a drawing room won't satisfy a court of law. You'd never get a conviction on that story. You wouldn't even get an arrest. As you said yourself, there's no evidence, as the law understands it. I saw to that, at all events. If you take this tale to the authorities, you'll only create a great deal of unpleasantness and achieve precisely nothing."

"But, Rona, you can't intend to do *nothing*?"

"But why should I do anything? I admit that a mistake —a blunder, if you like—is a crime; but to my way of thinking that's the only crime I've committed. I consider it a beneficial act to rid the world of a parasite and an incubus, which is what I intended to do. You may cling to the law if you like, with all your public-school mind; I admit no judge or jury but my own conscience. And my conscience clears me. Except, of course, for the blunder. That was unpardonable."

I was speechless, simply speechless. I had known that Rona's ideas were revolutionary, but this sounded to me like sheer Bolshevism.

Rona smiled at me in a pitying way.

"You're thinking I ought to be punished. That's in accordance with your code, isn't it? Well, my code doesn't approve of punishment. Punishment does more harm than good. It's barbarous. An eye for an eye, a tooth for a tooth, a life for a life, eh? I'm afraid you're terribly Old Testament, Douglas. Still, if it's any consolation to you, I have been punished, and shall continue being punished all the days of my life—unbearably. Don't you think that's worse than being hanged by the neck?"

"But . . . but that's different," was all I could find to say.

"Different, yes. And worse. No, Douglas, I can't see that, because I attempted to rid society of a useless member, a member who can still be useful should be exterminated, as your code demands. Nevertheless I'm prepared to make a concession to you. I'll undertake that my life shall be more useful to the community than it has been. There are plenty of openings. Yes, this decides me. I'll leave Glen and these petty activities here and go back to London. I need work anyhow now, real work. I'll let you know later what I intend to do." Rona smiled at me derisively. "You shall be my warder and watch that I'm working out my sentence properly."

"But, Rona——"

"That's enough, my friend." Rona cut me short with a firmness that took my breath away. "You may do what you like; I've told you what I shall do. We'll discuss it no further."

There was in any case no chance to discuss it further at the moment, for just then Glen appeared.

"Hullo," he said. "Been sticking on in the hopes of being offered a glass of sherry?"

"That's right," I said, pulling myself together. "And with the intention of asking for one if not offered. I feel I need one."

3

Well, that was eight days ago.

I have not seen Rona since, I have done nothing, I have not said a word to anyone, not even to Frances. And the reason is simple: for the life of me I can't decide what to do.

This morning Harold informed me, with much excitement, that Rona was going to leave Anneypenny for London again. He said she was taking up a post in a big charity organisation for helping destitute children —an unpaid post, added Harold, his eyes bulging. No doubt Harold's information is correct; it usually is.

But things can't be left like that. I must do something, Mere justice demands it—though Rona is, of course, right, and justice would never be done. But that does not shift my responsibility.

I feel I really ought to do something.

But what ought I to do?